DIESELFUNK!

....

EDITED BY
MILTON J DAVIS
AND
BALOGUN OJETADE

MVmedia, LLC

Fayetteville, Georgia

MVmedia, LLC
PO Box 1465
Fayetteville, GA 30214

Publisher's Note: This is a work of fiction. Names, characters, places, and incidents are a product of the author's imagination. Locales and public names are sometimes used for atmospheric purposes. Any resemblance to actual people, living or dead, or to businesses, companies, events, institutions, or locales is completely coincidental.

Book Layout ©2017 BookDesignTemplates.com
Cover art by Paul Sizer
Cover design by Uraeus

Ordering Information:
Quantity sales. Special discounts are available on quantity purchases by corporations, associations, and others. For details, contact the "Special Sales Department" at the address above.

Dieselfunk -- 1st ed.
ISBN 13 no.: 978-1-7372277-3-1

Contents

SOAR: Wild Blue Yonder By Balogun Ojetade 9

Power Play: The Very True and Accurate Story of Eunice Carter, Mob-Buster By Day Al-Mohamed 38

The Girl With The Iron Heart By S.A. Cosby 47

Into the Breach By Malon Edwards.. 75

Angel's Flight: A Tale of The City By Joe Hilliard 89

Unusual Threats and Circumstances By Ronald T. Jones 106

Bonregard and the Three Ninnies By Carole McDonnell 135

Down South By Milton J. Davis.. 151

Big Joe versus the Electro-men By James A. Staten......................... 172

THE DIESELFUNKATEERS 198

To the Dieselfunkateers!

A PEOPLE WITHOUT THE KNOWLEDGE OF
THEIR PAST HISTORY, ORIGIN AND
CULTURE IS LIKE A TREE WITHOUT ROOTS.
—Marcus Garvey

SOAR:
WILD BLUE YONDER
BY
BALOGUN OJETADE

One

First Lieutenant Jasper Ross pulled at his khaki tie as he slowly turned his head from side-to-side.

The woman sitting beside him in the back seat of the *Ford GP* stared at him chuckling. "Hot under the collar, Jazz?"

The men and women – well, *woman* – of the 555th Parachute Infantry Battalion called Lieutenant Ross "Jazz" – short for Jasper because according to his peers Lieutenant Ross was, like jazz, cool and free, yet deep.

At least, that's what he told everyone who asked.

"Dad-blamed right," Jazz replied. "How is the driver gon' stop *three times* to do the number two? We were supposed to be here twenty minutes ago!"

"Sorry sir . . . ma'am," the driver said, peering over his shoulder. "I had a hamburger last night. It ain't agreeing with me."

"That's the problem, private," Jazz said. "Do you have any idea where hamburgers are from?"

"Um . . . I . . ." the driver stuttered.

Jazz leaned forward. "Hamburg, Germany, private! *That's* where. Eating that burger means you *bought* that burger, which means you supported Germany, which means you supported Hitler. Do you support Hitler, private?"

"N-no, sir!" the private stuttered.

"But you love hamburgers, right? Especially with pickles and juicy tomatoes on top?"

"Well, yes, sir," the private replied.

"Then you love Hitler," Jazz said. "It's bad enough you love *any* peckerwood that ain't your mama or your daddy of course, but Hitler?"

"I didn't say I love Hitler, sir," the private croaked.

"Actions speak louder than words private; right?"

Sweat dripped from the driver's forehead, falling onto the steering wheel. "Well, I . . . I . . ."

"Well, what *is* it, private?" Jazz said, feigning impatience. "Do actions speak louder than words, or not?"

"I . . . I suppose so, sir!"

"You *suppose* so?"

The woman sitting beside Jazz nudged him with her elbow. "Leave that man alone Jazz, or you are going to make him have to hit the head again."

"I'm just having fun with him, Ronnie," Jazz whispered. "Besides, we're here now; he can number two 'til the cows come home!"

The Jeep came to a halt. Jazz grabbed his duffle bag and leapt from the Jeep. Ronnie grabbed her bag and followed suit.

The driver snapped his right fingertips up toward his brow in a crisp salute.

Jazz and Ronnie returned the salute.

"Thanks, Klaus," Jazz said, lowering his hand.

"It's Barber, sir," the driver said, pointing at the name tag on the breast of his shirt. "Edwin Barber."

Jazz nodded. "Whatever you say . . . Klaus."

Ronnie pushed Jazz toward the two formations of soldiers who stood at attention a few yards from them. One group wore olive drab side caps, an olive-drab gabardine, spread-collared shirt worn with a khaki worsted wool tie, an olive-drab wool four-button tunic with leather belt, khaki wool trousers, and russet-brown leather shoes – the common Class-A uniform of a U.S. Army officer. The other platoon was dressed nearly the same, except most of the men wore the olive drab trousers of enlisted men. Five of them wore officers' khaki wool pants. All of the soldiers in the second platoon wore combat boots with their uniforms, indicating their elite airborne status.

Jazz and Ronnie dropped their bags and took their places with the officers of the second platoon.

"Looks like the First Lieutenant has pulled rank and doesn't have to show up for formation on time like us other lowly GIs," a soldier standing beside Jazz shouted. The rest of the men in the platoon laughed.

"Your mama just didn't wanna let go, Allen," Jazz said.

"Hey, I understand," Second Lieutenant Clifford Allen said. "You were winin' and dinin' mama and Rhonda's fine self." He peered past Jazz to Ronnie and crooned "Hey, Warrant Officer Wilson.

Ronnie rolled her eyes.

"He still ain't gettin' none, though," a soldier shouted from the back of the formation. "Except, of course, from *Allen's* mama."

The soldiers in both formations laughed.

"Yeah, 'cause he's too short for the job," Allen said.

More laughter echoed across the crisp morning sky.

"And he's still TWICE as tall as you," Ronnie said.

The soldiers roared, laughing heartily.

"All that noise must be coming from the Nickles," a voice boomed.

The soldiers fell quiet.

A bullish man stepped before them. Jazz noticed that his skin was just half a shade darker than his khaki tie. He also noticed that the man's name tag read 'Woodbine'. Major Roy Woodbine's name was legend. He was secretly the brains behind the formation of the 555th Parachute Infantry Battalion – the fierce and feared *Triple Nickles* – and the 332nd Fighter Group – the highly decorated *Tuskegee Airmen*.

"No sir," Jazz replied. "I think it was a flock of seagulls flying overhead, sir."

"Those goddamned Tuskegee, Alabama seagulls at it again, huh, Lieutenant?"

"Seems so, sir."

"Uh-huh." Major Woodbine stepped a bit closer. "My name is Major Roy Woodbine. All of you know my name; some of you know me. Kinda like Jesus, hooah?

"Hooah!" the soldiers replied in unison.

"And like our good Lord and Savior, you will find that, while I am filled with joy and mercy and light, I also come with a sword dripping blood up to the horse's bridle – a sword I will use against anyone who stands in our way, white or Black; red, green, yellow, purple, pink or polka-dot. Hooah?"

"Hooah!"

Major Woodbine pointed toward his right. Here, you *had* the 332nd . . . the Tuskegee Airmen . . . the deadly aces that shot the Nazis *lightly* and they died *politely*."

"Here, you *had* the 555th – the mighty Triple Nickles – the twenty-three coldest soldiers in this man's Army. The nation's first all-Negro parachute infantry test platoon, company, and battalion."

The Major paused, perusing the troops before him. He went on. "Notice I said 'had.' You *were* the 332nd; you *were* the 555th. And you will be again. But right now; at this very moment – and until our mission is complete – you are SOAR: The Special Operations Air Regiment. Hooah?"

"Hooah!" the soldiers boomed.

"We are going to take this war to the Land of the Rising Sun and give Hirohito a new asshole in the center of his forehead, courtesy of a Colt M1911," Major Woodbine said, pacing back and forth before the troops. "A defeat in their country – at the hands of Negro soldiers, no less – will totally demoralize the Nipponese and weaken their resolve as you are only as invincible as your smallest weakness."

Major Woodbine raised three fingers in the air. "I have three months to work with you. Just three months to make the best better. But like I said I'm like Jesus and Jesus is a miracle worker. Hooah?"

"Hooah!"

"Work with me these three months and I promise you the same three things Jesus promised his disciples," Major Woodbine said. "That they would be completely fearless, absurdly happy . . . and in constant trouble."

The soldiers laughed.

"SOAR . . . dismissed!" Major Woodbine bellowed.

The soldiers saluted. Major Woodbine returned the salute, turned on his heels and then sauntered off.

"This should be interesting," Ronnie said to Jazz.

"Very," Jazz said. "Drink?"

Ronnie raised an eyebrow. "You buying?"

"What? Your money don't spend?" Jazz asked.

"See . . . that's why we never dated," Ronnie said, shaking her head.

"We never dated because I never asked," Jazz said.

"Then ask," Ronnie said, batting her eyes. "You know you want to."

Jazz laughed. "Why? So, you can reject me loudly in front of everyone? Shit, you ain't setting me up for *that* one!"

Ronnie bent over laughing. "You know me well."

"Too well," Jazz said. "I gotta get better friends!"

* * *

Jazz and Ronnie sat at one of the circular oak tables in the Negro Officers' Club, sipping their favorite drinks – *Ron Merito Puerto Rican Rum* for Jazz and an ice-cold *Schlitz Beer* for Ronnie.

"Nice place," Ronnie said, perusing the club. The polished hardwood floors and hand-carved mahogany ceiling fans were a nice touch. "Nicest Negro Officers' Club I've ever been to."

"Yep," Jazz murmured, staring over her shoulder.

"Not *half* as nice as that white Officers' Club we snuck into back at Fort Huachuca, though."

"Mm-hmm," Jazz hummed.

Ronnie snapped her fingers in front of Jazz's face. Jazz blinked rapidly, his focus returning to the table.

"Huh? What's up?" he said.

"Stop worrying about those fools," Ronnie said, nodding her head back toward three Airmen who sat at the bar. "They have been staring since we came in. They probably think you're cute."

Ronnie laughed.

"I know you heard them whispering about your booty," Jazz said. "I'm not the one they're checking out."

"Yeah, I heard them," Ronnie said, dismissing them with a wave of her hand. "Talkin' about it looks like two turkeys fighting under a blanket and all that."

"They're crackin', but they're fackin'," Jazz said. "It *is* nice."

Ronnie sucked her teeth. "Boy, please. Half these Negroes lose their minds when Miss Anne bumps them with her ol' ironin' board backside. It ain't about the booty, it's about the boy. *Men* know there's much more to a woman."

Jazz's eyes fell to Ronnie's chest. "Mm-hmm."

Ronnie smacked Jazz on the side of his head with her palm.

Jazz laughed. "You'd better stop being so rough. These Zigaboojies like 'em soft and prissy, with baby-makin' hips."

Ronnie laughed. "Zigaboojie...I like that," she said, admiring Jazz's play on Zigaboo – *slang for Negro* – and boojie – *a Negro who apes the dominant bourgeoisie class*. "But I already told you, no baby for me until I'm at least 37; and that's *baby*, as in one – un; uno; eins; daya; moja."

"Okay, I recognize the French, Spanish and German," Jazz said with a raise of his eyebrow. "What were the last two?"

"Hausa and Kiswahili."

Jazz shook his head. "Show off."

"Hey, our Companions enhance our natural gifts and interests," Ronnie whispered. "I've always had a love for languages."

"Well, get ready to learn Japanese real soon," Jazz said.

"I'm more interested in learning the languages where *we* are," Ronnie said. "So, I can communicate with my people wherever I go."

"Planning to finish what Boukman, Dessalines and L'Ouverture started, huh?"

Ronnie shrugged. "Our Companions enhance our natural gifts and interests."

"No wonder I keep going after those pitch-toes," Jazz said, smiling.

Ronnie sucked her teeth. "Please . . . you just like those Creole-lookin' gals 'cause they're siddity. They don't care about the quality of your character or your convo . . . just the *quantity* of your connections and your cash."

"Isn't your mama Creole?"

Ronnie nodded. "Yep . . . and she married my daddy because he was the first Negro doctor in Ruleville, not because she loved him. I think maybe she loves him now . . . maybe."

Three Airmen sauntered into the club. Jazz recognized one as Captain Benjamin Davis, Jr. – commander of the Airmen and son of Benjamin O. Davis, Sr., the first Negro General in the Army.

"Marry him and you'll do your mama proud," Jazz whispered.

"Shut up," Ronnie whispered back.

Jazz smiled.

His smile faded, however, as the trio of Airmen strode toward his table.

Captain Davis stopped inches from the table. The two other Airmen stood at his flank.

"Hello, Lieutenant," Captain Davis said with a nod. "Warrant Officer Wilson. I'm Captain . . ."

"Benjamin O. Davis, Jr.," Ronnie chimed in. "Your reputation precedes you."

Captain Davis chuckled. "More like my *father's* reputation precedes us both."

"You've made your own name," Ronnie assured him. "Your skills in the cockpit are spoken of with high respect among us pilots. And call me Ronnie."

"Kind words, Ronnie," Captain Davis said with a smile. "Call me Ben. And since you're so kind, we'll let you stay here instead of going to your designated Non-Commissioned Offic-ers' Club."

"Didn't mean any disrespect, Benny," Jazz said, stone-faced. "In the 555th, we don't make any distinction between Commissioned and Non-Commissioned Officers. We all chew the same dirt."

"It's Ben, for the *lady*, Lieutenant," Ben said, his gaze still locked on Ronnie. "Not Benny. *You* will continue to address me as Captain."

The men standing behind Ben laughed.

Jazz sucked his teeth.

"My brothers here are Lem and Charlie," Ben said point-ing his thumbs backward over his shoulders. "That's Lieutenants Lemuel Custis and Charles DeBow to you, Lieutenant Ross."

"Roger that, sir," Jazz said rolling his eyes.

"Now, would you care to dance, Ronnie?" Ben asked.

"There's no music," Ronnie replied. "Besides, I doubt you could hang."

"I'm the best dancer on this base," Ben said, thumping his chest with the palm of his well-manicured hand. "Hey, Clyde . . . Claudine . . . give us something to juke to!"

The old bartender and the nearly-as-old waitress shuffled over to the baby grand piano that sat along the far wall. The man sat down, stretched his crooked fingers and then held them in place over the yellowed keys.

Claudine belted out in a strong alto:

"Patience and fortitude
Patience and fortitude
Patience and fortitude
And things will come your way."

Clyde's fingers jumped across the piano keys like crick-ets on a hot-plate. A fast jazz tune erupted from the piano and shook the club floor.

"When you have solitude
Can make life dull and crude

Patience and fortitude
Things will come your way."

Ben extended his hand. "Dance?"

Ronnie smiled and took it.

Ben pulled her to the dance floor.

Custis and DeBow sat down at Jazz's table.

"Have a seat, gentlemen," Jazz said, rolling his eyes.

"The Triple Nickles, huh?" Custis said, resting his chin on his fists. "I keep hearing how tough the Nickles are. Hell, I thought y'all would be giants who beat craters into the earth when you marched and shit, but y'all don't look so tough to me."

"And they shol' ain't smart," DeBow said, slapping Custis on the shoulder with the back of his hand. "Who the hell spells nickels N-I-C-K-L-E-S?"

Custis and DeBow laughed.

Jazz leaned forward and, smiling, directed his gaze from Custis to DeBow, back to Custis. "It's the Old English spelling, dummies," he whispered. He sat back in his chair. "Now, *what* college did you go to?"

DeBow leapt to his feet. "What?!"

Jazz leaned back in his chair with his fingers interlaced behind his head. "Sit down, boy, before you get yourself hurt."

The music stopped.

Ben and Ronnie rushed over to the table.

"What's going on?" Ben asked.

Custis rose to his feet. "This grunt just called us dummies," he said. "DeBow was about to teach him a lesson."

"DeBow was about to get his ass whooped," Ronnie said, cracking her knuckles. "You, too, if *you* jump, Lem."

"Woman, you'll get the spankin' your daddy should have given you messin' with me," Custis said.

"Nothin' between us but air and opportunity," Ronnie said, pointing her fingers between her and Custis' chests.

"Hold on," Ben said, raising his hand high above his head. "There won't be any fighting among us. Understood?"

"Yes, sir," Jazz and Ronnie said in unison.

Ben snapped his head toward his friends, glaring at them. "Understood?"

"Yes, sir," they murmured.

"Now, around here, we settle disputes like civilized men," Ben said. "Care to arm wrestle one of my boys, Lieutenant Ross?"

"Naw," Jazz replied.

Custis and DeBow exchanged glances, smiling wryly.

"Thought so," Custis said. "I knew . . ."

"I want to wrestle all three of y'all," Jazz said. "At once."

Ronnie tapped Jazz on the shoulder. He looked up at her. She shook her head.

"*You* must be the dummy, DeBow said. "There's no way you can win."

"Try me," Jazz said.

Ronnie pressed her fists to her hips, tilted her head and glared at Jazz with a raised eyebrow.

"I got this," he said to her with a smile.

Ronnie shook her head and released a sigh.

Jazz placed his elbow on the table and then opened his hand.

Custis, the largest of the three Airmen, took Jazz's hand in his. DeBow placed his hand on top of Custis' and Ben put his hand atop DeBow's.

The patrons and staff in the club gathered around.

"If I win, any time it is my turn to clean the barracks, y'all do it," Jazz said. "If I lose, I'll take each of your days."

"Get ready to get calluses from all that sweepin', boy," Ben said.

The club erupted in laughter.

Jazz laughed, too.

Ronnie shook her head.

"Go!" Ben shouted.

The Airmen laughed as they pushed, expecting to slam the back of Jazz's wrist into the table, but his arm did not move.

"What the hell?" Ben said.

He leaned his weight in a little, as did DeBow. The veins in Custis arms looked as if they would burst from the strain.

Still, Jazz's arm did not move.

Jazz smiled. "My turn."

Jazz inhaled and then pushed hard.

Custis screamed as his knuckles struck the table with a loud *bang*. DeBow and Ben went tumbling away from the table. Both men landed on their sides with a dull thud.

The gathered crowd clapped.

Jazz stood and took a bow. "I guess I should have let them know that I was arm wrestling champion of Chicago three years in a row." He winked at Ronnie.

Ronnie shook her head.

DeBow and Ben scrambled to their feet. Custis leapt from his chair, pounding his fist on the table. "Damn this arm-wrestling nonsense! Wrestle me for real and let's see how *that* turns out for you."

Jazz drew back, half smiling. "Dang, Custis! You like rolling around on the ground with strong men, huh?"

"What?" Custis took a step toward Jazz, his fists balled at his sides.

Jazz smiled.

Ben stepped between the two men, placing a palm on each of their chests. "That's enough, fellas. Save it for Hirohito."

Custis nodded, but kept his gaze locked on Jazz.

Jazz continued to smile as he shouted an enthusiastic "Yes, sir!"

Ronnie grabbed Jazz's arm. "Come on, champ." She pulled Jazz away. Jazz continued to smile at Custis over his shoulder.

"Ronnie . . . how about dinner tomorrow night?" Ben shouted.

Ronnie looked back at Ben and waved her free hand. "It's a date." She then yanked Jazz out of the club and onto the sidewalk.

"Dang, Ronnie!" Jazz said, rubbing his forearm.

"You're lucky I didn't snatch it off!" Ronnie hissed. "You know better than to show off like that. You could have exposed us all."

"Those pretty boys are going to learn about the Companions and what they allow us to do soon enough," Jazz said. "We *are* one big, happy family now, after all."

"The existence of the Companions – and the Nickles' possession of them is top secret, sensitive compartmented information," Ronnie said. "Above the Airmen's pay grade."

"I can go back in there and make them all a gold star in their mamas' windows if you want," Jazz said.

"You're just woofin'," Ronnie said. "Besides, I kinda like Ben."

Jazz rolled his eyes.

"What?" Ronnie said, smiling.

"Let's go," Jazz said. "Beatin' pretty boys makes me hungry."

Two

The Airmen and the Nickles stood in their respective platoons, dressed in olive drab herringbone twill uniforms. On their feet, the Airmen sported M43 combat boots; the Nickles wore the status symbol of paratroopers: Corcoran jump boots.

Major Woodbine paced back and forth before the elite soldiers. He stopped dead center of both platoons and turned to face them. "Good morning, SOAR!"

"Good morning, sir!" The soldiers shouted in unison.

"The law of inertia states that an object at rest tends to stay at rest, unless acted upon by a greater force," Major Woodbine said. "You had a full day off . . . and since a day to the Lord is like a thousand years and I am just like good Baby Jesus, you had a full lifetime of rest . . . and there's nothing like a run at dawn to get you moving again; Hooah?"

"Hooah!" The soldiers thundered.

Major Woodbine sniffed the air and then closed his eyes and smiled. "Mm . . . smell those pancakes, eggs, bacon and grits?"

"Yes, sir!" the soldiers replied.

"The first platoon with all their soldiers to complete the run gets to savor that scrumptious breakfast," Major Woodbine said. "The losing platoon gets oatmeal, or whatever the hell that gruel was in that pot I peeked in. Airmen . . . you have a ten-mile run this beautiful morning."

"Yes, sir!" the Airmen shouted.

Major Woodbine snapped his head toward the Triple Nickles. "Nickles, you have fifteen."

"Yes, sir!" the Nickles replied.

"Go!" Major Woodbine commanded.

Both platoons took off.

"*They're* the dummies," DeBow said. "They looked happy they're running five more miles than us. They can't win."

Captain Davis snickered. "Not unless they can sprout wings and fly."

* * *

When Lieutenant Yancey Williams came jogging in, his fellow Airmen cheered. Not one Nickel was even in sight.

"We all broke our previous times," Ben said. "Yancey, you clocked in at 45 minutes, 52 seconds."

"Dang!" Yancey said, between huffs and puffs. "Ten seconds faster. What was your time, Captain?"

"44 minutes, 24 seconds," Ben said.

"Those boys are gonna be wonderin' how we finished so fast," Custis said.

"Maybe we'll fill them in about the Companions one day," Yancey said.

"But not today," Ben said.

The Airmen laughed and then marched toward the mess hall. Upon stepping up to the large cafeteria's front door, they were greeted by the delicious smell of hot maple syrup and freshly squeezed oranges.

Ben smiled as he pulled the mess hall's door open. "Let's go, brothers. I can't wait to toast the Nickles with a crispy piece of bac . . ."

"Bacon?" Jazz said, holding a crisp piece high in the air as he leaned back in his chair. The other Nickles followed suit. Stacks of steaming pancakes sat before them.

Captain Davis' jaw fell slack. "How?"

"Enjoy your gruel," Jazz said.

The Nickles laughed as they returned to their plates of food.

* * *

Three soft knocks came from the other side of Major Woodbine's door. The Major looked up from his morning newspaper. "Come in."

Ben Davis opened the door, took three strides toward the Major's desk and then snapped to attention.

"At ease, Captain," Major Woodbine said.

Ben assumed a stance with his legs shoulder length apart and with his hands behind his back.

"I figured you'd come see me soon after breakfast," Major Woodbine said. "But damn, Captain Davis . . . *two minutes* afterward?"

Ben frowned. "Sir, when the Airmen agreed to your experiment to become one with these alien things connected to our brains and our nervous system . . ."

"Companions," Major Woodbine said, interrupting him.

"These *Companions* were supposed to make us the elite of the elite; the best soldiers in the history of warfare."

"You *are* the best," Major Woodbine said.

"Seems like the Nickles are *more* best," Ben said.

"No, they're just different," the Major said. "The Companions provide enhancements to their hosts based on the hosts' most frequently performed duties and how they train."

Major Woodbine opened his desk drawer and pulled a mahogany pipe from it. He lit the pipe's contents with a match he struck on the piece of flint on the top of his silver matchbox and then took a puff before speaking again.

"You Airmen are fighter pilots, so your apperception and metacognition are many times greater than that of normal humans. The Nickels have . . . other gifts that are the perfect complements to yours once you learn to work together; once you become a single link."

"You mean the strongest link in the chain," Ben said.

"No, smart-ass, I mean a single-freakin'-link," the Major said. He blew a ring of smoke toward the ceiling.

"Why a single link, Major?" Ben asked.

"Because a single link *never* breaks."

Three

An almost funereal silence permeated the room as the soldiers entered and took their seats. Each Airman wore his olive drab AN-S-31 flight suit and was decked out with all his gear except his parachute. Each Nickle wore olive drab battle uniforms and carried backpacks and belts with pockets for extra ammo and survival gear. On each Nickle's helmet was the illustration of a black panther crouched atop a white parachute, with the numbers '555' surrounded by golden wings. All of this was on a crimson background.

Training briefings routinely began with crude jokes and occasional horseplay, but there was none of that now, as this would be the Airmen's and Nickles' first training mission working together as SOAR.

Major Woodbine sauntered through the door and took his position at the front of the room at the blackboard.

"Gentlemen," he began. "Three days ago, the 187th Glider Infantry Regiment of the 11th Airborne Division landed on the Treasury Islands — here, about 50 miles south of Bougainville." He pointed to a tiny pair of islands of Papua New Guinea on the map with a wooden baton. "Resistance has been minimal, but the landing site is within easy reach of the Japanese airfields at Kahili, Kara, and Ballale, here on the southeastern end of Bougainville. The enemy's main forces have been pushed northward in the past few weeks, but there are still sufficient contingents at these bases to threaten the soldiers. Nickles, you will eliminate these contingents. Airmen, you will ensure that no Japanese patrols pester our troops on the ground."

"Yes, sir!" the soldiers shouted in unison.

"Airmen, your run up will be at 200 knots and you'll fly a ten-by-three-mile oval over the target at 20,000 feet," Major Woodbine continued. "Nickles, the B-29 Superfortress will also run up at 200 knots, but at 5000 feet. Airmen, you will cover the Superfortress until the Nickles jump. Nickles, you won't be doing static line jumps; you have to actually do a little work and pull your own ripcords, for once."

Laughter filled the room. Normally, paratroopers' ripcords were connected to a cable in the plane. The paratrooper would jump and the weight of the paratrooper would cause the ripcord to tear and the parachute to open automatically. Of course, normal paratroopers jumped from a height of 1200 feet, not 5000 feet, but the Nickles were not normal.

"Nickles, if you don't make contact during the patrol, the B-29 will land and then it will extract you. We have been authorized to then make strafing runs on ground targets of opportunity upon retirement."

A chorus of excited murmurs filled the ready room. Once the noise settled, the Major continued. "Take note of the reminder on the bottom of the board. In the event you encounter enemy fighters, do not press an attack if you don't have an altitude and speed advantage. Your P-51 Mustangs are maneuverable as hell, and so is that B-29 in Ronnie's more than capable hands, but a Zeke or Oscar will outturn you in a low-speed dogfight. Do not try to turn with it, or you *will* die. Whenever possible, attempt a high side run with the sun behind you. If you don't make a kill on the first pass, don't get greedy and start playing around with him. Use your speed advantage to regain altitude *and* I don't want anyone getting combat-happy and breaking off on his own."

All eyes and ears now hung on the Major's every word. Anticipation spread through the room like a contagion.

"This is what these last two months of our training has been about, so I don't expect any screw-ups," the Major continued on. "This is your last training mission before we send you into the heart of the Land of the Rising Sun. If you get hurt, you're nearly 200 miles from home. You can head southeast to

Munda or Ondonga if you're in bad trouble, but you may end up stuck there for a while if your plane's not flyable."

"It sounds like a milk run to me," Ronnie said. "Our Companions have adjusted to us working as a team and everyone is sharper and more powerful because of it. We're gonna tear those Nipponese boys up."

"You won't be bored out there, if that's what you're worried about, Warrant Officer Wilson." Major Woodbine said, smiling. "Now, let's mount up and open a can of whoop-ass on that Wild Blue Yonder. Hooah?"

The soldiers of SOAR leapt to their feet, snapped to attention and boomed: "Hooah!"

* * *

Outside, a few brilliant stars still speckled the midnight blue sky, though golden glows painted the eastern horizon like a watercolor wash. A gentle ocean breeze swept over the beach and through the camp. For this final training mission, SOAR had relocated to Hawaii and Jazz had spent as much time as possible enjoying the sand and surf – quite a different life from Tuskegee and a whole different world from his native Chicago.

Jazz made his way through the dark morning to the first of the waiting jeeps and then climbed into the back. Ronnie hopped in next to him.

"Morning, Beautiful," Ronnie said, smiling.

"I'm supposed to tell *you* that," Jazz said, shaking his helmeted head.

"Then, tell me," Ronnie said.

"Good morning, Beautiful," Jazz crooned. "Marry me?"

Ronnie clapped her hands together. "Let's do it!"

"I'll invite Captain Davis to be our Maid of Honor," Jazz said.

Ronnie laughed. "Leave my future ex-boyfriend alone."

"Ex-boyfriend?"

"Yeah," Ronnie replied. "Ben is a nice guy and all, but he's no fun. Our relationship is like doing pushups on your knees . . . it's just not working out."

Jazz burst out laughing.

The overweight jeep bounced and sloshed down the muddy track toward the revetments. As the vehicle approached the line of P-51 Mustang fighters and the B-29 Superfortress, Jazz spotted a pair of fuel trucks pulling away and several Army Air Corps crewmen scurrying back and forth among the planes. The smell of gas had replaced the tang of salt in the air, and the roar of diesel engines thundered above the grinding of the jeep motor.

Jazz hopped out of the jeep and strode toward the B-29. He noticed that the immense bomber's tail had been painted red just like the Airmen's planes. "One big, happy family," he whispered as he climbed into the B-29.

Ronnie followed him inside, but as Jazz sat on a long bench in the bomb warehouse, which was converted into a transport for the Nickles and their equipment, Ronnie strode past him without a word to the nose of the plane and then strapped herself into the pilot's seat.

Jazz was used to Ronnie's aloofness right before she flew the B-29. Her Companion was preparing her to take up all 11 crew positions; increasing her already exceptional apperception, metacognition, speed, accuracy and ability to multitask. "I'm my own damned co-pilot," she was fond of saying. Ronnie was also the plane's bombardier, engineer, radio operator, navigator, radar operator and gunner on the three 12.7mm cannons and the 20mm machinegun.

Ronnie tightened the seat harnesses and made sure none of them were twisted behind her. She pulled on a pair of snug gloves and then looked over her instruments, which glowed warm red in the solid black panel in front of her. Finally, she pulled her goggles over her eyes and glanced back to ensure all of her fellow Triple Nickles were strapped in and ready to go. Satisfied, she pushed the throttle forward, feeling the plane shiver and shake as power built up. The Superfortress lumbered out of its revetment and onto the apron, where Ronnie steered to the right and then taxied her plane to the northwest end of the runway. She pushed the throttle all the way up. The B-29 shuddered with an explosion of power and began to move. The Superfortress gained speed quickly, and when the airspeed indicator read 75 mph, she nudged the stick forward to raise the tail-wheel; at 90 mph, she pulled the stick back, lifting the plane smoothly from the ground and into the air.

Now clear of the ground, she pulled up the landing gear and then made a slow, climbing turn to the right, out over the ocean. She watched her instruments and listened to the smooth roar of the engine. When the altimeter indicated 1,500 feet, Ronnie glanced over her right shoulder and saw the black silhouette of a P-51 lifting off the runway and turning to follow her. She continued southward, climbing until she reached 5,000 feet and then she veered to the left to begin a slow orbit as the rest of SOAR came up to form on her wings.

Their destination – Kahili – was forty-five minutes away at the southeastern end of Bougainville. For many months it had been the most heavily defended enemy base south of Rabaul. In conjunction with its neighboring airfields, Kara and Ballale, Kahili presented a formidable bulwark against allied air and sea forces. In the last few weeks, however, allied concentrated assaults had come tantalizingly close to breaking the enemy's back in the region, and the name Kahili no longer inspired quite the degree of terror it once had. Still, flying to Bougainville remained a risky endeavor. Even though the threat from Japanese fighters had diminished, the antiaircraft guns at the Ballale airfield boasted legendary status and enemy shipping in Tonolei Harbor, which supplied the Bougainville bases, continued virtually unchecked, despite the allies' frequent – and deadly – antishipping raids.

The Airmen ascended until they were 15,000 feet above the B-29, but flying in time with the Superfortress.

SOAR flew in silence the entire distance to the target, which Jazz first glimpsed through a heavy cloud layer just a few minutes after sunrise. Their approach brought them over Bougainville at its southernmost end; the island extended some one-hundred fifty miles to the northwest, and to the left, Ronnie could see a line of distant green mountains – *the Crown Prince Range* – jutting up through the clouds like the heads of watchful giants. The B-29 veered slightly to the right to begin its orbit above Kahili.

Ronnie flipped on her gun switches, charged the guns, and squeezed the trigger on the control yoke to fire a few test rounds. With the sound of a jackhammer, six orange streams of tracers sliced through the air in front of the plane, three more came from each wing, and another volley came from the tail. All guns were working. Taking Ronnie's cue, the Airmen followed suit and fired their test rounds, the very act of which bolstered everyone's confidence.

At 200 mph indicated airspeed, the first ten-mile leg of their orbit took three minutes to complete. The entire flight then made a gentle left-hand turn in unison to swing back in the direction they had come. For the next hour and a half, SOAR flew this pattern high above Kahili, all of the pilots scanning the sky, the clouds, the sea, and the airfield below, their eyes never ceasing to roam, their necks growing sore from constantly turning their heads. During that time, none of them saw the first sign of enemy air activity, though a few flak bursts dotted the sky several miles to the northwest, at a lower altitude – probably in response to a raid on Kara by dive bombers based at Munda.

By 0910, it seemed certain that no enemy fighters intended to challenge them, at least not at that altitude. It appeared the Japanese decided that flying up to engage American fighters was not worth the risk just to attack a single bomber. The chances of getting any kills today were looking slimmer and slimmer.

At 0920, Ronnie began a 1,500-foot-per-minute descent eastward, beyond Kahili and out over Tonolei Harbor. The Airmen followed. Since they had been authorized to strafe ground targets, SOAR intended to make the most of the opportunity.

As they passed over a small flatland between two mountain ridges, the radio silence was shattered by an excited voice. *"SOAR, we've got bogeys at our ten o'clock, heading west."*

Jazz and the other Nickles exchanged glances. "Looks like it's time to jump, Nickles," Jazz shouted over the roar of the plane's engine.

"Why in the hell did I ever agree to jump out of a perfectly good plane?" Allen said, shaking his head.

"And over fifty times, no less," Jazz replied.

The men laughed.

In the cockpit, Ronnie stared out to the left and forward of the flight. She looked about the skies but saw nothing.

"This is Red Leader," Captain Davis' voice croaked through the B-29's speakers. "We got what looks like two yellow-green masses at our nine o'clock high, coming in fast. We're breaking' left and into 'em, SOAR."

Jazz tapped the side of his helmet to adjust his radio. He must have heard wrong. *Yellow-green masses?*

"Red Leader, repeat that last transmission," Ronnie said. "I did not copy the…"

"Red three and four, take the starboard mass!" Captain Davis' voice exploded from the radio, interrupting her. "It's starting to turn."

"Red three, roger!" DeBow said.

Ronnie snapped her head to her left and right. "*Red Team . . .*" Her transmission was interrupted by another excited radio call.

"Red three, this is Red Leader, you still got a visual on your mass?"

DeBow's voice came over the radio. *"I got it in sight."*

"Red two, this is Red Leader," Ben Davis said. *"Let's clean 'em up and engage. The port-side mass is at our eleven, going left to right."*

Custis' scream came through the radio. *"The mass! On me! Looks like a man's seed!"*

The mass looks like sperm? Jazz shook his head. *Flying sperm? What in the hell are we fighting?*

Again, Ronnie began her radio transmission to the flight, voice crackling with apprehension. *"SOAR, this is Blue Leader. Keep a good lookout and report anything you see."*

"Blue Leader!" Red Leader snapped. *"Stay off the air unless you see something. The flight's engaged by monsters!"*

"Sperm monsters," Jazz corrected, whispering. Allen, who sat to Jazz's left, shook his head.

The rebuke angered Ronnie, but she let it slide. Whatever was out there had Ben shook and he was losing his cool. She resolved to talk to him after they got back on the ground.

And then she saw it – the "sperm monster" – as it rocketed toward the B-29. The creature, nearly a yard longer than the Superfortress, had a massive, oval-shaped head that ended in a circular maw filled with hundreds of needle-like teeth; the rest of its body was a sinewy, cable-like tail that ended in a wicked hook of what appeared to be bone. The creature's pulsing flesh was sickly chartreuse in color and the slick film that covered it shone in the light of the moon.

"Bogey at nine o'clock low," Ronnie said, aiming the machinegun. She pulled the trigger.

A barrage of bullets stormed down upon the creature, shredding it into large hunks of yellow-green flesh.

A sound like heavy hail fell upon the top of the B-29.

"You've got spermoids all over you, Blue Leader!" De-Bow's voice shouted through the radio. *"Red three, assisting."*

"Spermoids?" Jazz said, unhooking the straps across his chest. "I'll be damned if I let the Airmen and Ronnie have all the fun!"

A smile spread across Allen's face. He unhooked his straps. "Come on, Nickles, we're going up top!"

Jazz slipped on his face mask. *"Negative, Red three,"* Jazz said into the microphone embedded in the mask. *"This is Black Leader; the Black Team will deal with the spermoids on the plane and then jump to ground. Any unoccupied Reds cover us on the way down."*

"Copy that, Black Leader," DeBow said.

"Welcome to the party, Black Leader," Captain Davis said. *"This is Red Leader. When you touch ground, let's try to locate the home base of these bogies."*

"Copy that, Red Leader," Jazz said. *"Blue Leader, open the door, please."*

"Copy that," Ronnie replied.

A hooked piece of bone burst through the steel-plate roof of the B-29 and then hooked into the ceiling. A moment later, a jagged piece of the plane's roof was snatched off and tossed into the clouds by a spermoid's tail.

The air turned cloudy and ice cold. A gale wind ripped through the plane.

"We've got explosive decompression," Ronnie said into her masks microphone. "I'm taking her down."

Jazz spun on his heels away from the door-sized hole in the ceiling and dashed toward the wall facing him. He slapped the holsters on both thighs and then drew his dual Colt M1911 pistols just as he leapt toward the wall. He bounded off the wall, his powerful legs driving him toward the ceiling. He torqued his hips, turning to face the jagged hole. He flew up through the hole, firing his pistols at the three creatures that surrounded him.

The spermoids released shrill cries into the cold night air as bullets chewed into their slimy flesh.

The plane descended. Jazz continued his ascent into the night. He looked down and saw his fellow Nickles following suit. Each of them leaping through the hole and firing into the spermoids as they rose, like Black angels, into the sky.

The spermoids fell, one-by-one, from the plane. Their lifeless husks tumbled toward the ground below.

Jazz pulled a cord that hung from the pack on his back, releasing its parachute. The other Nickles did the same.

The Nickles fell to earth. The chutes, designed for low altitude opening, so paratroopers could get to the ground quickly before ground forces could use them for target practice, slowed their fall just enough to prevent injury or death.

Jazz's feet hit the earth with a loud thud. He relaxed his body, going with the force of the fall and collapsed onto his side. He quickly rose to his knees, disengaged his parachute, stuffed it into his pack, tossed the pack over his back, leapt to his feet and then sprinted toward a line of trees, using the shadows to conceal him. He perused the area, his Companion allowing him to see in darkness as if it was the bright of day. His fellow Nickles had landed and were running toward him. He looked up. The B-29 was making a fast descent about a mile away. The P-51s had descended low enough to be seen. Orange lines streaked through the sky. The Airmen were firing at something in the distance.

The Nickles rallied around Jazz.

"The Airmen are firing at something in that direction," Jazz said pointing. "I'm betting it's whatever sent those spermoids at us."

"Must be one hell of a big ding-a-ling," a Nickle named Biggs said.

"Big enough to put a smile on your mama's face and a tear in your daddy's eye, Biggs," Jazz said.

The Nickles snickered, forcing back their laughter.

"Let's get over there and help our winged brothers kill that big giggle stick," Jazz said, drawing his pistols.

The Nickles drew their weapons – M2 carbines, mostly and one or two M1A1 "Tommy" machineguns – and then jogged behind Jazz through the dense forest.

Four

"This is Blue Leader," Jazz breathed a sigh of relief as Ronnie's voice came through his helmet's radio. *"I have landed safely. Headed three clicks northeast to assist Red Team who has a big bogey at their twelve."*

"Copy that, Blue Leader," Jazz whispered into his mask. "Black Team en route."

"Copy that," Ronnie replied.

"Red Leader, Black Team will rendezvous in five mikes," Jazz said. "We're about four clicks south of your location.

"Hurry, Black Team," Captain Davis' voice croaked through the radio. *"Please."*

Jazz sprinted through the forest with the rest of his team on his heels. Though the Nickles wore heavy boots and carried over 20 pounds in gear and weapons each, their movement was silent, almost supernatural.

Overhead, a massive flock of birds flew in the opposite direction of where the Nickles were headed. After a minute, Jazz saw why the birds were fleeing the forest.

The beast crossed the hills in a single stride. Though its shape suggested a towering mass of writhing squid arms, it had an outer shell composed of ossified dermal scutes covered by overlapping, keratinized epidermal scales, connected by flexible bands of skin. The creature had no head that could be made out, just more tentacles. Its short, thick trunk, like its hundreds of arms, was a viridian blue-green. It moved on a mass of longer, thicker cephalopod arms than the upper ones. From each of those "legs," grew a myriad of tentacles that skittered across the ground as if in search of something. From the top of its skull jutted a dozen thick cephalopod arms that looked, to Jazz, like a huge, twisting, crown of snakes.

"Medusa," Jazz whispered into his mask, giving the monster a name.

With a second stride, Medusa was halfway across an open field of high grass. The earth shook and cracked.

"Lord, Jesus!" One of the Nickles gasped.

"Let's keep it together, Nickles," Jazz said, peering over his shoulder. He inhaled deeply and relaxed as much as he could. His Companion did the rest, lowering his blood pressure, slowing his heartbeat and releasing endorphins and dopamine into his system.

The air shuddered with the simultaneous fire of dozens of 12.7mm machineguns from the Airmen's P-51s. The bombardment, thunderous at ground level, was reduced to insignificance when it hit Medusa. Streaks of fire became tiny blossoms against the articulated shell of the immense monster. Medusa snapped upward with several of its arms, plucking three planes out of the sky. The arms encircled the planes and then squeezed. The planes exploded. The monster dropped the wreckage to the earth and then continued its forward march.

The Airmen flew in circles around Medusa, firing into it as they evaded its flailing arms.

The creature stopped. Its trunk quaked furiously. A moment later, spermoids flew from the tips of the arms that comprised Medusa's "crown." The spermoids swarmed one plane. The rest were shot down by the Airmen.

"Attack the thing's legs," Jazz shouted over his shoulder as he ran toward the beast. "Get between them, so it can't grab you with its arms!"

The Nickles followed Jazz, weaving to avoid Medusa's legs, which the creature raised and then slammed downward rhythmically, beating jagged chasms into the earth. One of the Nickles, 2nd Lieutenant Warren Cornelius, tripped after leaping one of the chasms. He rolled to his feet, but it was too late; one of Medusa's legs came down on Lieutenant Cornelius' head. He screamed and then disappeared beneath the enormous limb.

The rest of the team ran for mirages of cover past the creature's legs, right beneath its trunk. It felt to Jazz as if they were now in the eye of the storm.

"This bastard killed Corny," Corporal McKinley Godfrey, the youngest Triple Nickle, cried. He aimed his Tommy gun at one of Medusa's legs and fired. The bullet ricocheted off the limb with a whistling noise. A moment later, Corporal Godfrey collapsed. A stream of smoke rose from a hole in his forehead.

"Damn it!" Jazz shouted. "Look, I know this is some otherworldly shit we're dealing with right now, but if we panic, we die. Rely on your training and your Companions!"

"Yes, sir!" the Nickles said in unison.

Jazz tapped one of the creature's legs with his palm. It was hard and cold, like steel. "This thing is gigantic and covered in armor," Jazz shouted above the roar of machinegun fire in the sky. "It's so powerful; it doesn't even realize we're here. But nature always provides a balance. An ant can lift thousands of times its body weight, but it is miniscule in size and weight; man is highly intelligent and the most adaptable mammal on earth, but is also the physically weakest in comparison. This monster *can* be killed!"

An explosion shook the ground. Jazz looked up. One of the P-51s has turned into a fireball. Jazz noticed something else – a puckered orifice in Medusa's trunk. He pointed at it.

"Look," he shouted.

"The monster's bunghole," 2nd Lieutenant Allen said. "Let's hope it don't take a dump on us."

"I'm not worried about what's gonna come out," Jazz said.

Allen raised an eyebrow. "We're not going in there . . ."

Jazz smiled.

"Damn it, Jazz!" Lieutenant Allen shouted.

"Follow me!" Jazz said, sprinting toward a limb. He leapt upward and then rebounded off a limb, which drove him higher. He continued to climb that way – bouncing from leg to leg.

The Nickles followed Jazz upward; all the way into Medusa's orifice.

Ronnie felt the heat of the exploding plane over her head. She bit back a cry of agony as hot casings from her carbine jumped down the collar of her fatigues as she fired round after round at the creature. She had discovered that the flexible folds of skin between the bony plates on Medusa's limbs were vulnerable to gunfire and she was doing enough damage to distract the creature and to keep it from moving while Jazz and the other Nickles entered the thing. Unfortunately, her mask's microphone was damaged when she landed, so she could not tell anyone what she was doing or her position. She knew Jazz would find a way, though. He had to, or they – and soon everyone else on the island – would be dead soon.

Ronnie fired her last round.

Silence fell on the field. Ronnie stared at the creature. Medusa stood there, seemingly looking down on its work. The debris from the fallen planes were encased in flames. The field was wounded by dozens of chasms from which clouds of dirt rose. Trees had been rendered splinters and the sky was blanketed with smoke.

Medusa stood triumphant, raising its arms to the night sky. And then it pointed an arm in her direction. Somehow, the eyeless beast had seen her.

Ronnie's heart beat a rapid song in her chest, but she knew there was no escaping this monster; nowhere she could hide from this gargantuan thing, so she seized the only weapon left to her: provocation. She raised her carbine and shook it at Medusa as she shouted "Yo' mama!"

Medusa raised two arms high.

Ronnie roared.

Medusa shook violently. Its arms fell slack. The creature's trunk swelled and then a flood of gray-green fluid and hunks of black flesh poured from the bottom of Medusa's trunk, filling the chasms and coating the grass in putrid muck. The creature stiffened and went still. Thankfully, held aloft by its stiffened limbs, which spread out acres across the field in all directions, it did not fall.

A moment later, Jazz crawled out of one of the chasms covered in ichor. The other Nickles followed. Jazz fell onto his haunches and then busied himself wiping muck from his hair and off his face.

Ronnie ran to him.

"Hey, Beautiful," Jazz said, forcing a smile. "Kiss me?"

"When you clean up, I will," Ronnie said. "You earned it."

Jazz's smile faded. "Save the kiss for later; we have a problem."

"Worse than *that* thing?" Ronnie said, pointing toward Medusa.

"Maybe," Jazz replied. "Inside Medusa's gut we found something attached. A tracking device, I think."

"What?" Ronnie collapsed onto her haunches beside Jazz. "That thing is owned by somebody?"

"Somebodies," Jazz said, correcting her. "The device had two flags engraved in it. One was the rising sun."

"The Japanese," Ronnie said. "Must be some biological weapon they planned to unleash on the allies, but it escaped their control. Good! Who's the other culprit, the Fuhrer?"

Jazz shook his head.

"Who, then?" Ronnie asked.

"Uncle Sam," Jazz said. "I think the Japanese and American governments were testing this thing and we were the test subjects.

"Damn," Ronnie said. "Dispensable Zigaboos."

"Yeah," Jazz said, rising to his feet. "I don't know if Major Woodbine is behind this; I don't know how far up the chain this goes, but I intend to find out."

Ronnie leapt to her feet. "You know I'm with you."

The Nickles rallied around Jazz.

"Let's inform the surviving Airmen and then come up with a plan," Jazz said. "We were supposed to die tonight. Let's show them it takes more than a souped-up squid to kill the Nickles and the Airmen! Hooah?

"Hooah!"

The End (for now)

POWER PLAY:
THE VERY TRUE AND ACCURATE STORY OF EUNICE CARTER, MOB-BUSTER
BY
DAY AL-MOHAMED

Assistant District Attorney Eunice Carter fought to hide her surprise. Her star witness had just lied. She risked a quick glance at the Special Prosecutor. It was Thomas Dewey's case after all, a career-maker he'd called it and he'd been willing to follow her suggestion, a colored woman's suggestion, to put the robot on the stand. Dewey's face was calm but she could see the faint blush of red at his collar. She could feel the sweat at the nape of her own neck.

A blue-painted robot whirred and clicked on the witness stand, completely unaware of the chaos it had just caused in the case. Eunice gave in to the urge to glance over at the defendant.

Luciano smirked, his lips pulled back crookedly. He leaned back in his chair, seemingly at complete ease. His hair was slicked back with some natural wave showing, as was the fashion, and his London drape suit was a dapper midnight blue. It may have been 1936 and the rest of the country was battling the Great Depression, but the mobster could still afford the finest.

For a brief moment, Eunice wondered if he really was "lucky." Her gaze went from Luciano to her boss. Dewey hated Luciano. Eunice could feel it; like a cold wave, the hate rolled off the man. And yet he stubbornly stood by her as his choice as Assistant District Attorney, even when the other eighteen white men had quit in protest. Now, she and Dewey were all that remained - "Two against the Underworld." Eunice took a deep breath and faced Judge McCook.

"Your Honor, I'd like to request a recess to address this change in testimony."

Judge McCook leaned forward and peered nearsightedly at Eunice.

"Listen missy, I wasn't keen on your new-fangled ideas. You wanted me to allow technological testimony and now-" He waved a hand in disgust.

"Yes, Your Honor." Eunice said quickly, hoping that the judge wouldn't be too upset as she cut him off before he began another luddite-inspired tirade. "However, a change, just as with a flesh-and-blood witness, would require the prosecution to address the deviation."

The judge looked at Dewey, clearly not willing to take her word on the matter.

"You agree?"

"Absolutely. I have the utmost faith in Assistant District Attorney Carter."

Eunice heard a snigger from someone in the court. Obviously other people didn't have quite as much faith in her. Whether it was because she was a woman or colored, it didn't matter. All that mattered was that she was different. And that meant "not good enough."

Eunice fought to keep her shoulders from slumping. Because of her recommendation, Luciano would likely get away. Luciano or one of his cronies had to have gotten to the witness; altered the robot's memory or programming. That was the only explanation for such a drastic change in testimony. She took a deep breath. Then another.

The judge affirmed Eunice's motion for recess with a resigned sigh and newspapermen dashed from the room to file their latest updates on the case. Judge McCook was a stickler for no live wireless telegraphy, or photography, or in fact, any diesel-driven or gear-powered technology in his courtroom. The robot had been a ground-breaking exception. And now it had likely sunk their case. No doubt the photo phone lines would be hot with the most recent testimony. Unfortunately, the reporters were the only ones who seemed excited by the break.

Dewey himself pulled out his baudot-phone and powered it up. It chimed, indicating it was ready.

"Well?"

Eunice met Dewey's gaze, "We're losing them. I lost them," she corrected. "The jurors don't even try to pretend anymore – "

"Yeah. "Lucky" Luciano, Public Enemy Number One; trial of the century; no living witnesses; and we're going down in proverbial flames."

Dewey's grand jury had spent weeks hearing testimony. But the hours and hours of minutiae, endless interviews of minor enforcers and whores, forensic details, statistics, probabilities, had not convinced them of his guilt. What was worse, they didn't even care about a verdict anymore, they just wanted back to their homes and their families.

"I'm sorry."

"Sorry doesn't fix it." Dewey snapped. He leaned his elbows on the smooth wooden table and rubbed his eyes. The baudot-phone chimed again. Dewey pulled it out of his pocket and opened it, reading the tiny raised brass pins, translating them instantly in his head.

"Extension denied." Eunice said. Her words came out as a statement rather than a question.

Dewey flicked a switch on the side of the device, dropping the pins and erasing the message; and blew out an exasperated breath. He began rewinding the power coil.

Eunice continued, "We were lucky McCook let us call the automaton as a witness. Perhaps we could call the maid?"

"She's gone. Likely swimming in the river in concrete overshoes."

Eunice blanched. "The other prostitutes?"

"Already recanted their testimony. As far as they're concerned, there is no Bonding Combination racket. They weren't being forced into prostitution, and there's no such thing as the Cosa Nostra."

Eunice sat fighting back tears.

"Now Mrs. Carter," Dewey said, handing her his handkerchief, "This is your area of expertise." Though his voice was soft and words innocuous, Dewey's anger was clearly visible as he snapped shut the baudot-phone's brass clamshell body. "Tell me how Luciano could have done this."

Eunice shook her head, her black hair tightly coiffed under her hat. She was aware of how much was at stake, not only for Dewey, but for her as well.

"I don't know."

Automatons weren't supposed to lie. Automatons weren't supposed to recant their testimony. Someone had to have gotten into its programming. But the automaton had been under tight police custody for the past three weeks.

"Then perhaps we'd best find out. Come on." Dewey said. He stood abruptly, knocking his chair back into the railing that separated the public from the Prosecution - those without power, from those who did; those who merely observed Justice from those who meted it out. Eunice had been so proud the day she had been able to step from one side of the rail to the other, an attorney, and a colored woman. She couldn't fail.

"You were trained as a Telemechanical Specialist?" Dewey asked as he stalked through the courthouse's dim hallway. Although not a large man, he strode as if he owned the building, a living legend with a snappy comment, a crisp grey suit, and a smile that never wavered.

He already knew the answer, but Eunice responded anyway.

"Harlem Gearworks Court." Her words were slightly breathy as she struggled to keep up him; hat askew, too tight shoes, and fighting for balance on the freshly waxed floor. But the discomfort was nothing compared to the stares from the other attorneys, half envy, and half hate.

Dewey slowed. "Don't let them get to you." he said, his voice only audible to her.

Eunice opened her mouth but was quickly cut off.

"You're the best for the job. I only work with the best. So, don't waste my time on this. Or them."

Eunice shook her doubts. Focus on the case. "What is the plan?"

Dewey flashed his winning smile, teeth perfect.

"Still have your kit?" Dewey wove through the crowd effortlessly, his fingers tapping out messages on the baudot-phone at a speed one of Bell's telegraphers would have been proud of – the office, his wife, notes on two other cases, and a nasty message to his chief agent about some overdue information. The baudot-phone chimed almost continually with incoming and outgoing messages and ticked and whirred as the gearworks spun to keep up. The stream of information didn't slow Dewey in the least as the crowd instinctively parted for the predator in their midst.

Eunice swallowed nervously. "I do." She had hoped that this new position would be a chance to move on to a new career, but it looked like her old electrengineering skills wouldn't let her go.

"Good. If someone has interfered with the automaton, I'm going to need someone I trust with the skills to understand what has happened." Dewey's expression turned both shark-like and grim with unspoken promise.

It was less than five minutes later when they arrived at the small room that operated as a private interrogation room. Small, grey with concrete walls and institution-tile floor, it looked little different from an average prison cell but for the industrial metal table at its center and the bright steel automaton, a Personal Companion 1934, designation female, seated on the far side. In this case, its name was Flo, "Cokey Flo."

Eunice watched with some skepticism as Dewey, after taking a moment to make sure he was positioned so the room's photo transceivers caught his "best" side, slammed his briefcase and baudot-phone onto the table with a loud bang.

"Explain yourself." His tone was firm and authoritative.

Eunice's expression remained serious but the corners of her eyes crinkled for a moment. Dewey, it *is* an automaton; theatrics aren't likely to make any impression.

Dewey's baudot-phone chimed, as if in agreement with Eunice's silent thoughts.

The metal irises in the automaton's eyes shuttered but it didn't move. Dewey hadn't asked "Flo" a direct question.

Eunice pulled out small lead wires and opening up the automaton's shell, clipped them to the main punch-wheel. She pushed a couple of buttons and reviewed the oscillation pins and transistor panels, taking care to pause over the electromechanical teleprinters. This was just a preliminary scan; she could reattach the leads for a deeper search once the questioning began.

"Flo, why did you lie?"

"I do not understand." The automaton responded placidly.

Eunice shook her head. No signs of reprogramming. The pins were clean and the teleprinters didn't seem to have been tampered with. Her gaze flickered between the dials and meters on her scanner, and the internal moving mechanisms inside Flo.

"What you said today, in response to my questions – it was untrue." Dewey fumed.

Eunice kept her attention on the robot. Every minute that went by was another that gave Luciano time to further "erase" what had happened. She had seen too many live witnesses recant or go missing.

Dewey's baudot-phone chimed; he ignored it.

"I repeated the events as matched my recollection of the events." The robot responded.

Eunice added more wires, connecting them to a Beat Frequency Oscillator. The device was small and sleek, more electronic than mechanical. With its sensitive filters and detectors, if there was any suspicious programming, the BFO would identify it, demodulate it, and then provide a detailed output using a perforator. It was Eunice's favorite tool.

She frowned as the punched tape began to whirr from her machine. Eunice turned various dials and knobs. Everything seemed normal, no unusual electro-encephalitic activity.

"You recorded a different story three weeks ago." Dewey snapped open the briefcase, pulling out the transcripts, "Mr. Luciano was present at the event. Mr. Luciano stated that he would organize cathouses just like the A&P supermarket chain."

"I do not recollect those statements." Flo said.

Dewey glanced at Eunice, his confident look slipping. The baudot-phone chimed twice in quick succession.

Even from across the table Eunice could see it already needed the internal power coil rewound.

"Slippage." Dewey muttered. He slammed the "Off" button and the clicks and whirrs from the internal mechanisms ceased immediately. The baudot-phone chimed one last time in protest. "Third time this month."

Eunice shook her head. It didn't matter how frustrated Dewey got, there was still nothing, no evidence of tampering.

"Who has accessed your programming?" Dewey bit out.

"My programming has not been accessed."

Dewey leaned closer, his body bristling with intimidation, "Who accessed your punch-memory?"

Flo didn't move; the automaton's copper had a faint greenish tinge, likely from neglect while in federal custody, "My punch-memory has not been accessed."

Dewey threw the transcript pages at Flo. They fluttered around the room like half-dead moths.

"Nothing," Eunice said. And as dramatic as Dewey's theatrics were, they didn't exactly make her job any easier. Losing his temper wouldn't help. Eunice raised an eyebrow and nodded towards the photo transceivers.

Dewey smoothed back his hair and with an immaculate smile for the photo transceivers (and anyone else who might be watching), sat down in the other chair.

"Can we use the prior testimony? The transcript?"

Eunice's smile was tight, "We cannot use written testimony if the witness is available and competent to testify in person."

Dewey leaned back in the chair, disgust clear on his face. He shuffled the pages on the tabletop, "And Flo here seems to be just fine."

Eunice's grip tightened on the BFO, "It's my fault. Demanding the automaton testify."

Leaning forward, Dewey tapped the table. "I took a chance on you, Mrs. Carter. Don't prove me wrong. Find the answer."

Eunice closed her eyes. She couldn't pull answers out of the air. Opening them again, she repeated Dewey's question to the automaton, "Your programming has not been accessed?"

"No."

Eunice paused as an idea came to her. She gestured to Dewey. "Ask that again."

Dewey's body tensed, "Your punch-memory has not been accessed?"

"No."

Eunice was suddenly a small flurry of activity as she pushed buttons and gazed into Flo's whirring shell body. Her expression changed through a variety of emotions before finishing at inscrutable. Maybe, just maybe . . . one more time. She made a "continue" motion towards Dewey.

Dewey sat back and lifted his hands in an *it's all yours* gesture.

Eunice looked up from the interior of the automaton and rephrased his question, "Has your *system* been accessed?"

"No."

Eunice set down the scanning equipment. She stood and stepped around to the table by Dewey, "Has your power coil been rewound?"

"No." Once again, the automaton offered its placid response.

"When was your power coil last accessed?" Eunice's voice was soft, almost melodic. Dewey opened his mouth but she raised a hand, stopping him.

"My power coil has not been accessed," responded the automaton.

Eunice glanced quickly at the room's camera. The answers would be recorded. "When was your last coil diagnostic?"

"I have not had a coil diagnostic."

Eunice nodded towards Dewey's silent baudot-phone where it lay on the table.

Understanding, Dewey's shark-like expression returned.

Eunice felt her own smile. The PC1934s – Flo would have needed its coil rewound regularly, at least weekly to maintain power. No activity, tasks, memory, or movement could take place without it. The automaton should have responded with a date within the last week. Whoever had removed the memory of Luciano's activities had also removed every other memory from Flo.

Picking up his baudot-phone, Dewey turned it on and waited as it warmed up and its regular ticking began.

Just to be sure, Eunice asked the question again, "When was your coil last wound?

"My coil has not been wound."

Dewey gazed down at his baudot-phone and watched the coil tighten as he patiently rewound it, "Thank you, Mrs. Carter."

Eunice looked smug, "Slippage." With proof that Flo had been tampered with they could now use the previous testimony. Luciano was going to jail.

The baudot-phone signaled its readiness to transmit the news with a cheery chime.

THE GIRL WITH THE IRON HEART

BY

S.A. COSBY

This isn't my world.

I wasn't born here. My DNA is not on file in the Central Data Bank. My fingerprints are not recorded in the City Master File. I'm a stranger in a much stranger land.

I was pulled into this world three years ago. I suppose it was three years. I could have been traveling through the rift for a hundred years even though it felt like five minutes. Relativity and all that jazz. Once I had been a soldier assigned to protect some scientists for the US of A at a lab in the middle of the desert near Area 51. No one ever looked for the lab because they were too busy looking for Area 51.

The scientists had been working on a complex machine that they spoke about in hushed tones. I never really knew what it was supposed to do. What it did was open a hole in the universe and create a portal to alternate dimensions. The whole facility was sucked into a swirling whirlpool light and fury and deposited in the desert in the same spot where the lab had been in our world. The building landed in a pile of rubble and everyone inside was dead except yours truly. The trip didn't kill them but the landing did a number on them. I survived by sheer luck. Whether it was good or bad depends on your point of view but landing in a pile of hazmat suits saved my life. The world I entered as I escaped the wreckage of the lab was one different from the one I had left but tantalizingly familiar.

America was now called the North American Federation with a fully annexed Mexico as a member. World War Two was still being fought, in a fashion, forty years after it started. The Germans and the Japanese had invaded Canada from the west through Alaska and taken over the country. The Italians over threw Mussolini but the Axis powers never gave up in Europe. They kept everything east of Poland up to Russia while France brokered a non-aggression pact. England, Sweden and Norway kept up the good fight but France and Spain played the neutrality card. Without support from the motherland, the British Colonies fell and the land returned to the native Africans, who quickly discovered the wealth of natural minerals that existed right under their feet. The war ebbed and flowed as the Axis Alliance West and the Axis Alliance East waxed and waned in their war efforts.

This world had an Africa that was a superpower under one national government, a Jewish homeland in Italy instead of Israel and a Kaiser in what I would have called Canada. It was enough to make a Tea Party member eat his red, white and blue pajamas. I had landed in the midst of one the ebbs where tensions between the Federation and the Alliance were at an all-time low. This was like saying the temperature had dropped from Hell to the surface of a star.

One of the major differences I first noticed was that nuclear energy was verboten here. Apparently, there had been a catastrophic accident in the Big Empty with atomic power leaving much of the Southwest a wasteland. Where our lab landed was just outside the massive Borderwall, an enormously hideous structure that stretched from the tip of Idaho to the bottom Arizona. It was two hundred feet tall and covered with gun ports and barbed wire. It looked like the worst fence around the worst junkyard in the world.

Electromagnetism was the magic that drove this place. Diesel was its blood and iron and steel was its skin. Hovercars bounced off the earth with glowing magnetron engines lighting up the night sky as they flew among the skyscrapers. Diesel powered twin turbine hoverbikes zipped through alleyways and up and down boulevards past luminescent billboards. I had walked out of the desert and entered one of the soot covered cities that crackled with eldritch lights at night and shimmered with an art deco aesthetic filtered through a hallucinogenic prism during the day.

I found out a few other things pretty quickly. One, I was an anomaly. I didn't have a government ID number. Nor did I have a DNA profile that was mandatory for all citizens of the Federation. Nor were my fingerprints on file anywhere. That was also mandatory. As far as the government was concerned, I was a ghost. No, not even a ghost because a ghost had once been alive. I was nothing, a nowhere man from somewhere no one believed existed. Little by little I learned how to navigate these dark streets. I had been born in Compton and trained by Special Forces. I had a specific set of skills that when coupled with my anonymity gave me a certain cache with some segments of this brave new world. I could go places that most citizens couldn't without worrying about their DNA being picked up by the cops or worse the Sentries. Slowly but surely, I began to eke out a living. Back home I would have been called a mercenary or a hired gun. Here in the city of New Sanctuary I was an operator.

All things being equal I think I adjusted to my new circumstances fairly smoothly. I didn't waste time asking "how "or "why" I had ended up here. I just focused on living, eating, drinking and occasionally sharing the company of a lady. Occasionally I had nightmares that unnerved me. The nightmares were wretched, filth covered things that climbed out the pit of my subconscious and grabbed hold of my soul with a madman's grip. I saw . . . things in those nightmares. Things I wanted to forget all together or remember completely.

I would see flashes of light and then the faces of the scientists melting or my mother growing old and crumbling into dust waiting for me on the porch of our house. Other things so horrible that I'd rather not discuss right now thank you very much. There were times I was tempted to go to a speakeasy to imbibe something stronger than alcohol in hopes of quieting my dreams. But I was afraid of getting hooked on Zanaire. I didn't want my disturbing dreams to become waking nightmares. So, I stuck with gin and whiskey. Places like Slow Jim's, The Tornado and The Steel Jack were my therapy clinics.

I had just entered the Alchemy Club and ordered my first drink of the evening when I got a line on a possible job. It was a rainy Friday night and I was in a mood to see how tough my liver was. I typed "gin and tonic/double" on the touch screen with one hand while I tapped a short cigar out of the pack with the other. I was just about to insert my debit square into the bartenders pay slot when the droid slid down the magnetic rail. His chrome torso floated above and greeted me. He wore a brown suede vest over a shimmering chrome chest and white suede gloves that covered his metal hands. His face was a smooth metallic mask with narrow slits that simulated a mouth, eyes and a nose.

"Hey Traveler, some military types were in here earlier looking for you," the droid said. His voice sounded like an asthmatic speaking through a harmonica. His technical designation was a Hospitality and Libations Android. HALA. Most people bastardized the acronym and added a gender. Hollowmen were what they were commonly called. I dug my lighter out of my pocket and lit a shorty cigar.

"They say what they want? "The droid turned its chrome plated head from side to side.

"Negative. They instructed me to tell you they were looking for you," he said in his quiet monotone.

"How'd they know I'd be coming in here?" I asked.

"Where else would you be on a Friday night, Traveler? According to our records you have come into the Alchemy Club every Friday night for the past year and a half. Probability dictates —"

I held up my hand and the droid stopped talking. He was right. Where else indeed. A man with no family, no real friends. A bar is exactly where I would be. Only where I come from the bartenders didn't have logic circuits.

Military types looking for me could only mean one thing. They needed a job done. The kind of job only a man who didn't exist on paper or in the central data banks could do. The man some people called Johnny Traveler. The Borderwall patrols who found me among the ruins of the lab started calling me that before I escaped. It was just as good a name as any. My mind was a dichotomous paradox. I could remember what my mother looked like but couldn't recall my given name. Maybe my head got scrambled coming through the portal. Or maybe I was laying somewhere in a hospital in a coma. That thought crossed my mind more than once. As we talked the droid made my gin and tonic and slid it to me across the lacquered bar top.

I finished my drink and put my debit square in the pay slot on the bar.

"Thank you, Mr. Traveler, for you purchases of . . ." The droid paused for a second. "25 dolseos of alcohol and the . . ." Another pause." Five dolseo tip." The hollowmen announce your tip or lack thereof out loud. I didn't mind but some of the more frugal patrons of the bar hated it. They would get irate and belligerent. Then the hollowmen would escort them out forcefully without that quiet monotone ever changing its pitch.

"Don't mention it," I said. I took a drag off the shorty and moved to a table near the back of the bar and sat in a chair against the wall. The bar wasn't full and the denizens that were there were hidden behind a fog of cigar and cigarette smoke. I pulled my fedora down over my eyes and waited. Every now and then I patted the handles of my Tesla eight charge plasma pistols. Here Tesla won the feud with Edison. He lived to the ripe old age of 109 and was still making discoveries and inventions right up to the day he checked out.

Plasma pistols weren't cheap and mostly illegal but in my new world just like in my old one you could find anything for the right price. Those military types would be back in here sooner or later. I figured whatever they wanted me for it would be dangerous and totally illegal but I needed the money. The dollar and the peso had been combined like their parent countries and I went through them like a bullet through butter. I drank too much, I smoked too much, and I dealt with women of ill repute or more accurately no repute. Anything to distract my mind from the Alice in Wonderland on acid story my life had become. So, I sat and I listened to the house band sing songs that lamented lost love and lost life as the customers drank themselves into a mental oblivion to take their minds off the threat of annihilation. Everyone in the bar had their ears pricked waiting for the wail of an air raid siren while they laughed and talked and pretended they didn't have a care in the world.

A few hours dragged by like a snail crawling through glue and I was just about to hang it up for the night and return to my little dingy apartment above another even seedier club when a tall, ramrod straight military guy walked up to my table dressed in civilian clothes trying desperately to not look like a military guy in civilian clothes. He had a close-cropped graying buzz cut and pale watery blue eyes. His face had a ruddy countenance and I pegged him for Air Corps. Maybe a gyropilot or more likely a yeoman on a flying fortress. He had on a black turtleneck and a ratty old blue blazer that would have looked better on a dead man.

"You Traveler?" he asked. His voice was deep and gravelly. It sounded like he gargled with battery acid. I pushed my hat out of my eyes and gazed up at the man.

"Naw, I'm the Easter Bunny," I said. The military type frowned. He put his hands on the table, leaned forward and growled.

"Either you are or you aren't, but don't get smart with me ya schwarz," he said as spittle flew from his lips. In this world the German word for black had taken the place of the n-word as an insult for people of color. I sipped my drink and leveled my eyes at the military man.

"Trust me buddy, I don't think there is any possible way I could get smart with you," I said as I stared at him. A mottled red flush began to spread across the military type's face. He made his hands into fists and I put my hand around the heavy glass ashtray on the table.

"Come now Lt. Jarrell, no need to be rude to our associate," an urbane voice said from my right. I glanced over my shoulder and saw Mr. Green standing there holding a martini glass. Green was a spook with the FIS, Federation Intelligence Service. They ran spy networks, completed black box missions and organized wet works here and abroad. They were a Frankenstein made up of the worst parts of the CIA, FBI and the NSA with some psychopaths and brainwashed assassins thrown in for good measure. Green was a slight man with a sharp aquiline nose and a thick shock of black hair that he combed straight back and slicked down with some god-awful pomade. He wore a tight black suit with a black and white floral print tie and black shirt. He was thin but wiry and moved with the grace of a dancer that had been trained by ninjas. He had an engaging smile but to me it was the grin of a shark. I had worked for and with Green before and I had no doubt he was the deadliest man I had ever had the misfortune to meet. I had once seen him kill three Alliance agents with a spoon. Yes, a spoon.

He sat down at my table and motioned for Lt. Jarrell to do the same. He sipped his drink then motioned toward my temple.

"As evidenced by your exchange with Lt. Jarrell I see your ability to irritate the hell out of people has not lessened since the last time I saw you," he said. I shrugged.

"It's a gift. What can I say?" I said. Green smiled again.

"The shiner or your attitude?" he said and I laughed.

"This is the guy you think can help us? A schwarz with a smart mouth?" Lt. Jarrell asked.

"Say "schwarz" one more time and I'm going to put my foot so far up your ass when you burp, you'll be spitting up shoe polish," I said not looking at Jarrell. He started to get up but Green reached across the table quick as a hiccup and grabbed his wrist. He squeezed a spot near Jarrell's thumb and the larger man went limp.

"Sorry about that. My superiors insisted I bring him along. Some interdepartmental posturing from the Air Corps since it was their incompetence that has necessitated our government's need for you services," Green said as he took another sip from his drink.

"I get it. He's a racist's jerk who is pissed off because his boys messed up," I said. Gray shook his head and took another sip.

"I have made arrangements with the owners of the establishment for use of a room in the back so that we may discuss how we will compensate you. Follow me," he said as he rose from the table. I jerked my thumb toward Jarrell.

"What about him?" I asked. Green smirked.

"I'll wake him up on my way out," he said as he smiled.

Green and I entered a cool well-lit room behind the bar. Full cases of liquor and boxes of napkins lined the walls. A heavy, roughhewn wooden table held court in the middle of the room. I sat at one end and he sat at the other. Green still had his martini and he took a sip as he removed a telescreen from his jacket. Telescreens were what cell phones would be if they had appeared a hundred years earlier. Green's was a small metal coated rectangle about the size of a deck of cards. He opened it like an old flip phone and I saw a smooth clear glass in the center. Green touched the glass and suddenly a holographic image began to float above the table. It appeared to be some sort of file floating in midair. The letters floating above the file spelled. FEATHERTOP. A picture of a fairly attractive woman appeared next to the floating file. Green touched the screen again and a disembodied voice began to speak.

"FEATHERTOP: Protocol Seven Nine Seven Alpha Delta Sigma. Operation FEATHERTOP is a program jointly authorized by the FIS and the Federation Air Corps. President Galen White has authorized this program in accordance with his powers under the War Act of 1947. All information contained in this file is level XPD." I raised my hand. Green nodded.

"XPD?" I asked.

"Expedited Demise," he said plainly.

"Oh well that's good to know," I said under my breath. The voice continued.

"The FEATHERTOP initiative was the first program to succeed in creating a viable cybernetic agent. This agent, code name "Lily," has a fully functioning artificial intelligence which allows her to be self-aware, to rapidly assess numerous variables in her immediate environment and create an organic personality outside of the confines of her mission protocols. These attributes were intended to give the agent more flexible operating parameters during the course of assigned missions." I held my hand up again.

"This thing is saying 'supposed to'. What actually happened?"

Green put down his drink and touched the telescreen. The hologram disappeared. He put the telescreen back in his pocket.

"What happened was that this thing totally ignored its operating protocols, refused to go on missions and escaped Air Corps custody on its way to being destroyed," Green said.

"So, she kicked some Air Corpsman ass. Nice. If I meet her, I'll shake her hand," I said as I pulled out another shorty cigar. The Air Corps were the elite members of the Air Force for the Federation. These were the guys that carried out assaults on flying fortresses with only TM-25 machine guns and a jet pack. They were also to a man monumental assholes with a Viking like fascination about dying with honor.

"She didn't kick their asses. *It* killed them. A week ago. Four Air Corpsmen and one Special Ops agent," Green said. For the first time I heard the faintest hint of anger in his voice. Couldn't have been about the Aircorpsmen; he had as much disdain for them as I did. Maybe the Special Ops agent was a friend? Was Green violating the cardinal rule of espionage? Was he taking this mission personal?

"So, if this thing single handedly killed four highly trained operatives, how the hell am I supposed to help you?" I said. Green leaned forward.

"We just need you to find it," Green said. I took a puff off my shorty.

"I don't know Green. I don't need some robot showing me what my insides look like," I said.

"It is a cyber Traveler, not a robot. It's a biological entity with a metallic endoskeleton and advanced diagnostic and strategic software uploaded into an artificial intelligence that achieved self-awareness in a body powered by an incredibly dense atomic battery encased in lead and iron in the center of her chest," Green said. He tapped the table with his index finger every three syllables for emphasis. I knocked some ash off my shorty.

"Atomic power is illegal in the Federation isn't it Green?" I asked. The government man smiled and his thin lips parted showing his babyish teeth. He interlaced his fingers and placed his hands on the table.

"Hence our need for your particular skill set. We will provide you with a tracking device. Place it on the body and we will do the rest. For this you will be rewarded handsomely," he said softly. I rubbed my chin.

"I'm thinking about it, Green. But this is way outside my usual wheelhouse. Whatever you were thinking of paying me would have to be tripled just for me to consider it. This thing sounds like the Terminator," I said. Green raised a quizzical eyebrow.

"Never mind. It's a movie where I'm from. But seriously I'm going to need more than our regular going rate to chase this thing down," I said, taking another puff on my cigar.

"What if I told you we were prepared to offer you something more valuable that money?" Green said.

"Oh, you planning on paying me in gold doubloons?" I said. I stared at Green's martini glass. I was suddenly dying for another drink. Or ten. This deal sounded bad. It felt bad. I didn't have any idea what Green was planning on offering me but I was beginning to doubt it would be enough for me to take this job.

"No, not gold, Traveler. What if I told you our scientists had been studying the phenomena that brought you here? That they think they can replicate it. That's what we are prepared to offer you, Traveler. A ticket home," he said.

Green was good. He feinted with the seriousness of the job then sucker punched me with the thing he knew I wanted more than money. For a second it threw me off balance. I had no pithy rejoinder, no smart-ass comment. Going home. I had long ago put the thought out of my mind. A man could go crazy pining for home when home was on the other side of a wormhole. Green could read the shock on my faces like a school kid going over his first primer.

"They just need the battery Traveler," Green said finally.

"Nice story Green. Next, you'll tell me Santa Claus has a present just for me in his sack of toys," I said but Green saw the hope in my eyes.

"This isn't a fairy tale. Find the cyborg, Traveler and we will try to send you home," he said.

"And then you can chop it up and hide your little mistake from the Federated Congress since using atomic energy is in direct violation with the International Nuclear Treaty the Federation signed with the Allies, right? Kinda killing two birds with one stone huh?" I said.

Green didn't respond. He reached in his jacket again. I had the not so irrational thought he was going to pull out a weapon and grease me right then and there. My hands moved toward my plasma pistols. But he didn't have a weapon. He pulled out a small black box and a cheap plastic telescreen. A throwaway.

"You proposing to me, Green? Why this is all so sudden." I placed my hand over my heart. Green slid the box and the throwaway toward me.

"It's the override control for its operating systems. It looks like a ring with a red stone. However, when you get close to it the stone will change to orange. It's like a mini Geiger counter. The closer you are the more intense the orange color. If you are less than five feet away it will glow. Touch the cyborg anywhere it has exposed skin and its operating systems and AI will reboot. At that time, it will be susceptible to your suggestions. Tell it to follow you. Touch the engraved eagle on the side of the ring and that will engage a tracking device. We will send a team of Air Corpsmen to retrieve it. The throwaway has a file with pictures and a detailed description of its appearance. Commit the details to memory then toss it."

He rose from the table. I stared at the box. If Green was telling the truth that box was my first step toward going home. Back to a world where I wasn't thought of as a freak or a mental case. Where people knew what the Terminator was. Where the West Coast wasn't a radiation filled wasteland. Where I had a name. I picked up the box. Green started to leave.

"Green," I said. He stopped and turned around.

"Any idea where I should start looking for this thing?" I asked.

"Start at the speakeasies. Before it escaped it had become fascinated with being a showgirl. We would like you to start looking for it immediately," Green said in a business-like tone, like we were talking about a crate of bananas that had been shipped to the wrong grocer. A showgirl? Who designed this thing? Josephine Baker?

"Yeah sure. Getting right on it, boss," I said in an exaggerated rural accent then instantly regretted it. He had no context to understand the joke. Slavery hadn't taken hold in this world the way it had back home. Before their Civil War, an incredibly virulent boll weevil infestation destroyed 85 percent of the cotton fields in the South. Slaves were released or escaped as plantation after plantation fell into oblivion. By the time hemp was introduced as a replacement for cotton the country had moved past enslaving its citizens. The history books I borrowed from the library still painted a pretty bleak picture of life for people of color. But I got the impression it could have been much worse for a longer period of time if not for Mr. Boll Weevil.

"Yes . . . well, I will be in touch. Goodnight, Traveler," Green said.

He left the room. I put the box and the throwaway in the pocket of my trench coat and left the room as well. I watched as Gray walked past Lt. Jarrell and flicked him on the ear. Jarrell awoke with a start and jumped up so fast he fell out of his chair. I stifled a laugh and motioned toward the hollowman.

"A drink before the war my good man," I said as I typed my order on the touch screen. The droid floated toward the liquor bottles on the shelf behind the bar. An inebriated patron who was barely able to stand poked me in the shoulder. I turned and faced the man. By the look of the broken veins in his pale nose he was an experienced drunk.

"There ain't no before the war. The war ain't got no beginning and it won't have no god-damn end," he said. His voice slurred like he was swallowing a mouthful of marbles.

"Gee, thanks for the newsflash Nietzsche," I said. That seemed to confuse him and he wandered back into the smoky haze of the club. I knew he was right of course. Wars don't end or begin. They just have brief intermissions.

I left the Alchemy with Green's presents and headed for my car. I had some misgivings about this whole job. I wondered why they didn't just build the damn thing with an internal tracker but who was I to question the intelligence of the Federation? As I walked into the cool air, I craned my neck upward and saw a few hovercars zipping by like hawks among the arc sodium lights that illuminated the night sky. One hoverbike flew by well under the minimum altitude that the government said they had to maintain. The person on the bike was wearing a bulbous chrome helmet and a billowing black leather jacket. If the hovercars were eagles then the hoverbikes were hornets zipping through the steel and iron forest of the city. Hovercars were expensive and usually only the wealthiest or the most corrupt citizens could lay claim to one. I was neither wealthy nor corrupt enough so I drove a car. A burgundy Tucker. Its cycloptic headlight stared at me like an angry lover inquiring about my whereabouts. I climbed in and fired up my old jalopy and eased into the heavy Friday night traffic.

I thought about what Green had said. About sending me home. Part of me wanted to dismiss it out of hand. Another part of me, the part that had seen this world and the wonders it held had a small glimmer of hope. But hope is a dangerous thing. It can blind you. Lead you astray. Hope could get you killed. I also thought about what Green had said about this thing and how it wanted to be a showgirl. Speakeasies were the easiest place for an aspiring dancer to get a job. They were also the most dangerous places in the city of New Sanctuary. In my line of work, you couldn't help but wander into places like that from time to time. I know what you're thinking. Why are there speakeasies if alcohol is legal here? Well speakeasies didn't sell alcohol. They sold Zanaire. What is Zanaire you ask?

It was the magic potion that made all your dreams come true.

I drove out to an abandoned cathedral near the industrial area of New Sanctuary. I passed the Verona Iron Works then turned left at the Geuaxton Ammunition Plant. Another left turn and I saw Our Lady of Perpetual Peace looming ahead of me. Composed of gray and charcoal colored brick, it towered over the factories that surrounded it like a feudal lord standing over his serfs. I pulled into a parking lot across from the cathedral and trotted across the street. The rain had stopped but the stench of oil and petroleum and gun powder filled the air. Off to the west I could see the spotlights from the Air Corps base near the Great Lake that bordered this fair city. Across the lake the Axis Alliance waited like a junkyard dog ready for the slightest provocation to send their flying fortresses across the border. I tried not to think of what would happen if this job went ten toes up.

There were a few cars parked up and down the street. One shiny black hovercraft with red velvet seats and gold trim sat on its landing gear near the cathedral. That was the only hint about the true nature of this former house of God. I walked up the granite steps and entered the building. The light from a few weak street lamps shone through the cracked stain glass windows and cast weird shadows across the overturned pews. I went to the decrepit confessional and opened the door. The small bench had been stripped of its padding long ago.

I put my hand under the bench and pressed a small metal button. The screen between my confessional booth and the other one slid aside. I saw the silhouette of a man sitting there wearing a priest's stole. He was definitely not a priest.

"The harvest is plentiful," he said.

"But the workers are few," I said. The man nodded and pushed a button under his seat. My bench began to descend at a leisurely pace into a hidden elevator shaft. When I reached the bottom, I stepped out onto a wooden platform. On the other side of the platform was a stone covered wall with a heavy iron door in the center. I walked up to the door. A small hatch slid open and a pair of baleful eyes stared at me.

"To truly enjoy the harvest," he said.

"You must have labored in the fields," I said. The eyes disappeared and I heard the clang and grind of the door locks being opened. I stepped through the door and walked past the guard into the den of iniquity.

On the street this particular speakeasy was called the Church but nothing holy was taking place here. I'm no prude by any means but The Church was on another level. It was an abattoir of inhibitions. Anything and everything could be found within these worn wooden walls. The Church had been a bomb shelter built by the Catholic Church when World War 2 reached the Canadian shores. Twenty-foot ceilings striated by heavy teak beams soared above my head. Two rows of leather-bound booths ran down both walls to my left and my right. The row of booths on the left was interrupted by a bar with a stolen hollowman and a large stage. A brass band was chugging away on stage at a frenetic pace. Wide octagon shaped tables filled the space between the rows. Someone had pushed a few of the tables to the right to give the patrons room to dance. And dance they did. Bodies gyrated and bucked like wild stallions and mares. The blackjack table and the craps table in the back were surrounded by men and women throwing money around like confetti on New Year's Eve. I made my way to bar. I passed a table where a cop still wearing his uniform was receiving a handy from a socialite wearing a fox stole with the fox's head still attached. In a dark booth near the bar two couples had cleared their table and were coupling furiously. Then they switched partners.

Zanaire was the fuel that fed this bonfire of the moralities. Part absinthe, part Ecstasy, Zanaire was a sparkling blue liquid that one could imbibe or spray from an atomizer and inhale. Incredibly potent and highly addictive, it put its users into an incredible state of euphoria. How powerful the euphoria depended on the dose. A couple of shots you might forget where you parked. A half a liter and you could forget to sleep. Or eat. Hence, its street name; Blue Amnesia. This got shortened to Blue A.M.

Which then inexplicably became Blue Morning. One of those etymological anomalies, I guess. Blue Morning had been illegal for a decade but that didn't stop people from consuming it or gangsters from selling it. Guys with names like Tony "Clockwork" Flaubert and the Russian and Sam "The Brighton Butcher" O'Bannon and their gangs fought for control of the lucrative Zanaire market. The Federation was stretched thin paying for the war effort and so individual municipalities were on their own when it came to fighting the gangs. Pitched gunfights on the sidewalk were as common as cookouts in the summertime.

I never tried Blue Morning. Oh, I was tempted. When you wake up four or five times a night from nightmares the idea of not sleeping is sort of appealing. But the vacant eyes and perpetual grins of some of the hardcore users kept me away from the "blue fairy." I would stick with alcohol.

I made my way to the bar and ordered a gin and tonic. The bartender offered to put a shot of Blue Morning in it but I politely declined. The band stopped playing and the stage went dark. Sparse techno music began to fill the speakeasy. The stage lights came up and there were five scantily clad women standing there in sheer white gowns and long sheer scarves. The women began to glide over the stage in time with the techno-beat.

I pulled the box out of my pocket and put on the ring. The gaudy red stone stared back at me. I picked up my drink and edged closer to the stage. I passed a table where a woman was spraying her companion in the face with an atomizer full of Blue Morning. The ring remained as red as a spring apple. I slowly edged a little bit closer. Nothing.

"Well cross this one off the list," I murmured. The crowd was so loud I could barely hear myself. I finished my drink and was turning to head for the exit when I heard a roar come from the crowd. Pierre "Pig Iron" LaPointe had entered the place. Since this was his speakeasy that wasn't unexpected. LaPointe was a big man who looked more Arabic than his Gallic surname would suggest. A large man with long, wild black hair he tied back in a loose pony tail, LaPointe ran this part of town and its Blue Morning market. Rumor had it that he kept a pen below his club full of half-starved feral pigs. If LaPointe thought you had betrayed him or misled him in any way you went to the petting zoo. Or if you wore purple socks. Pierre was funny like that.

He was flanked on either side by two gorgeous women, one dread-headed sister and one blonde. Neither one looked anything like the picture in the file on my phone. I decided to have one more drink before I left. As they passed me, I held my hand up to get the hollowman's attention.

The ring had gone from red to orange.

"Shit," I whispered.

The three of them went to a booth all the way in the back of the speakeasy. His guards surrounded them. I cursed a few more times under my breath then tried to think. It made sense that it had come here. This was the biggest underground club in the city. Apparently, the tin man didn't want to dance anymore. It wanted to be a gangster. I'd have to come up with a reason to get close while avoiding the petting zoo. Did cyborgs have to use the bathroom? I didn't think so. I got up from my stool and tried to casually make my way over to where LaPointe was holding court.

I slipped through the crowd trying to look as nonchalant as I could. LaPointe's guards were two coiled snakes on either side of their boss. I'd have to be quick and I had to be prepared to take some lumps. As the band struck up a new song I pretended to trip and fall into LaPointe's booth. As I fell, I tossed my drink at his bodyguard. There was a mad scramble as LaPointe jumped up and showed a total lack of chivalry. He grabbed the blond and tossed her toward me with one meaty hook hand. As I lay sprawled across the table I reached out for the dread-head's right arm. It was incredibly fast. It gripped my hand and I could feel my metacarpals grinding together.

That was when I touched its forearm with the ring that was on my other hand. The effect was instantaneous. Its eyes became completely white. Its head snapped up and it appeared to be staring straight ahead. Seconds after, hands pulled me away from the table but moments before they started pummeling me, I was able to shout out a command. I didn't know if it would work but things were moving fast and it was the best plan I had.

"Help me escape!" I screamed. Then a fist slammed into my jaw.

My own programming took over. Somewhere a capricious god was laughing. I couldn't remember my own name but I could remember my Green Beret hand-to-hand combat training.

The first guard reared back to sock me again while the second guard held my arms. As the first guard hurled his fist at my face, I snapped my head back and to the right. My fedora provided a little bit of protection for the second guard, but his nose still met the majority of my skull. He instinctively released my arms. I surged forward. As the first guard's right fist slid over my left shoulder I reached up and trapped his elbow with both my forearms. I pulled down on his arm while raising right knee. His face slammed into my knee cap and I felt a soft explosion of flesh that told me I had broken his nose. The big man dropped to his knees.

I spun around just in time to see the second guard pull out his .45 and aim it at my face. His mouth and jaw were coated in his own blood from his bleeding nose. I was quick but he had the drop on me. While I contemplated whether I would end up in heaven or hell a blur came into my field of vision from the right. It was the cyborg. It kicked the second guard in the wrist and his gun went flying through the air. I heard a dull snap and realized it had broken his forearm. As he grabbed at his shattered radius and ulna bones, it chopped him in the windpipe and the big man fell like a redwood.

Without saying a word, it grabbed me by the wrist and then dragged me along for the ride as we slammed through the crowd. Patrons were tossed aside like bowling pins. We reached the platform in front of the heavy iron door. The guard that had let me in had his piece out and fired it right in the cyborgs pretty face. It didn't even slow down. One punch to the solar plexus and then another one to the throat and that guard joined his co-workers in La La land. It released me for a moment while it used both hands to rip the lock off the door and open it. The sound of metal scraping filled my ears drowning out the screams chasing us out the club.

The empty elevator shaft seemed to mock us. I was staring at it when I heard a mechanized voice devoid of any emotion in my ear.

"Jump . . . on . . . my . . . back," it said in a stilted monotone. I dared to look over my shoulder. More guards were shoving their way through the crowd. Pierre LaPointe was leading them. He had an EMRG in his hand. An electromagnetic rail gun rifle. It fired a small dime-sized shot. Using magnetic resistance instead of gunpowder, the ball bearings came out of the gun at two thousand feet per second. I had a feeling that would do me and the cyborg in quite effectively.

"Fuck it," I said and jumped on its back. I guess I shouldn't have been shocked to find that it felt like a real woman. It was soft where it was supposed to be and firm where it needed to be. Its hair smelled of lilacs, not oil or that innominate scent computers and sterile plastic gives off. It stepped into the shaft and seemingly effortlessly began climbing up the shaft with me on its back. It spread its legs and arms wide until all four limbs had a point of contact with the shaft. Then it began to scuttle up the tube like a spider. We were moving incredibly fast. But not so fast I couldn't hear someone mutter "What the hell?"

We reached the top of the shaft and the cyborg punched through the floor of the confessional. Splinters rained down on my fedora. It pulled itself out of the hole and I jumped down off its back. I didn't see the priest who wasn't a priest.

"Follow me!" I said. We both took off running for the door.

"Hold it, you sons of bitches!" It was the phony priest. He came around the confessional brandishing a shotgun. I dropped to my knees and turned as I slid along the old wooden floor. I pulled out my plasma pistols. I was just about to fire on him when I saw a pew fly over my head and slam into him as he stepped off the pulpit. Yes, an entire pew. I glanced at my companion then hopped up and ran out the door. It followed me and we jumped in my Tucker. I roared out of the parking lot and we escaped into the night.

A pew. It threw a pew at him. What the hell had I gotten myself into?

I drove out to my place on Decatur Avenue above the Tin Can, a bar that lived down to its name. It was the roughest legal bar in the roughest part of town near the Pilcher auto plant. On my side of town, the smell of diesel was so prevalent after a while you stopped smelling it. The streets were soot swept roadways bathed in the plant's vaporous jetsam. I pulled my car up to the curb.

"Get out and follow me," I said. The cyborg complied. We had to walk up a staircase on the side of the bar to get to my apartment. As we passed, a man was thrown through the door. He hit the sidewalk with a thud. He groaned as he rolled onto his back like an intoxicated turtle.

"Y'all ain't shit, man! Forget your raggedy ass place. I've seen outhouses with more class!" the man screamed. A wiry figure appeared in the door carrying a cricket bat. The man's dark face was a black cloud of fury. His bald head gleamed under the street lamps. He had a gold hoop in his right ear.

"Get out of here Willie. Or I'll beat the gin out of you," the bald man said. He noticed me and my guest passing by with our heads down.

"Hiya Traveler," he said. His voice was low and smooth like a sleek coupe.

"Hey Boiler," I mumbled. Boiler nodded and turned his attention back to the drunk. Most apartments here required your date of birth, DNA (to make sure you were not a foreign agent), job history, first born son and an oath of never-ending fealty. Okay, I'm kidding about the last two. Maybe. But Boiler was used to living on the outskirts of society and off the grid. He rented me this place with no questions asked as long as I had the rent every month.

My apartment was as sparse as a Spartan's. I had a Murphy bed on the left side of the room and patio door without a patio on the right. I didn't open the door a lot because of the stench from the plant. In the morning the sun would cut through the oily haze that always seemed to permeate the air and wake me up from my latest drunken stupor.

I pulled the Murphy bed down and lay across the bed. I eyed the cyborg warily. It was getting harder to call it an it instead of a she. The black dress it-she wore had torn during our escape and one firm thigh peeked at me through the rip. Her reddish-brown dreads were a tangled mess just the way I liked a woman's hair to be. Green had said it would revert back to its standard operating parameters after five minutes. It had been a lot longer than five minutes.

I don't know why I touched her with the ring again. It just popped in my head and I did it. I had seen her carrying on a conversation with LaPointe. So, I know she could be reasonable. I'd like to say it had nothing to do with being lonely. I'd like to say I didn't consider her a machine and therefore something I could control. I'd like to say those things. But I won't. I stood up and walked over to her. I touched the ring to her shoulder. This time I noticed a circular pattern of light that appeared on her skin where I touched her. Her pupils reappeared and she punched me in the sternum so hard I flew through the air and landed on the Murphy bed. If it hadn't folded up at that very moment, I think she would have killed me. As it happened the bed fell into its recessed spot in my wall. When she pulled the bed back down, I was holding my plasma pistol and pointing it at her face. It was charged and the cyclotron was emitting a high whine as it charged a small pressurized capsule of gas.

My mouth was full of blood. I spit a globule on the floor. My sternum was aching like an elephant had tapped danced on my chest. I could barely breathe. Every time my abdomen drew inward a sharp pain shot through my chest.

"Stop. Just stop," I panted. She stared at me impassive-ly.

"That's a Tesla 229 particle charging plasma pistol," she said. Her voice was soft, subtle really. She started to move forward. It killed me but I straightened my arm.

"Bullets might not go through your head but this plasma particle will cut right through you and fry you up like a piece of chicken," I said. The pain in my chest was troubling but not as troubling as what she could do to me if she got her hands on me.

"You are working for Green and Jarrell, aren't you? "she said. I nodded. She laughed. The astonishment must have shown on my face. She crossed her arms and cocked her head to the side.

"I wouldn't be a very good assassin if I couldn't assimi-late into various social settings with a passable sense of humor. I laughed because you have no idea what is really going on here," she said. My arm started to quiver. The pain was a living thing devouring my body like some wild beast.

"W-w-what are you talking about?" I stammered. She uncrossed her arms and squatted down so we would be eye level as I sat on the bed.

"Green and Jarrell are playing you. They were a part of the team that was escorting me to Central Command in Olde York. The scientists who designed me gave each member of that team an override chip hidden in that ring. Green and Jarrell killed the crew and started flying me across the border," she said. I stared at her.

"They were going to sell you to the Alliance," I said. She nodded.

"After they killed the crew that engaged my override. I heard the screams of those dying men and I could do nothing to help them. When the override protocols are engaged it's like I'm in a lucid nightmare. I can only respond to commands. It's like I've been kicked out of my own body. It's disgusting," she said. My arm was killing me.

"How'd you escape?"

"Jarrell. The pervert couldn't stop touching me while I was under. Ugh, it's was horrible. Before he could get his penis inside me his ring brushed against my bare thigh. He accidentally released me," she said. I could guess the rest.

"You didn't want to be a showgirl, did you?" I said. She laughed again.

"No. But I knew I couldn't legally get past the city limits without a profile in the city data banks. I headed for the speakeasies to find a member of the criminal underground. There was a 74% probability they would have access to alternative methods of leaving the city," she said

"Why don't you look like the picture in the file? I mean you're beautiful and all but you're definitely not the pale redhead in that pic," I said. She smiled. She had a lovely smile.

"My exterior is composed of billions of transmorphic nanobytes. They can change shape and color. It was an original part of my programming. It evolved over time as I evolved," she said.

"I'm going to put my pistol down. I think you broke my sternum. Please, I'd appreciate it if you didn't kill me," I said. I put the pistol on the bed. I spit another blob of blood on the floor. The cyborg didn't move.

"So, they don't have any way of using your power source to open an inter-dimensional doorway," I said.

"No such procedure exists to accomplish such a task," she said. I nodded my head.

"Where were you going if you left the city?" I asked.

"Somewhere out west. Near the Borderwall. As my AI programs evolved so have my consciousness. I have desires that do not align with my operating directives. I wish to explore these desires. I do not believe my designers anticipated my AI would evolve so quickly," she said.

"You just wanna be yourself," I said. My voice was barely a gasp. I felt stupid and dirty. I couldn't turn this . . . creation over to Green just so the Axis Alliance could dissect her. I felt like a hood turning over a runaway to a pimp.

"Help me up," I said. She grabbed my hand and pulled me to my feet like I was a baby instead of a six-foot-tall two-hundred-pound man. As I reached in my trench coat, I noticed it had blood on it. It wasn't mine. I pulled the throwaway out that Green had given me.

"What are you doing?" she asked.

"I'm calling Green and telling him you left the city. That should give you a little bit of a head start," I said. She stood straight up and stared at the patio door. She turned back to me.

"No, it won't. He and Jarrell are approaching in a gyrocopter. They must have tracked you when you activated the ring to override my systems," she said.

"But they said I had to — oh right they were lying. Well let's leave the ring and I'll get you out of here," I said. She shook her head.

"They are already . . ."

My patio door/window exploded inward as projectiles shattered the glass. I fell to the floor and screamed in pain as my sternum slammed against the carpet. My arm and my leg were burning. I guessed I had been hit. Either that or my arthritis was acting up. Lily, as I now thought of her, did a back flip out of the line of fire, then dropped to a crouch near the card table where I usually ate dinner.

I heard a loud WHOOSH and Jarrell was flying through my window wearing a jet pack. The jet pack user was wearing brass and leather goggles and an oxygen mask, but it had to be Jarrell. Lily ran toward him like a synthetic polymer lioness. Jarrell was holding a metal box of some kind. It was about the size of a drink cooler. He dropped the cooler and pulled some type of collapsible staff from the pocket of his flight suit. As Lily leaped into the air, he extended the staff. It was then I saw a glowing orange jewel on the tip of the staff. Jarrell jabbed it into her neck. She fell to the floor then hopped up and stood at attention. Jarrell removed his mask.

"Get in the box," he said. Lily bent down and flipped open the latches on the lid. She twisted her arms and legs into shapes that would have crippled a human being. She climbed into the box and folded herself like a piece of origami. Jarrell closed the lid. He turned and pulled on a cable that was attached to the box. I watched as the gyrocopter ascended into the night sky, pulling the box out of my window. I rolled under the Murphy bed.

"I'm gonna kill ya, Traveler! Ya hear that, ya dusky schwarz?" Jarell growled. I saw his legs directly in front of me. I had seconds before he flipped the bed up and I would be as vulnerable as a turtle on its back. I pulled my pistols and fired at Jarrell's legs. Plasma pistols fire a small shot about the size of a pea that is surrounded by a plasma bubble. When the shot leaves the glass packed barrel the plasma bubble is hotter than the surface of the sun. The plasma tore through Jarrell's shins ripping them to shreds while cauterizing them at the same time.

Jarrell screamed and fell onto his knees. I pushed up on the bed with my back and stood in front of him. I put the barrel of one of my pistols against the lens of his goggles. The pistol was a gaudy looking thing with an industrial gold-plated surface and an exaggerated grip that had a bit of a flourish at the bottom. Jarrell had dropped his weapon. A TM-25 dual cylinder machine gun. It sat as a mute witness to our final conversation.

"I told you don't call me that," I said as I pulled the trigger. That close the plasma melted the lens and sliced through Jarrell's skull like a rapier. The back of his head exploded like a piñata. The smell of broiled flesh filled my apartment. Jarrell fell face first onto my carpet. I looked out the window at the rapidly retreating lights of the gyro.

I looked at the jet pack that was strapped to Jarrell. When I was first hit the city, I spent most of my time in the local libraries. I stayed until they closed, then I wandered the streets until they opened in the morning. I educated myself as much as I could on this place of androids and flying cars. I could fly that jet pack. I had no doubt in my mind about that.

But I didn't have to. I could let Green take Lily across the border and go get some much-needed medical attention and a drink. And not necessarily in that order. I thought of her in that box twisted up like a pretzel. A body that was no longer her own. I couldn't leave her in that state. And then there was the matter of Mr. Green. He had played on my greatest desire and made a fool of me while I risked my life for a ticket home that didn't exist.

There were some debts that needed to be settled.

I knelt down and flipped Jarrell over on his back. I started undoing the buckles of the jet pack. I slipped my arms through the harness rig and latched my buckles. There were two rubber coated throttle cables on each side of the jet pack. These cables ended in fingerless gloves. On the palms of the gloves were the throttle controls. I slipped my hands into the gloves and slipped the oxygen mask over my mouth. I didn't have goggles so I grabbed some old sunglasses off what was left of the night stand. After a second, I took them off and tossed them on the floor. The sky was still dark. I didn't want to fly into one of the massive skyscrapers that dotted the city's skyline. I reached over my shoulder and flicked the choke switch. I backed up to the Murphy bed.

"One, two, THREE!" I screamed. I ran toward the window and jumped. I plummeted like a brick for a few seconds. I felt my gorge rising and I was sure I was going to vomit. I pressed my fingers into the palms of the gloves. The thrust from the jet pack sent waves of pain through my chest. I straightened my legs and angled my torso up like I was doing a Hindu push up.

I rose through the night air like a broken-down comet. I saw the gyrocopter. The box was hanging from it like a lamprey eel on a shark. It swung wildly as the copter headed north. I hit the throttle and zoomed toward the copter. The wind was scratching at my eyes. It felt like every piece of debris and dirt in the world was being rubbed into my face. As I streaked toward the copter, I realized too late I was going to pass it. I zipped right over its huge set of twin rotors. I banked up and then did a barrel roll as I came around to face the copter. Green saw me and I swear I could see him smile. The two rotating barrel machine guns came up and Green aimed them at me. I cut the throttle on right turbine and rolled to my left just as Green opened fire. As the sound of two massive .45 caliber machine guns tore through the night, I passed the copter on his right.

As I slipped by, I pulled out my plasma pistol and unloaded my six remaining shots into the cockpit. I didn't see them hit Green, but I watched as the copter started to list to the right, then back to the left. The nose dipped like a commoner curtsying and the copter fell to the earth. I banked to the left and the hit the throttle in my right turbine, but I had waited too late. I couldn't right myself. I saw the stars and the streets lamps swirling around me like a kaleidoscope as I rolled over and over. I cut the throttle in both turbines and then I did vomit as I saw the street racing up to meet me. I hit the throttles again and screamed as I skimmed the pavement at a height equal to a politicians moral standing. I cut the throttles again and this time I crashed into the asphalt. I felt something in my chest burst. Blood filled my throat. I rolled over and over again until I landed near a parked sedan. I pulled off my oxygen mask and vomited again. Gin, blood and yesterday's lunch splashed across the street. I heard a thunderous explosion toward the north. I turned my head and saw an orange and blue fireball streak across the sky.

"Get up. Get up," I told myself. I tried and fell back down to the street.

"Come on Traveler, get up!" I thought. I pulled myself up by holding on to the door handle on the sedan. I caught a glimpse of myself in the window. My face was sporting some road rash and my shirt was covered in blood and vomit. I had lost my hat. I stumbled toward the explosion. The copter had crashed into a Woolworth's. Fire greedily ate the ladies' coats and gentlemen's shoes. I saw the box in the gutter. I fell down and crawled toward it. My hands felt numb but I fought with the latches until the lid opened. I felt lightheaded and my legs were cold. I reached into the box and touched her on the shoulder with my ring.

A five-foot six jack in the box popped into the air. Lily landed next to me. She turned her head from side to side and her twisted limbs went back to their normally scheduled positions. She knelt beside me.

"You risked your life for me," she said. Her voice was even and calm.

"Not . . . just you. I really needed to kill Green. Jarrell's dead too. Just so you know," I said. I felt very tired. She laid a cool hand on my forehead. Her eyes went totally white again.

'You are very badly injured. You need medical attention," she said.

"I could have told you that and I'm not even a cyborg," I said. She laughed. It was too loud and too raucous but it made me smile. I pulled the ring off and tossed it toward the storm drain.

"Go on. Get out of here. If the cops catch you here there will be too many questions," I said. She watched the ring roll into the storm drain. I thought I heard it clang against the sides of the drain as it fell. Lily ripped my shirt open and traced her hands over my chest. It felt so good I wanted to go to sleep. Until she pushed on my rib cage. I howled like a banshee. I felt a strange sensation. It was halfway between a tickle and a pinch.

"I transferred some of my nanobytes to your body. Your injury will temporarily be repaired. You will still need medical attention. The nanobytes will degrade rapidly in your blood stream," she said. Quick as a snake she leaned forward and kissed me on the cheek.

"Goodbye Traveler," she said. I nodded and gave her thumbs up. I closed my eyes as I heard sirens approaching. I hope the coppers don't find Lily. I hope she gets what she wants. The same thing we are all want. A life of our own.

I closed my eyes and sighed.

It was enough to melt your heart. Even if it was made of iron.

INTO THE BREACH
BY
MALON EDWARDS

I'm off my bunk and into my jodhpurs, knee-high leather boots and flight jacket the moment the long-range air attack klaxons seep into my nightly dream about Caracara.

Muscle memory and Secret Service training kick in; I'm on autopilot (no pun intended) and a good ways down the hall buttoning up both sides of my leather jacket to the shoulder a full thirty seconds before I'm awake.

And just so you know, the ever so slight tremble in my hands and fingers is not fear. It's adrenaline. I'm cranked and ready to put my foot all up in it.

A door to the right opens and Pierre-Alexandre falls in on my right flank, his steps brisk like mine. Our boots echo down the long hallway as we make our way from the underground bunker at Soldier Field to the bunker at Meigs Field.

"What you think we got?" he asks.

My reptile mind—that wonderful, hedonistic thing of mine—notices how lovely his make-me-jump-up-and-dance-like-I-just-caught-the-Holy-Ghost-in-church dark skin looks in the red emergency scramble lighting.

And yeah, I know. I'm going to hell for that.

A door to my left opens and René-Bastien, better known as Pretty Boy, falls in on my left flank and matches our stride.

"My guess is fifteen bogeys coming in hard and fast from the south," he says.

His flight jacket is only half buttoned and he's not wearing his T.I. issued white tee-shirt (that's Tuskegee Institute for those that don't know). I flicker a glance at his beautiful, honey-hued, well-muscled chest and frown.

I bet he just left some police academy recruit in his bunk. Good-N-Plenty is going to smack him upside his head for entertaining unauthorized personnel after lights out. Lax discipline gets people killed. We've had enough of that, lately.

"It don't matter what we got," I tell them, throwing open the double doors leading to the enormous underground hangar at Meigs Field, as long as we finish what they start.

We hustle down the short flight of metal stairs and fan out to our respective bright-shirted handlers waiting for us at our outfit stations: me to Skittles, Pierre-Alexandre to Sour Patch, and Pretty Boy to Good-N-Plenty. Good-N-Plenty pops the back of Pretty Boy's neck with a comb before she hands it to him and buttons up his flight jacket.

Skittles catches my eye as I pull on thin leather gloves and stand shoulder-width apart on my platform, arms outstretched.

"You okay?" she asks as her fingers flow across her station console, manipulating my exo-suit into place from above.

I hesitate for a fraction of a second before I answer. "M byen. I'm cool."

Skittles tries to hold my gaze. She knows I'm still grieving hard. Instead, I look at the empty outfit stations scattered throughout the hangar. Once, there were thirty-six of us, including Caracara. I still can't bring myself to look at her station on my right.

Robotic arms lower the torso of my powered armor onto me and outfit my arms and legs with the rest of my sleek exo-suit. I feel all components lock into place, one by one.

"You're online," Skittles says, handing me my helmet.

"Systems check?" I ask her.

"All systems green, including weapons."

"What's the gouge?"

Skittles glances at a second console screen. "Thirty-one bandits, south by southwest. City-state airspace ETA five minutes."

Shit. This isn't just a show of force. The State of Illinois wants to crush us. Wipe us out. Smother us in the bed of our city-state infancy.

"Is the Sable safe?" I ask her.

She nods. "Safe and protected in an undisclosed location with Marie-Thérèse, Marie-Louise, Jean-François and the last CPD contingent."

(That's Chicago Police Department, for those that don't know.)

I smirk. "I told them they'd outlive us."

"We're not dead yet," Pretty Boy says, and his voice echoes as it carries to me from across the almost-empty bunker.

"We will be if you don't put down that damn comb," Pierre-Alexandre tells him.

I pat my tight and right Janelle Monáe before I wreck it with my helmet. "I'm taking the scissors to your hair when we get back," I say to Pretty Boy.

If we get back.

Pretty Boy shakes out his hair before he puts on his helmet. "Cut these beautiful curls," he says through our helmlink, "and you take away my power."

"Your power of bullshit," Pierre-Alexandre says.

I can't help but smile. Good thing they can't see it. They might think I'm getting soft.

"Scramble in thirty seconds," I tell them.

Skittles starts the countdown clock before she steps onto my platform and throws both arms around me.

"Kale je." Her voice is soft. Hesitant. I needed that hug. I don't tell her that, though.

"My eyes are always open," I say instead.

Except when Caracara died.

"It wasn't your fault," she says, putting on her headset and switching to our private commlink. Skittles is a good handler. She knows me better than I know myself.

"Tell that to my dreams," I whisper.

One hundred feet up, the roof of the bunker slides open, taking its sweet time. Skittles steps off my platform and goes back to her console. I watch the last ten seconds to lift-off flip down to zero on the huge digital clock affixed to the far wall.

"Anmize ou byen," Skittles says in my earcomm, her voice now normal-husky like far-off water over rocks. "Tandiske fè atansyon."

I laugh into our private commlink. "Both fun and careful are my middle names," I tell her before I touch my left thumb to base of my left pinkie.

The rocket pack molded into the powered armor Skittles designed and built for me roars to life. Not wanting to be left in my diesel exhaust—drawers down and ass-out embarrassed again—Pierre-Alexandre and Pretty Boy fire up their rockets, too.

I look over at them, and then up at the so small dark sky.
"Men m la pran m," I tell them.
Catch me if you can.

*   *   *

I didn't think that day would be our last together.
I didn't think that would be our last sortie.
I didn't think I would never see you again.
You gave me no reason to think that way.
You were fierce. You were bold.
You didn't take shit from nobody.
You never doubted yourself.
At least, that's what I thought.
You'd always said if we doubt, we die.

I often wonder if you'd ever thought, I just may die today.

But then, I shake those thoughts away. And I put on estipid bravado along with my armor.

Like I did just now in the hangar with Skittles.

Yeah, I was frontin'.

Tankou si ou. Tankou granpè nou.

Just like you. Just like our grandfather.

We must have gotten it from him. And look where it got you.

I wonder if I'm going to die today.
I hope I don't die today.
I'm afraid of dying today.
But not if that means I get to see you again.

* * *

Not that I didn't believe Skittles, but I'm still surprised to see ten Maybach 62S exo-fighters escorting twenty-one Conquest Knight XV shit shells over the south suburbs, just miles short of city-state airspace.

Well, I did tell Skittles fun is my middle name.

And careful, too. But to hell with that.

Bèl Flè, grann mwen—my grandmother—used to say, kapon antere manman l. Cowards bury their mothers.

Or in my case, their sisters.

I don't want to be a coward today.

"Get your guns ready, boys," I tell Pierre-Alexandre and Pretty Boy as we tease out the sound barrier to play with us over Park Forest, Illinois.

"Ready to go hard and fast," Pierre-Alexandre answers.

"I hope you didn't tell her that last night," Pretty Boy lobs to him.

I can already see where this is going. Pierre-Alexandre has never been that bright. Strong and reliable, yes. But a neg sòt, too.

"Tell who?" he asks Pretty Boy.

"Palmetta."

There's a brief pause, and then Pierre-Alexandre says, "You just mad 'cause it's gon take you five hours to get your butters back done up after this."

Pretty Boy kisses his teeth, sadness in his voice. "You ain't said nothing but a word."

I clear my throat. "While you boys are mourning Pretty Boy's hair, I'll just go defend our Sovereign State and its freedom."

I touch the tips of my thumbs to the tips of my middle fingers, as if I'm about to meditate for enlightenment. Not quite.

Side-mounted Browning M2 .50 caliber machine guns unfold from a compartment in my exo-arms. One hundred and seventy-five rounds each. My radar shows me that Pierre-Alexandre and Pretty Boy are now armed and have done the same.

Our guns and ammo don't leave room for much else, but they do go well with our exo-suits: my Mercedes Benz S-Guard 600 powered armor, also known as Lark; Pierre-Alexandre's Audi Attack 8 powered armor, also known as War Eagle; and Pretty Boy's BMW 7 Series High Security powered armor, also known as Peacock.

Yeah. You heard right. Peacock.

Just know I didn't hand out code names when I first assembled this outfit.

"We doing the usual maneuvers?" Pierre-Alexandre asks me.

No. The usual got Caracara killed.

Out loud I say: "No. Fall back. Let them think we're buggin' out because we're surprised by their numbers."

I pull up and hover. Pierre-Alexandre and Pretty Boy flank me. White, wispy-thin clouds broker the distance between us and the Illinois National Guard's shit shells.

I am surprised by their numbers. And somewhat cowed.

But I lift my chin at our enemy, my voice flush with that estipid bravado I inherited from granpè mwen (Jean-Baptiste Point du Sable, for those that don't know). The same estipid bravado he had when he seceded Chicago from the State of Illinois, established the City-State of One Hundred Fists and named himself Lord Mayor.

The same estipid bravado that killed Caracara.

When their shit shells open their hatches to let loose their turds, I tell my dwindled team, move into position beneath and blow them straight to hell.

* * *

Before the air attack klaxons sounded, I'd been dreaming I was five years old again, sitting on my grandfather's knee. Michaëlle-Anicia was sitting next to me, on his other one.

"Tell us again where the gold is, Grandfather," I'd said to him.

"And the silver! And the diamonds!" Michaëlle-Anicia piped up.

Grandfather chuckled and kissed the loose, dark curls at the crown of our small heads. "The gold and the silver and the diamonds," he told us, "Are in the same place when I first settled in Chicago many coffee harvests ago."

"San rekòt kafe?" Michaëlle-Anicia asked him.

Grandfather pulled us close and laughed again, so deep and so rich that his big belly shook both our backs. "Ti chouchou," he asked my twin sister, "do I look that old to you?"

"Wi, Granpè," she answered, and pushed on his big belly with her tiny fists. I giggled, both hands over my mouth.

"Non, non," Grandfather said, shaking his head, "I have seen nowhere near one hundred coffee harvests. Now, your grann, Bèl Flè mwen, she has seen many rekòt kafe. I bet she has seen more rekòt kafe than you can count."

"Nuh uh!" Michaëlle-Anicia flared, sitting up straighter with challenge.

"How many has Grann seen?" I asked.

"Can you count twa san rekòt kafe?" Grandfather asked us.

"Wi!" Michaëlle-Anicia answered, and she could. So could I.

"Grann is not that old," I said, my mouth pursed in disbelief.

"Oh, but she is!" Grandfather assured us. "Bèl Flè mwen, lanmou cheri mwen—your grandmother—she saw the bombs drop and scorch the land, many, many coffee harvests ago."

Our eyes widened with wonder and pride and fascination as Grandfather told us again the story of Chicago's history and our family, a story we could never get enough of.

"But remember, ti chouchou," Grandfather went on to say, "it was also grann ou who rebirthed Chicago. It was she who purified the soil and cleansed Lake Michigan again. It was she who put the gold and silver and diamonds—and the copper and the uranium, too—deep down in the earth, and called it the Gold Coast. All so we could rebuild and thrive and live."

"And the big bad State wants us to give it all to them!" Michaëlle-Anicia shouted, her fists clenched angry.

"Just like the big bad wolf!" I shouted with her.

"Ah, but ti fi cheri mwen yo," Grandfather said, "we should always share with those who are less fortunate."

"Why?" Michaëlle-Anicia asked, her fists still angry. "They take and take and take, and they never give anything back!"

"E vre!" I shouted, wanting to be louder than my twin sister. "They will take until we have nothing left!"

"No, they won't," Grandfather told us, his voice deep and calm. "We will only share until they have enough. Until they can rebuild and thrive and live. Just like us. And when they are finally able to do so, we shall share no more, and they will take no more."

"Non, Granpè!" Michaëlle-Anicia said. "Ou fè erè! They will always take and take because they are bigger and because they are bullies!"

"Ah, ti chouchou," Grandfather tutted, "but I am right. The State of Illinois will take no more than we give them because you and your sister will not let them."

Michaëlle-Anicia turned to face Grandfather and looked up at him, her eyes narrowed, and her head cocked to one side, so I did the same.

"And if the day ever comes where they try," Grandfather continued, kissing the crown of our small heads again, "Senyè, lonje men ba yo."

DIESELFUNK!

* * *

It's as if the Illinois National Guard knows what we're doing. Their shit shells hold and hover as well. Standoff.

Not that this was ever meant to be a complex plan.

"What now, bòs?" Pierre-Alexandre asks me.

Kounye a, my grandfather, is somewhere hiding in a deep, dark basement—afraid—waiting for the city he rebuilt from its ashes to fall on his head.

I never thought I'd see the day granpè mwen would cower. From the time I was ti fi, I always believed he feared nothing.

He is a gwo nèg. A bon nèg.

He is the rebèl who gave the Land of Lincoln the double middle finger. The politisyen who made Chicago a Sovereign State, and gave Kreyòl and English equal legal weight. The innovateur who manufactured the armor that seduced me and Caracara with its sleek, sexy power—a power manman nou, our mother, never forgave us for embracing.

Not even on her deathbed.

Caracara is supposed to be here. Caracara is supposed to be doing this.

I guess it's up to me now.

I look at Pierre-Alexandre and then Pretty Boy. "Back to the usual maneuvers," I tell them. "I'll take the point. Follow my lead."

She did always say: go big or go home.

* * *

I never call her Caracara in my dreams. It's always Michaëlle-Anicia.

And she never calls me Michaëlle-Modeste. It's always Lark.

So, when Caracara said to me, "Lark, love of my heart, if you die today, I will kick your ass," I knew my dream had changed and we were no longer five years old sitting on Grand-father's knee.

"Grandfather shouldn't have made me head of his Secret Service," I'd told Michaëlle-Anicia. "He should have chosen you."

Michaëlle-Anicia took both my hands in hers. We stood, facing one another. My mirror. Her mirror.

"He chose you," she said, "because he knew I would die. I am foolish. You are not."

"Non," I told her, shaking my head. "I never wanted this. But I put on my armor because you put on your armor first. I wanted to do everything you did. You were born for this. Not me."

"Non," Michaëlle-Anicia countered, shaking her head harder than my head-shake so her loose, dark curls flew. "You were born for this, just as much as I was. Bèl Flè—grann nou—made you strong, just as she made me strong."

"I don't believe in Bèl Flè," I said, dropping her hands, my voice small. "We are no longer ti fi," I went on. "We no longer have short curls and skinned knees. I don't believe Granpè's tall tales anymore."

Michaëlle-Anicia scowled at me. She looked disgusted. "Because you are afraid, they are true."

"Non," I said, "because—"

But Michaëlle-Anicia shouted me down, challenging as always. "Because you are afraid to embrace Bèl Flè's legacy! Because you are afraid to lead! Because you are afraid everyone knows your flawed decisions killed me and almost every single one of your team members!"

Her shouts bounced all around us before they were swallowed by a white, loud silence that rang in my ears. Never before had my twin sister said anything like that to me. Not in my dreams. Not when she was alive.

I turned away from her, from my mirror, so she couldn't see me struggle not to cry. "Se pa vre," I whispered at the whiteness all around me, "that's not true at all."

But Michaëlle-Anicia didn't answer because the air attack klaxons sounded, shattering my dream, taking her away from me.

* * *

"You're stressing your armor," Skittles says in my earcomm, her voice calm and quiet, as it always is during battle. "A lot. Any faster, and Lark will break apart."

"Mwen pa bay yon mèd," I say, my voice just as soft, and I push even further past the sound barrier, toward the Illinois wedge of exo-fighters and bombers.

"Michaëlle-Modeste!" Skittles scolds, shocked by my language. That's the loudest I've ever heard her speak. And the most pained.

"Well, I don't care!" I scream at her, just as loud, and la pou la, I wish I could take those words back.

I check my heads-up display radar to make sure Pierre-Alexandre and Pretty Boy are still flanking me before I apologize. "Eskize'm," I tell her, my voice small and five years old again. "Really, I am."

"That armor is my life," she whispers.

"I know," I tell her.

"I've devoted more time to Lark than I have to manman mwen ak sè mwen," she says.

"I know," I say again.

"I love Lark as much as I love you."

"I know," I repeat a third time, because I don't know what else to say.

"Stop saying I know," she yells at me again, "and start respecting her! And while you're at it," she goes on, "stop feeling sorry for yourself because your sister is dead, and go bust some Illinois ass!"

She doesn't have to tell me twice.

As I streak toward the Illinois wedge tankou moun fou-- like a crazy person--I line up the ten Maybach 62S exo-fighters and twenty-one shit shell bombers in my sights, fists outstretched, Supergirl-style. My .50 caliber Brownings tear through five of the ten Maybachs. Jagged, black pieces of exo-suit go flying, end over end.

I'm not surprised. They're just fodder. The shit shell bombers are the ones with the heavy armor. They do all the damage.

The return fire is hot. I point my toes and roll onto my back, dodging most of it with my usual grace as I watch the five Maybachs spin away from their wedge and fall to the earth, limp and broken.

Just like Caracara fell.

But I'm not graceful enough. Blazing pain rips into my left shoulder and right hip.

"How bad is it?" Skittles asks, la pou la.

"Se pa mal, I lie," as my blood streams out to mix with the thin clouds. "Se pa anyen ditou."

"You never were a good liar," she chides, her voice softer than usual.

"Yell at me when I get back," I tell her, my voice just as soft, and then I say louder into my helmlink: "How are you doing out there boys?"

"Eight bombers down," Pretty Boy answers, "but they're starting to shit all over the world."

"Well, we can't have that," I say, my voice wavering yon ti kras, "now can we?"

"You keep those Maybachs busy," Pierre Alexandre tells me, "and we can finish off these shit shells in about di minit."

"Knowing you and Pretty Boy," I say, rolling onto my stomach, "I'll be done here in five and have to save your asses."

I'm channeling Caracara big time now, talking shit and everything. Wish I would have known wedge busting was this fun before she died.

"How's the armor holding up?" I ask Skittles, forcing strength into my voice.

She doesn't buy it. "Better question is," she says with all the gravity in the world (no pun intended), "how are you holding up?"

"M byen," I tell her, "good enough to do this."

I put my arms tight to my sides for better aerodynamics and climb straight up to the dark edge of space, ak tout vitès. The Maybachs pursue, just as I expected. My teeth rattle as the g-forces try to tear me and my armor to pieces.

When I can't take it anymore, I bank left, hard. Two of the Maybachs go with me. The other three shake apart and tumble back to the earth.

My neck, my head, my lungs, my heart scream with pain as I try to circle behind the last two Maybachs. I'm too far up. The turn is too tight. I won't make it.

And then, the white-hot fire from their bullets rip my left side open.

I don't hear my crash avoidance alarms going off. I don't hear Skittles crying and screaming at me to right myself. I don't even hear the howl of the wind as I spin and fall. I push that all aside.

I just focus on the two Maybachs above, diving for me, arms at their sides.

And—after one revolution, two revolutions, three revolutions—I smile, let loose my guns, and blow both Maybachs straight to hell.

* * *

Michaëlle-Anicia had been our wedge-buster.

Lib-e-libè. Wild at heart. Our free spirit.

More than one hundred and fifty sorties. And hardly a scratch to Caracara.

She'd been badass that way.

Michaëlle-Anicia had also fiercely believed in Bèl Flè.

She believed Bèl Flè had been stricken with polio by Babalú-Ayé, the god of sickness and disease, who withered every last one of Bèl Flè's organs when she was ti fi.

She believed gwo grann, our great-grandmother, took Bèl Flè to a steam surgeon who specialized in metallurgy and glasswork, and told him to fix her daughter.

She believed the steam surgeon removed all of Bèl Flè's withered organs, gave her a steam clock heart and compost boiler, and then encased her torso with nigh-unbreakable glass.

She believed Bèl Flè's compost boiler, powered by the most high-quality coal dust, creates rich, dark, pristine topsoil every three weeks.

She believed Bèl Flè used that rich, dark, pristine topsoil to cover the scorched land and glowing ash left by the bombs and warheads.

She believed healthy and vibrant grass, plants and trees grew from Bèl Flè's rich, dark, pristine topsoil.

She believed the transpiration from the healthy and vibrant grass, plants and trees reversed the effects of nuclear winter, bringing fat, and cleansing raindrops not seen for years on the North American continent.

And she believed, after the war, Bèl Flè placed gold, silver and diamonds, and uranium and copper, too, deep within the earth beneath Chicago, called that land the Gold Coast, and left it all for Granpè to govern as Lord Mayor.

Those were the beatitudes of Michaëlle-Anicia.

But now, as I streak toward the earth tankou yon boul dife--like a ball of fire--I recite her beatitudes and make them mine.

And they give me strength.

ANGEL'S FLIGHT: A TALE OF THE CITY BY JOE HILLIARD

I was born to fly.

I was born to soar.

My grandfather was a Buffalo Solder. A sergeant in the Ninth Cavalry. Sergeant Pompey Fitz. My mom told me tales of his sojourn in the Badlands of the Dakotas. The herds of buffalos. His fellow cavalrymen. And the Sioux. Especially the Sioux. He had a mean old respect for the Sioux.

He claimed that in the winter of 1889 he fought the Spirit of the Buffalo. It was a long lean creature with the head of a buffalo, the wings of the great eagle, and the body of a brave. It pulled him up into the cold crisp air, arms bulging with the exertion. The snow tumbled around them as his lonely campfire fell away. His troop had been destroyed in a raid; he fought the Spirit alone, high in the midnight sky. Desperately, he grappled with It, wrestling It amongst the stars. The barren night grew longer. The Sergeant twisted behind It, his hands wrapped around It, an old wrestling hold maneuver learned in camp. The Spirit struggled; its muscles clenched tight. It would not yield. Its wings flailed in his face. The Sergeant remembered Jacob, and his struggle with God. "I will not let thee go; except thou bless me!" howled into the night. And he did not let go. The Spirit weakened. They fell to the ground, spiraling down into the snow. The Sergeant rolled away; reaching for his Springfield carbine, but the Spirit of the Buffalo jumped into the air, and slowly disintegrated into the rising sun. Forever after, the Sergeant claimed its huge shaggy head was outlined by a halo effect as it disappeared. He was only 24.

As soon as he could, Sergeant Pompey Fitz mustered out of this man's army. He never flew again. But the rest of us, his ancestors, we flew. I learned how to fly before I was born.

He decamped to Los Angeles. Home of perpetual sun. And no buffalo. Bought a home. Started a family. He died the week before my sister and I were born. No one knew how old he was, or even where he had been born. The Sergeant had been. Until he was not. My mom named us after him. Pompey Stanley Gilford. And my sister, Sinai Fitz Gilford.

I've seen pictures of him. A daguerreotype in his uniform. Black and white slick paper photographs in front of the house. I do not look like the Sergeant. He was tall and broadshouldered. He had the wingspan of the great California condor.

Me? I'm tall too. But I'm thin and narrow. All legs, as my father is wont to say. The Sergeant, even in his old age, looked like he could take on the Spirit of the Buffalo. Me? I look like I might be able to outrun it. If I got going fast enough. If I ever got going fast enough.

I was running now. As fast as my sixteen-year-old legs would carry me. Pounding down the pavement on Grand Boulevard. The Angel's Flight towered above me. The black metal lunch pail jabbed against my thigh, over and over, with each stride. I would have a terrible bruise tomorrow morning. But it wasn't tomorrow morning. It was past 4pm. Past starting time for the swing shift of the Angel's Flight. My father had already started his shift. And he'd left his lunch sitting on the table when he left.

It was unlike my father. He rarely forgot things. He knew everyone's birthdays. Mom's. My sister and I's. Twins made it easier. Not that much easier, but easier. And every July 20, flowers for their anniversary. But today, he had forgotten that battered metal pail filled by mom. The September sun was hot. Los Angeles, what you going to do? The heat came hard and early. No snow here. I'd only seen snow in photographs. I sure didn't have the Sergeant's antipathy to it. We were sweltering. The idea of cold from the sky sounded just the relief we needed. I wouldn't have cared if the Spirit of the Buffalo had brought it. Mom begged an extra block from the ice truck this morning. I think he doubled the normal price for it. It was worth it.

There had been a juicy sweet orange in my father's lunch. I devoured it on the Red Car on the way. He wouldn't mind. "Riding the rails is hungry work." He said that himself. It kept him at the table on the weekends, pouring over schematics while eating barbecue roast and hush puppies. Mom made the best hush puppies this side of the Mississippi. Least that's what they said. I knew I'd never had finer.

I stopped across the street from the base of the Angel's Flight. The late afternoon crowd from the Grand Central Market enveloped me. I waited for the signal, banging the lunch pail against my thigh now. Double time. And I heard cursing in Spanish behind me.

A fleet-footed kid, almost as fleet as I, darted out into the spread of cars. An older Latino man started out after him. Just then, a beige Nash Ambassador shot through a gap in the cars. I grabbed El Viejo by his white starched guayabera and hauled him back. The Nash leaned on its horn and nasal arrogant voices hurled insults about our parentage down on the two of us. Must have been some trash out of Hollywood. Only place that could afford new wheels these days. The kid had disappeared into the crowd at the base of the Angel's Flight. El Viejo stood next to me, panting. He scowled from underneath his fedora. Same crisp unearthly white as his shirt. It was hot. And he wasn't sweating a bit. Not even from the exertion. My button-down was soaked. My t-shirt was soaked. My collar could have been rung out, twice, and given you a good glassful of salty water. Not him though. He was one cool cat. He looked me over, and then nodded to himself.

The light changed. The crowd swirled around me to cross Grand. I looked. El Viejo had disappeared.

I let the crowd carry me across the street. I stood at the base of the Angel's Flight. I don't know if it is the shortest funicular in the world. My dad would say, "look it up," if I asked him. That was his answer to most issues. Look it up. Even if he knew the answer. Especially if he knew the answer. He felt expanding your mind was more important than simply knowing the answer. I'd spent more than one afternoon in the giant LA Public Library down the street from the Angel's Flight, sitting in front of the fountain with a book on my knee. Looking it up.

He seemed to have a second sense, my father. He was at the little door underneath the uphill tracks as soon as I knocked. His hand smoothly pulled his lunch box out of my hand and closed the door behind him with the other. I'd never even had a glance inside his job. I had no idea what went on inside the Angel's Flight works.

Archibald Gilford, my father was the opposite of the Sergeant. He was a City man through and through. He'd been born in Los Angeles, and, God willing, he would die there too never having known another home. There was too much to see in the City. He loved the Jewish delis that dominated Boyle Heights. He lived on pastrami and rye. He loved baseball and his Hollywood Stars. Somewhere in his travels he latched on to a cap and wore it everywhere. No fedora for my father. I know it frustrated my mom when they would go someplace fancy, him in his pinstripe suite, a pale blue tie – and his bright Stars cap. My mother was always trying to entreat him to change. I had a crisp Panama she bought him for Christmas of '38 that she had hoped would transplant that cap. But no luck. So, I was the only kid in school that had a fancy Panama with a black felt band.

I pushed it back off my head as I talked to my father. He leaned back against the door, suspiciously eyeing the orange peel on top of his corned beef. The wax paper wrapper was sticky with its juices.

"You should be more careful with the trash, son." He smiled at me. My father. "I know riding the rails is hungry work, but there's no reason to leave a mess."

"Sorry, dad. I had my mind on other things."

He pulled the Panama off my head and tousled my low-cut kinky hair. "I'm sure you do. And what's going on in Pompey's head today?"

"I'm going to soar. I was born to soar!" I was staring up into the sky. One of the City's dirigibles was floating overhead. An LAPD blue shirt swung off the bottom in a stainless basket, a bullhorn in his hand. If he was yelling at anyone, we couldn't hear him. It was headed off towards City Hall.

My father spit on the ground. He never did that. I stepped back. But he smiled over at me. And tossed me my Panama.

"So? You want to soar, do you?"

"Yes, sir!" I mock saluted him like I'd seen the soldiers saluting down in front of the school. Not like those sloppy ones you saw in westerns at the movie theatre. There had been a lot more soldiers lately. And a cadre of sailors too, just the other day.

My father's face sobered. "Knock off that madness, Pompey. It will come soon enough."

"Yes, sir." I lowered my eyes.

He smiled again. "You really want to soar? You really think you can fly?" He bit his lower lip. "Don't tell your mother. But come back tomorrow after school. Same time." He laughed. "You won't need to bring lunch. I'll pick up the tab." And he laughed even louder. I wondered what was going on behind those pale amber eyes of his. They were lit with a fire I had never seen before. Like he had caught the tail of that Spirit of the Buffalo.

And just like that, it switched off. He gave me a quick pat on the shoulder, opened the ornate copper door into the Angel's Flight, and disappeared into it.

I sighed and made my way back to the Red Car. My father met my mom riding the Red Car. You could say I was fated to ride the rails even more than I was meant to fly. You'll see what I mean soon enough. The Red Car was one more fascination of my father's. Shortly after I was born, my dad started taking engineering classes at the Frank Wiggins Trade School. He was in the first class accepted when it opened in 1925. I don't know how he finagled it. He was the only black student in that class. I think his boss, Frederick Thompson, pulled some strings. Thompson's father had been a young trooper under the Sergeant's command at the end of his service. He followed the Sergeant down to Los Angeles, settled in the same East Los Angeles neighborhood. Pacific Electric beckoned, and young Thompson answered the call. My father followed soon after, the lure of technology too strong. He'd already been working nights on the Red Cars at the Pacific Electric yard at Seventh and Central when he started school. And within months of graduating, he moved over to the Angel's Flight. He knew, somewhere in his mind, he would make it. He named my sister after one of the twin cars that ran up and down the tracks each day. Sinai and Olivet. I supposed if we had been twin girls, I would have been Olivet. But instead, I was destined by the Sergeant.

Sinai was sitting in front of the radio when I came in. I heard the cackle of the Shadow as I threw myself on to the floor next to her. I didn't realize it was that late already. I had taken longer talking to our father than I had thought I would. Sinai looked up from the floor. She had several Meccano toy sets laid out in front of her. She had arranged the gears in a crude geometric pattern around what was obviously an airplane fuselage.

I threw myself down on the floor next to her. I pulled the gears towards me. Sinai shook her head and pushed them away. She gave me several sheets of graphing paper. I raised an eyebrow at her. Only our father had expensive paper like that. She must have stolen some sheets from his desk in his office in the back room. She shrugged her shoulders, rolled her eyes, and giggled. "I couldn't help myself, Pompey."

"Of course, you couldn't. So, show me what you got, little sister."

"Only by three minutes. Don't think that gives you any call to boss me around."

I laughed. "Never said it did." I looked over the schematics she had doodled on the graphing paper. They were good. Real good. Almost as good as mine. I looked again. Better than mine. Sometimes I really hated my sister.

And sometimes I loved her more than life itself. The front of her Meccano airplane had a huge buffalo head where the propeller would normally have been. She moved the propellers to the wings. She gently twisted the key on the back, starting the gears in motion.

"Is that really aerodynamic?" I reached out and touched the buffalo head. It was warm to the touch. Like it was alive. I pulled my hand back with a start. And at that moment, Sinai let her airplane fly.

"Watch, big brother. Watch and learn."

It swooped high and almost bumped into the ceiling before looping itself over and diving back down towards us. It flew down low, knocking my Panama off my head.

"How do you control it?" I yelled. It swept back up toward the ceiling before shooting toward the doorway from the living room into the kitchen. I jumped up to chase it. At the last minute, it swerved back across the wall. "I'm not funning, Sinai! How do you control it?"

Sinai was sitting on the floor assembling gears into a concentric circle. She looked up into my face with a goofy smile. "I may be a genius, but I can't think of everything."

And the plane crashed into the radio, silencing the Shadow in the midst of his cackling laughter. Who knows what evil indeed? Sinai and I were going to be up all night fixing the radio before our father got home.

I stood in front of the ornate door to the Angel's Flight works promptly at 4pm. I had stood in front of this door hundreds of times over the years. I'd never been inside. And I never noticed the intricate patterns etched into the door. The US Ninth Cavalry logos circling up and into the stars, like constellations of soldiers. Of Buffalo Soldiers. All the stars in the sky. I reached out to trace a face that looked just like the Sergeant. The deep furrow of his brow. The high cheekbones. The stiff cavalry collar. Just like the buffalo on Sinai's Meccano airplane, it was warm to the touch. I pushed harder on it…

The door swung open. My father stood there. His Hollywood Stars baseball cap was pushed far back off his forehead. Sweat glistened on his forehead. He flashed a smile at me.

"Good to see you, son." He stepped out onto Grand and closed the door behind him. I heard the lock click into place behind him. I'd never noticed the automatic lock before that moment. What else had I not noticed ... about my father?

"Are you hungry, son? I've been having a busy day. And I could sure use some good grub. It's not your mother's cooking, but it's pretty darned good? What do you say?" He put his arm around my shoulder and pushed my Panama down over my eyes.

It was a quick trip across the street to the Grand Central Market. Even though it was only a few hours to closing, the Market was still bustling. Chinese and Mexican farmers haggled over the price of kumquats and avocados with each other, and the men from the swank restaurants pulling delicacies for tonight's menus. I saw two guys wearing Pacific Dining Car jackets looking over the daikon. And a Brown Derby crew sifting through the purple carrots. I eyed them all with some trepidation. It had only been last year that the restaurant wars spilled into the streets. At least one place had been burned to the ground in Beverly Hills, nearly killing the actor Franchot Tone in the process. My father must have noticed my nervousness. He put his arm around me and smiled faintly.

"Scared, son?" I nodded. "Don't be. I'm with you. I'll always be with you." I leaned against him. I could feel his muscles under his rumpled blue button-down. He still had the physique of a man working on Red Cars in the yard. I don't know how he managed it, cooped up under the Angel's Flight all day and then at his drawing board at home all weekend. He barely took the time to toss the baseball at the park with Sinai and me anymore. And we hadn't gone to a Stars game all season.

The Grand Central Market was not an open-air market. It was like an auditorium with huge awning openings on the east and west sides. We had come in on the west side. Ringing the north and south walls were counters set up for food. We passed a hamburger stand. And a Chinese counter smelling of garlic and ginger. My stomach rumbled. It smelled so good. We had Chinese food once. I remembered the spicy bite of it. My father stopped in front of the next stand. Under the glass overhang were piles of delicacies in different steaming vats. Pollo. Carne. Al Pastor. Lengua. Sesos. Carnitas. Nopales. Chorizo.

I was startled to see El Viejo behind the counter. He had his back to us, flipping tortillas on a hot open griddle. But I recognized the sharply pressed guayabera and the fedora. He turned as he heard us pull up metal stools in front of the counter. He smiled at my dad, a deep full-faced smile. His perfect white teeth bothered me. Before he had seemed simply an old man on the street. Now, behind the counter, he was too perfect. But my father did not seem to notice. He reached over the glass and shook El Viejo's hand.

"Sesos tacos, por favor. And pile them high." My father's voice boomed out easily. "Sit down, son. Eat up." El Viejo tossed a plate down in front of me with four tacos piled high with meat and a sprinkling of onions and cilantro on top. I poked at one of them dubiously.

"What is it?"

"Sesos. Brains. Eat up. Never enough brains, son." I blanched. My father and El Viejo laughed. He took a huge bite out of one of his tacos. I pushed the plate away from me. Still laughing, my father pulled the plate over in front of him. El Viejo piled a plate high with pollo and started to put it front of me.

But I shook my head and pointed down to the end of the counter. The mess of green chunks floating in sauce. "Those. I want those."

"¿Nopales?" El Viejo raised an eyebrow.

"Definitely." I sat down on the stool and pointed again.

My father laughed. "I like that, son. Make up your own mind. And stick to it. Stick to your guns." He took another bite of his sesos. "The world needs men that make up their own minds. And follow their dreams. You understand that, don't you, son"

"I do. I want to soar."

"My radio seems to think otherwise. It did not look so good this morning. Perhaps the Shadow had some trouble with foreign spies last night?" Sinai and I had ended up stringing a spaghetti mesh of wires outside of the wooden radio box to get the signal to come back in. And the front speaker panel had been irreparably damaged.

I felt my face redden. "That was Sinai. Honest."

My father raised an eyebrow. "Hmmm. Perhaps I should have her here instead. I mean, if she is the better engineer?"

I shook my head. "No, sir. I am as good as Sinai." I puffed my chest out. "Better."

El Viejo laughed. I hadn't realized he had been listening. I bit down on my nopales taco and looked away from him. It was tart. But I liked the taste. I only wished I had some of my mom's hush puppies to go with them. Nopales and hush puppies. Maybe I'd open a restaurant like that. El Viejo stared at me over the counter. I couldn't read his dark black eyes. But he really didn't look so old, so frail, anymore. Not the man I had seen yesterday. I shook my head. It had been a long few days.

My father clapped my back. "Well, son, you certainly don't suffer from being humble. I don't know what I will do with you." He pushed his empty plate away from him. "But I need to know if you are serious, Pompey. I need to know if you are serious about this."

"I am, sir." I nodded my head vigorously.

"Let's walk." My father threw a dollar on the counter. Did I imagine it, or was El Viejo troubled to see us leave so soon? The crowd had thinned in the Market. All the vegetables had been sold for the night. A few office workers were straggling in for a quick bite before going home. I thought El Viejo was going to follow us, but an overly obese man in a black bowler threw himself down into one of the stools at El Viejo's stall. Dinner time.

"Have I ever told you that I knew about the Spirit of the Buffalo *before* I met your mother?" I shook my head. Like I said, my father was a city boy. Capital C city. How would he have known about the Spirit of the Buffalo? Not from those bad westerns he loved to go see in the theatre. I knew I had never seen Herb Jeffrey deal with that. He was too busy singing to worry about spirits.

"I did. When I was your age. I started dreaming about It. I was scared. I never told my parents. Maybe I should have." He shrugged. And looked me over, expectantly. After a few moments, he continued. This was the most he had spoken to me in a long time. Since he had read to me as a child.

"Not like your grandfather, the Sergeant, dreamed. Hell, like he saw. The older I get, the more I believe that damned story of his. But I saw the Spirit. Not like he did. Not as a man. But as a machine. It was the face mounted on the front of a train. Taking up the entire front. With smoke trailing from its nostrils. Not a steam engine. Not diesel. I knew. I knew it was something different. And that night, I took out my pencil. And I began to draw. I started to put together my thoughts."

We had crossed over Grand and were standing in front of the Angel's Flight. He reached out and touched the inlaid work I had noticed earlier.

"And I drew myself here. And now, it has drawn you here as well." He pulled a large key out of his pocket. The head was that of a polished smooth buffalo. I'd never seen it before. It fit perfectly into the lock in the door. My father ushered me in.

"It drew us all here."

I don't know what I was expecting. Last summer my mother had taken us to a showing of an old silent film, *Metropolis*. The workers were forced to work underground in a great labyrinth of gears and levers. Somehow that had seeped into my mind as where my father worked. The truth was both more mundane and exquisitely grander than I imagined. The Angel's Flight underground was massive. Like a great airplane hangar. We walked down a swirling spiral staircase several floors to the work floor. We passed flying machines hanging from the ceiling as we went down. Strange single-seater planes with the head of the buffalo mounted on the front of them. Like the model Sinai had built. Frederick Thompson looked up at us as we descended and waved.

"Come on down, fellows." He shook my hand as we closed in on him, clasping mine firmly in his large ones. "Young Master Pompey. Good to have you on board. I know your father could not be prouder."

I looked over at my father. Proud? I hadn't thought how he would feel. He stood smiling at me as Mr. Thompson put his arm around me and drew me close to him. He pointed up at the hanging creations. A strange version of a Red Car with stubby wings on the side, like a red and black bumblebee hung directly above us. Different takes on the funicular cars Sinai and Olivet. Not open air like the ones that went up and down the tracks outside, but sealed at the ends. Where the railroad wheels would be there were sled tracks. They had short stubby wings as well. And glittering among them, single-seater motorcycle flyers, as though someone had lopped the wheels off of an Indian motorcycle and then inserted batwings on the side. I double-checked. It even looked like they were designed to flap. At least some of them. Others were solid wing. I started running some drawings in my head. It didn't make any sense at all. I started to reach for my bag to get out some paper, but I realized I didn't have it with me. I'd gone home first and left it there.

Mr. Thompson laughed. "Working on a problem already, Master Pompey? Good. I like that. I like that a lot." He pointed over at the rows of desks and drawing tables lined with slide rules, drafting light boxes and sheets of creamy paper. Most of the desks were manned. Older men in heavy wool suits. Older than Mr. Thompson. Men my father's age with their sleeves rolled up and their ties loosened. And a few who looked my age, a young kid with huge Coca-Cola bottle glasses in a sweater vest over his wrinkled white dress shirt.

"Your peers, Master Pompey. Your co-workers. Your family." He spread his arms extravagantly across the expanse of the room. "This is your family. The generations born of the Ninth Cavalry, born of the Buffalo Soldiers." A few of the men closest to us glanced up from their work and nodded when they heard Buffalo Soldiers. One of the older men gave Pompey a quick salute. A real one. Not the half one he had given his father … yesterday? Had it only been yesterday?

"All of us here are beholden to the Buffalo Soldiers for our life. We are all of their blood." He shook his head. "Their power, their strength, flows through us. And with it, with it, we will fly. We will *all* fly!" He raised his voice powerfully. Every man in the room let out a cheer.

I lay in bed that night. I was exhausted. I was exhilarated. I wanted to sleep for days. I never wanted to sleep again. Never close my eyes. Mr. Thompson and my father had shown me to my desk. My name was neatly engraved on the side of it.

Pompey Gilford. I had spent a few hours getting acquainted with the other members of the Angel's Flight team. And working at my desk. My desk. I had started in on the batwings. They'd opened a whole slew of ideas in my brain. They were still running through my head as I lay there. I could reach up and touch them as they flowed over my head, twisting the sketches around. I had never felt more alive.

But I must have been more tired than I realized. It seemed as though the schematics suddenly vanished, and I stood facing It. The Spirit of the Buffalo. It came as the Sergeant had seen It. The sleek wings of the golden eagle. The shaggy head of the buffalo. And the lean hairless body of a Sioux brave. No, a Sioux chieftain. I could feel the royalty in his bearing. In his veins. He was chief. He was king. He was a god. He *was* the Spirit of the Buffalo. Of dreams. Of flight. I could feel it in my bones. If I grappled with the Spirit tonight, then I would fly. I would truly fly.

I knelt down in a wrestling position. I'd never paid a lot of attention to it in gym class at school. I was a runner, not a grappler. But I needed that knowledge now. I needed all of my knowledge and all of my strength. The Spirit feinted to my right. I fell for it. He lunged to my left and threw me easily over his shoulders. I landed on the ground with a thud. My whole body ached. I trembled. I could not lose. Not now. I scrambled to my feet and faced the Spirit.

I did not fall for the feint this time. Instead, I slid under Its arms and wrapped mine around Its knees. I knocked it to the ground. It grunted as it fell. It could be hurt. I could win. I could defeat the Spirit. It struggled to escape my arms, but I held fast. My mind raced. What had the Sergeant done? The words of my mother returned. Fast now. My mother would read the Book of Genesis to us after she finished the Sergeant's tale. Jacob held fast until the break of dawn. I had no idea when dawn would break. So, I held on, praying it would be soon. The Spirit must have sensed my determination. I felt Its eyes boring down into me. It worked Its fists together into a ball and began to hammer about my neck and shoulders as hard as It could. I felt the welts rising on my back. But I held fast.

And I repeated those words. "I will not let thee go; except thou bless me!" I did not expect a new name. But I wondered if this was when Pompey Fitz had truly become the Sergeant. And perhaps I would have a new title. With a burst of light, the Spirit of the Buffalo exploded and disappeared, leaving me dazed and seeing starts. The stars slowly congealed into patterns, the patterns into schematics, the schematics into a machine. A new machine. My machine. My ticket to fly. Peniel. The face of God. That would be my machine. Everything went blank. But the plans, the plans were written indelibly in my brain.

I slept through school the next day. My father had already left for the Angel's Flight by the time I awoke. Sinai was sitting at the base of my bed when I opened my eyes. Her face was twisted in jealousy. She threw a sheaf of papers in my face when she saw I was staring at her.

"What?"

"Those drawings! They're amazing! Better than my airplane." She pouted. I looked at the sheets she had tossed at me. The Peniel. Complete. Just as I had seen it last night. My eyes lit up.

"It wasn't just a dream!" I scooped the up the papers and threw them in my satchel. I jumped into my pants. Sinai looked at me like I had gone insane. I didn't care. I had to button my shirt three times because I kept missing a buttonhole and making my shirt sideways. I almost forgot my Panama. Sinai brought it to me at the door. I kissed her on the cheek and laughed. Then, she knew I had gone insane. She slapped my cheek.

"What the heck was that for?" she demanded.

"Because I love you, little sister. I love you because you lie. Your design is better than mine. And you know what? I am going to tell father that."

The sky was dark by the time I reached the Angel's Flight. The clouds were threatening rain. It was unusual for September. And especially after all the heat of the past few weeks. Only two days ago when I brought my father his lunch, it had been in the nineties. Maybe we would cool off sooner this year.

I pulled my collar up higher against the cool as I crossed Grand. I didn't want to get sick. Not now. Not when there was so much to do. I had been too busy with the cold when crossing the street to notice it, but as I drew closer, I realized there was a white streak in front of the Angel's Flight doorway.

El Viejo. His starched white guayabera had given him away. El Viejo was bent over the lock to the Angel's Flight with something in his hand. He had a large key similar to my father's that he was trying on the lock. Around his neck hung a slim camera unlike any I had ever seen. The flash bulb seemed to be an integral part of it rather than a separate mechanism. Without a second thought, I yelled out. "Hey! What are you doing?"

Startled, El Viejo dropped the key with a clatter. I ran at him, knocking him into the metal door. It made a loud clanging sound. El Viejo was definitely not nearly as frail as he pretended. He pushed back, hard, and knocked me to the pavement. As he started by me, I swung my arm out at his legs. It staggered him. The strap on his camera broke and it spilled to the ground, shattering. El Viejo cursed in Spanish as he leapt away.

The door opened. My father and Mr. Thompson stood framed in it. I pointed at the fleeing El Viejo. "He was trying to get in." I struggled to my feet. My father pulled me into the Angel's Flight and locked the door behind us.

Mr. Thompson was rushing down the spiral staircase. "Code One Emergency! Code One Emergency! We have been compromised!" The Buffalo Soldiers jumped into action. Pulleys lowered the batwing airplanes and the Olivet plane to the ground. My father leaped into the Olivet. I followed quickly on his heels. He looked at me; I could see his mind starting to ask me to get out in a few seconds. But I shook my head and strapped myself into the co-pilot seat. My father smiled and nodded back. He tossed off his Hollywood Stars cap and pulled on a pilot's helmet complete with goggles.

"You better do the same, son. It would be a shame to lose that Panama now!" And he laughed.

The ticket booth at the top of the Angel's Flight, on the Olive end, was slowly sliding open. I could hear the gears grinding. Rain splattered down on the roof of the Olivet. Several of the batwings swooped past us and up into the night air. I could see Mr. Thompson at the controls of one. He pointed north towards Chinatown. My dad nodded and kicked the engine of the Olivet into gear. We rose with a sudden rush of air. I *was* born to fly. I *was* born to soar. And this was only the beginning. I let out a whoosh as we barreled through the opening and up onto Olive. It took me a minute to get my bearings. Everything was so different in the night sky. But then I focused on the lights on City Hall only a few blocks away. With its night lighting on, it was a beacon of modernity. It looked much more majestic from above, not minimized from being above it, but magnified. My city. Our city. I patted my father on the shoulder. It was too loud in the flying Olivet to speak. He looked over and nodded.

One of the batwings flew by and wiggled its wings at us. The pilot pointed in the direction of City Hall. A gyrocopter was rising from the park next to it. Even from here, I recognized the white guayabera of El Viejo. The batwing broke from us, its speed much more ferocious than ours. I couldn't wait to build the Peniel and try its speed out against one of the batwings. I knew I could beat them. The Olivet fluttered after it, much faster than I would have imagined. The batwings were soaring after the gyrocopter.

A shadow obscured the Olivet. I looked up as best I could. One of the LAPD dirigibles was floating over us. I could hear the whisper of its engines over our own. I glanced at my father; he clenched his teeth and dove. This dirigible didn't have any officers hanging off the bottom. Too dangerous at night, I presumed. At least then none were dropping on our roof. It dove after us. We went right, suddenly, and hard. I would have been thrown against the Olivet window if not for the safety belting. As it was, I felt a huge pull on my stomach.

We spun back around. The batwings and gyrocopter were in front of us. The faster batwings were circling the gyro, trying to force him back towards the Angel's Flight. El Viejo made a correction to avoid one of the batwings, but he must have overcorrected. His system went wild. The gyro lurched to the left, and then plummeted straight down and burst into flames. On top of the LA Times Building on First Street. I wondered if tomorrow's morning edition would be late. And who would be on the front cover.

The dirigible pulled up from its dive and shot towards the blaze atop the building. I could see LAPD officers scrambling out of the basket in their web suits, waiting to pounce on the roof. The batwings scattered high into the sky.

The doorway under the Olive Angel's Flight station clanged shut. The Buffalo Soldier pilots were slapping each other on the back and yelling. My father leaned into me and whispered, "This was our first real test. We've flown them at night. When no one was watching. But never all at once. And never anything but speed trials and gauge checks. This . . . this was the real thing. This is what we've trained for. This is what we have dreamed of." And he yelled too, loud and strong.

Mr. Thompson came over. He stuck his hand out. "Welcome to the family, Master Pompey. You earned your stripes tonight." He nodded back at my desk. "And I've had a chance to look at those drawings. The Peniel? It's got merit. Real merit." He looked over at my father. "You should be proud."

My father beamed. I pulled at his sleeve.

"Yes?"

"And Sinai too?" I looked down at my shoes. "I've seen her schematics. She just might be a better designer than I. Maybe." I met his eyes. "And you can never tell her I said so."

"Look." My father led me over to the desk next to mine. Engraved on it was Sinai Gilford. "Already done."

1941 was drawing to an end. 1942 was going to be an amazing year. For all of us.

UNUSUAL THREATS AND CIRCUMSTANCES
BY
RONALD T. JONES

Bronzeville was pleasantly silent beneath a night time, star riddled sky.

Jericho Aldridge hopped off the streetcar, carrying case in hand. He wasn't exactly looking forward to the two and half block walk to his tenement. A long work day exhausted his body. Three hours of night school did the same to his mind, but the latter he embraced with enthusiasm. Four years after returning home from the war intact, mentally and physically, he was finally making a move toward his goal of being a lawyer. The thought infused him with fresh energy, adding vigor to his stride.

A black Ford Deluxe pulled up alongside Jericho, its front wheel scraping the curb. The car stopped.

Jericho's drifting thoughts snapped back to the moment. He halted, a wary gaze on the vehicle.

The driver's side door opened and a black man, short and stocky with a wide face, pencil thin mustache and eyes radiating contempt, emerged from the car.

The sight of the infamous Negro cop Two Gun Pete normally invoked fear in those he confronted, guilty and innocent alike.

The deadliest cop in Chicago, he was called.

Deadly to his own people, Jericho thought venomously. He had known plenty of Toms like Pete in the army and would have gladly put a bullet in each of one of them if given an opportunity.

Two Gun Pete swaggered up to Jericho. The plainclothes cop wore freshly pressed slacks, silk gray shirt with a dark gray silk tie. His polished black Stacy Adams gleamed luridly beneath a glazing street light. In accordance with his moniker, two 357 magnums were holstered to a pair of gun belts around his waist.

"Where you going, boy?" Two Gun Pete folded his arms, drilling diamond hard eyes into Jericho.

Jericho held the cop's gaze, forcing away the scowl forming on his face. "Home, sir."

Pete's eyes narrowed to skeptical slits. "Home? From where?"

"School. I'm taking night classes."

"Really? You one of them educated niggas."

Jericho stifled an impulse that would definitely have earned him the electric chair if he got caught.

Pete cocked his head. "Where do you live?"

"A couple of blocks that way," Jericho said, pointing ahead.

"That's interesting." Pete dropped his arms and circled Jericho. "Because I just got a report of a break-in just down the street. A witness spotted someone fitting your description at the scene."

Jericho didn't bother to express alarm. He knew sooner or later some two-bit cop would pull that fitting-the-description crap on him. "I just got off the street car, sir."

Pete placed a threatening hand on the grip of his right holstered magnum. "Shut up, boy! Drop that case, turn your ass around and put your hands behind your back."

Jericho let out a frustrated sigh, placed his carrying case on the side walk and turned as the cop instructed. "I don't have anything to do with a break-in . . ."

Pete wrapped an arm around Jericho's neck, which took a bit of effort. Jericho towered over the cop.

"I said shut up!"

Despite the cool touch of a pistol barrel pressed against his temple, Jericho felt not a shred of fear. He had faced much worse in the war than a pathetic blowhard of a cop. If anything, his simmering anger intensified, but he held it in check.

"If you don't want a hole in your head the size of my fist, you'll keep that damn trap shut." Pete holstered his weapon, and took out a pair of handcuffs. He cuffed Jericho, reached down and picked up the case. He unzipped the case and dumped its contents on the ground; two textbooks, four note pads and a half dozen pens and pencils. He grunted and walked back to the car, not at all worried that Jericho might bolt.

No one with an ounce of sense ran from Two Gun Pete.

Jericho saw the cop talking on his police radio. He groaned as the situation began sinking in like a mud stain in clean fabric. Was he really about to be railroaded for something he didn't do? Final exams were at the end of the week and he couldn't miss any days at work.

Pete finished his radio call and sauntered back to where Jericho stood. A cruel smirk marked his expression. "You in for a hard time, boy."

"There's no need for this," Jericho expressed, not caring if he got cracked in the skull or shot for mouthing off. "You know damn well I'm innocent. You know you have no grounds for stopping me!"

Pete's hand flicked out like a serpent's tongue, grabbing Jericho's collar and pulling. "Useless ass nigga! I got all the grounds in the world and all the authority to go with it! You got somethin' else to say?"

Jericho curled his lip. "No. I got nothing else to say, lawn jockey."

Pete rammed a fist into Jericho's gut.

Jericho doubled over; the breath knocked out of him.

At that second, another Ford Deluxe arrived on the scene, pulling beside Pete's car.

Jericho rose slowly, pain throbbing in his midsection.

Two uniformed white officers exited the vehicle, one shorter, but slimmer than Pete, the other tall and beefy, like a linebacker.

Pete acknowledged the officers with a curt nod.

Jericho detected an abrupt change in the black cop's demeanor. He seemed docile, almost fearful in the presence of his supposed peers.

Both cops ignored Pete, zeroing in on Jericho like a pair of hound dogs.

"Well, well, what do have here?" The short cop announced with a lopsided grin. He grabbed Jericho's bicep and squeezed. "You're a sizable buck, boy."

The tall cop clapped Jericho's shoulders and tapped his chest with the back of his hand. "Yeah. Solid, too. I'll bet you were an all-around athlete, like that Jackie Robinson sambo, huh?"

Jericho fluttered a nervous nod.

The tall cop smiled, but it was the oddest smile Jericho had seen anyone deliver. It seemed pasted on, as detached from any real sentiment as the dazed look in the cop's eyes. Maybe he was high on something . . .

The short cop removed Jericho's handcuffs and tossed them at Pete's feet. "Good job, Sylvester. We'll take it from here."

Pete hesitated before bending to scoop up his cuffs. Even as the black cop shot a glare at Jericho, humiliation burned beneath his bravado. He quickly strode to his car, got in and drove off.

Jericho gave no more thought of Two Gun Pete. The white cop removed his cuffs? Why? That wasn't exactly standard procedure for the police especially when dealing with Negroes.

The tall cop prodded Jericho toward the unmarked police car, opened the door, and pushed him into the back seat. Both cops got in the front and seconds later, the car pulled off.

Jericho rode the next five minutes in silence, despair nibbling at him. All his hard work, so much effort to walk an inconspicuous path, in hopes of avoiding situations like this . . .

The car turned down a narrow street leading into Washington Park, one of Chicago's larger parks.

The car stopped and the cops got out. The shorter cop opened the passenger side rear door and jerked a thumb.

"Out."

Jericho fought to keep his head from reeling. "What? I thought you were taking me to the station."

The cop clutched Jericho's arm and yanked him out of the car with impossible ease, as if the latter weighed a hundred pounds less than his 195. Jericho would not have expected that kind of brute strength from the cop's larger partner, much less an average size man.

"You're free to go," said the shorter cop.

Jericho's gaze shifted suspiciously between both cops. He knew this story. The cops would make a pretense of letting him go, then shoot him and claim he tried to escape. But the cops were unarmed. They weren't even carrying batons. Maybe they weren't going to shoot him . . . unless they had guns in the car . . .

"Go!" The big cop yelled in a grating bass voice that didn't seem like his own.

Jericho backed away, whirled and ran full sprint into the park's all-encompassing darkness.

For several feverish seconds, his hammering heartbeat, rapid breaths, and his thumping footfalls pounding the turf filled his ears. The one sound he expected to hear was the gunshot that never came.

Instead, a high pitch howl pierced the stagnant night air. A chill, cold as arctic frost, raced through Jericho, despite the heat and sweat of his exertion.

As he neared a stand of trees, he sensed a presence behind him . . . heard a slavering growl. He spun about in time to see . . . something . . . leaping toward him; glowing, moonlit eyes, lupine muzzle stretched wide enough to expose rows of dagger-like teeth, and rangy arms ending in clawed hands the size of baseball mitts.

Shock would have frozen anyone else lacking in the kind of instincts Jericho possessed . . . instincts he hadn't drawn upon since the war. He dove out of the creature's path and it let out a yelp as it collided with a tree. The creature was massive and bloated with fur covered musculature. Tattered remnants of a police uniform clung to its heaving body like banners.

Jericho's eyes widened in disbelief at the animal nightmare before him but he couldn't afford to hesitate for a second. He pulled up his right pant leg and slipped a knife out of its ankle sheathe. His co-workers carried razors for protection. Jericho preferred his trusty combat blade. Thank God that self-loathing Tom cop hadn't frisk him.

A second creature bounded at him.

Jericho swung his knife in as precise a stroke as his limited reaction time could manage. A brutal impact jolted his arm, followed by the all-too-brief give of hide, tough as iron links, being penetrated by cold steel.

The beast screeched in pain and flopped on its side. The other beast, recovered from its headlong rush into the tree, charged Jericho, swinging a clawed hand at his head.

Jericho stumbled backwards, barely avoiding a blow that would have shredded his face. He fell on his back and the beast crashed on top of him, saliva from its wide-open mouth dripping in gooey strands.

Jericho stabbed upward, plunging his knife into the beast's throat in rapid, piston strokes. The beast sank its claws into Jericho's chest, intending to tear out his heart. But Jericho kept stabbing, repeatedly, desperately, ignoring the searing bite of claws breaking his skin. Finally, the beast's deadly grip slackened and it collapsed on Jericho with bruising force.

Jericho scrambled from underneath the body as the second beast, driven to a mad frenzy by its injury, lunged toward him.

Shots rang out.

The beast's chest exploded and it flew backwards a good twelve feet before plowing into the ground. It gasped a final breath and lapsed into death.

Jericho shuffled to his feet, drunk with terror-induced adrenaline. An extra ounce of terror seized him when he watched the beasts' bodies reverting back to human form; the two white cops. What the hell was going on?

Then he turned, probing the park to see where those shots came from. Three figures doused in surrounding darkness approached him. They appeared human and they were armed. Jericho stared apprehensively, not knowing if these incoming arrivals were friend or foe. As they drew nearer, he saw that they were Negroes, two men and a woman.

"It's alright, we're here to help," said one of the men with a friendly smile.

After so much hostility directed at him within the past hour, Jericho needed a whole lot of friendly. His shoulders sagged in relief.

"You OK?" the other man asked.

Jericho nodded, his gaze drifting to the woman, a sepia-toned beauty with large chocolate drop eyes and lustrous black hair pulled back in a pony tail.

Like her partners, the woman wore black coveralls tucked into calf-length black leather boots. All three carried automatic rifles of a type Jericho had never seen before.

The man who first spoke was dark and lean with a processed Cab Calloway mane. He stood over the body of the cop/beast Jericho killed and whistled, impressed.

"You got him good. You just went toe-to-toe with a werewolf and won. That's the first time that's happened."

"A werewolf?" Jericho exclaimed.

The other man, broad-chested with a scar cutting across his chin, shouldered his weapon. "We'd better make ourselves scarce before the normal law shows up." He pulled some kind of spherical radio device from a pouch on his belt then spoke into it. Afterwards he gestured to Jericho.

"You can come with us . . . if you want."

The woman gave her partner a sharp look. "Hold on . . ."

"He killed a werewolf," the scarred man said insistently. "I think that warrants an audience with the professor." He turned back to Jericho. "Your choice. If you don't want to come with us, we'll bandage you up and send you on your way. But you'll have to swear not to reveal anything you've seen or experienced tonight."

Jericho quickly agreed to accompany the trio. He had questions and he could safely assume that these people, whoever they were, had answers.

* * *

Jericho found himself in the backseat of a navy-blue Cadillac Fleetwood. The two men sat up front, the woman beside him. Despite a stinging chest wound and being drenched in blood and sweat, he still felt massively self-conscious being in such close proximity to the woman . . . as if she cared what he looked like in the wake of his near-death encounter with . . . werewolves? He still couldn't believe it.

"Who are you people?"

The scarred man in the front passenger seat twisted around. "I'm Frank." He gestured to the driver and the woman with his chin. "That's Herb and Nadine."

"Nice to meet you Frank, Herb, and Nadine. I'm Jericho. Not meaning to be rude or ungrateful for your timely intervention, but you still haven't answered my question."

"Everything will be revealed to you when we reach headquarters," Frank said. The soothing tenor of his radio announcer's voice put Jericho somewhat at ease. He decided to have patience.

"May I?" Frank requested.

Jericho followed the man's gaze and realized that he was still clutching his knife. "Oh . . . yeah." He handed the knife to Frank, its blade slick with werewolf blood.

Frank hefted the knife, examining it with admiration. "A Trench Knife. Nice."

"You know your blades," said Jericho. "A souvenir from the war. I took it from a dead Nazi."

Frank nodded and handed the knife back, hilt first. "Where'd you serve?"

"France. You?"

"Same. Herb, too. He was a tanker with the 761st."

"If we weren't blasting Krauts to smithereens, we were mulching them beneath our treads," Herb added, clearly relishing the memory.

Jericho slid the knife back into his ankle sheath and glanced over at Nadine. She stared out of her window, oblivious to the war talk. He wondered what her story was.

* * *

Ten minutes later, Herb pulled over in front of a church and parked. Jericho regarded the large, spired structure curiously. A sign above the main entrance with fanciful lettering read: Ebenezer Baptist Church. The others got out of the car and headed for the church's side entrance. Jericho followed, his curiosity deepening, but he held his tongue.

The four, Frank in the lead, entered the building and descended a narrow staircase to a lower level. They boarded an elevator, embarking on another descent approaching two minutes. How far down were they going? Jericho thought, growing mildly alarmed. The elevator finally stopped and the doors opened. Jericho stepped out into a mid-size room with concrete walls and floor. Ceiling lights lit the room, bathing it in a harsh glare.

Frank, Herb, and Nadine stood in front of a wall facing the elevator.

Jericho frowned. "What now?"

A teeth rattling groan filled the room, providing Jericho's answer. He flinched at the discordant noise. A section of wall receded, developing a doorway size opening. An older gray-haired man, sporting a van dyke beard and wearing a superbly tailored tan-colored three-piece suit emerged from the opening.

Frank spoke to the man, recounting the night's events. The impeccably groomed man regarded Jericho with a grandfatherly twinkle in his eye.

"Impressive. Frank was wise to bring you here." The man spoke with a lyrical accent, possibly Jamaican.

"We don't know that yet," Nadine grunted skeptically.

The gray-haired man chuckled indulgently, focusing on Jericho. "You'll have to forgive Nadine's blunt manner. It takes her a while to warm to strangers. I'm Professor Harrison Neal." He thrust a hand out.

Jericho grasped the proffered hand and shook it. "Jericho Aldridge. You'll have to forgive my blunt manner, sir, but the only reason I'm here is so someone can explain to me what's going on. One minute I'm walking home, the next I'm being mauled by creatures I thought only existed in movies."
Jericho looked around. "Who are you? What is this setup?"

"We're part of the NAACP," replied Professor Neal.

Jericho's jaw dropped. "What?"

"Unusual Threats and Circumstances Branch to be precise," Neal went on. "We are a secret branch of the NAACP, so secret not even the membership, outside of a few dozen or so select persons, is aware of our existence."

At Jericho's astonished gape, the professor went on. "As you know, the NAACP's purpose has always been to address issues of racial discrimination and violence against the Negro. The methods we have used in an effort to achieve equality for the Negro has ranged from legal action to protests and demonstrations."

"Yes," Jericho said in recollection. "My uncle is a member. I've read a few issues of the Crisis."

Professor Neal brightened. "Ah. Very good. I contributed several articles to the magazine over the years. You may have come across one?"

Jericho squinted, searching his memory. "Uh . . ."

"Never mind." Neal threw up a dismissive wave. "I'm sure you have. Anyway, there exist threats to the Negro that no conventional, non-violent mechanisms the NAACP normally employs can cope with. Dr. Dubois discovered this during the second year of the NAACP's existence. There are plenty of whites in this country who hate the Negro with extreme venom and passion. Very few whites, however, possess the means or the sheer psychopathic intent to create terrors designed to kill us. In 1912, Dr. Dubois assembled the most brilliant Negroes in the nation and presided over a clandestine conference where he advocated a need to form an arm within the NAACP for the singular purpose of locating and eliminating threats to Negroes of an abnormal nature. It was from that conference that UTC was born."

"These . . . abnormal threats," Jericho began, trying his best to process everything Neal was telling him. "Are they frequent?"

"Not particularly," said Neal. "But when such a threat does arise, it is often truly horrifying. In '27 for example, a UTC team was sent to a small town in Arkansas to eliminate giant spiders that were feeding on the Negro residents. The team successfully eradicated the spiders as well as the scientist that created them. Two years later, a doctor in Mississippi created a Frankenstein-like monster and unleashed it on Negroes. The thing killed over seventy men women and children before UTC operators tracked it down and destroyed it. And of course, they made the doctor disappear."

Jericho shook his head. "Negroes victimized by spiders and Frankenstein monsters? I've never heard of this. This would've been in the newspapers, on the radio . . ."

"If it were white people being attacked by these creatures, it would certainly have been national news," said Nadine. "Negroes don't get that kind of press."

"In fact," Professor Neal interjected. "The deaths of those scientists and doctor, received a great deal of news coverage, with not a mention of the Negroes killed by their creations." He sighed. "Sad."

Jericho looked intently into the professor's eyes. "And now, we have werewolves to contend with?"

Neal nodded. "Up to twenty-five Negroes that we know of vanished within a three-month period on Chicago's south side. Who knows what the true number is? A good number of the vanished, I'm sure, were vagrants. Witnesses reported the presence of bestial man-shaped creatures in tattered police uniforms prior to five of the disappearances. That's why we're here."

"Of course, the disappearances of those Negroes received no press attention," said a scowling Frank. "This assignment brings us into uncharted territory. Going after those were-wolves means going full fledge after the police. We've never confronted law enforcement in a direct action."

Jericho perked up. "Maybe you won't have to. Maybe those dead werewolves in the park were the only ones. The threat may be over."

"Could be, but I doubt it," said the professor.

"I know of a person who might be of help to you," Jericho stated. His expression turned fierce. "If you don't mind, I really want to be there when you meet him."

"Which brings us to our next topic," said Neal. "Frank acted on his discretion to bring you to me. UTC is always in need of skilled operatives. We could use someone like you in the ranks."

Jericho grinned modestly. "I didn't do anything special, Professor. Hell, I'd be just as dead as those other Negroes if your people hadn't shown up in the park."

"You still killed a werewolf," said Frank.

Herb nodded in vigorous agreement. "That qualifies you, along with your combat experience."

Jericho dropped his eyes. He had goals, a well laid plan for his future. Was he truly prepared to abandon them to join a group he had never heard of until now? But then, being attacked by werewolves could be the ultimate impetus for life altering decisions.

"Think on this," Professor Neal quietly intervened. "In the meantime, our doctor will treat your wounds and then you can lead us to the person you wish us to see."

Jericho smiled in anticipation. "Fair enough."

* * *

Two Gun Pete sat in his car puffing on a cigar, staring out listlessly onto a dark street. Slim pickings tonight. Normally, punks, pushers, and dregs would be packing these corners at this hour. But the disappearances and rumors of what caused those disappearances kept most of the riff raff indoors. As an officer of the law, Pete appreciated a quiet street. On the other hand, streets that were too quiet had begun to make his job a bit difficult. Maybe it was time for his 'colleagues' to operate in another part of town until the fear died down.

A Negro male walked past his car.

Pete watched him for a few seconds and then snuffed out his cigar, reveling in his good fortune. He hopped out of the car.

"Hey, boy!"

The man stopped and turned around.

"Where are you going?"

"Nowhere, just out for a walk."

Pete scoffed as he approached the man. "Boy, ain't no niggas ever just out for a walk. Especially after midnight. I think you're up to no good." He took out his cuffs, dangling them. "Get your hands behind your back."

The man obeyed without protest. Pete preferred he mouthed off. Not that the cop ever needed a pretext to beat the snot out of whoever he detained.

Before Pete could slap the cuffs on his latest quarry, a voice from behind stopped him short.

"Get your hands up, Two Gun."

Pete couldn't believe his ears. "What the hell . . ."

A gun barrel poked the back of his head, and Pete's hands shot up in compliance. He dropped the cuffs.

"Let's take a walk to your car," the voice ordered.

Pete turned to find himself facing two men and a woman. The man and woman were armed with heavy duty heat. The other man carried no weapon, but he looked familiar. When recognition kicked in, Pete's eyes radiated shock. "You! You're supposed to be . . ."

"Dead?" The unarmed man finished with malice on his face and in his voice that sapped Pete's arrogance like a mosquito sucking blood. "Sorry to disappoint you."

"Let's go," Herb prompted, aiming his Tuskegee 5 automatic at the black cop's head.

Frank snatched Pete's guns from his holsters and grabbed the cop by the back of his neck, shoving him roughly toward the car.

The woman opened the driver's side door and pointed to the radio. "Call your wolf pals."

Pete tried to put on a tough face. "Do you have any idea who you're messin' with?"

"Do as the lady says," Jericho ordered with a smack to the side of Pete's head. How immensely satisfying that felt. Peevishly rubbing his head, the cop reached for his radio and made the call.

Afterward, Herb and Nadine scattered to their places of concealment.

Frank handed Pete's guns to Jericho. "More souvenirs."

Jericho smiled his thanks and scurried into hiding behind a parked car across the street.

"You damn fools got death wishes," Pete snarled. "Y'all just some common ass niggas that don't know who they're dealin' with."

Frank cut an amused look Pete's way. "Think about it. Do we come across as common to you?"

Before Pete could answer, a car turned a corner and pulled to a stop next to the curb.

Frank kept his hands folded behind him, pretending he was cuffed.

Three white cops exited the vehicle, two in uniform, one plainclothes.

The plainclothes cop wore a navy-blue suit with a tan fedora. Stark blue eyes peered out of a narrow, deep-socketed face. He adjusted his fedora, looking Frank up and down like he was choice vittles.

"You got a healthy one, Sylvester. That's good."

"Thank you, Detective," Pete said abruptly.

The detective's head pivoted back and forth. He sniffed the air. "I smell more meat." He glanced at the uniformed officers. "You mugs catchin' a whiff?"

Both uniforms nodded.

"Must be some drunk laid out in the alley," Pete offered with a jittery grin.

"Must be," said the detective through hooded eyes. "You know what else I'm smellin' besides the usual nigger scent?" The detective stared at Pete; his florid face lined with suspicion. "Nigger fear and it's coming from you, Sylvester." His gaze slid down to Pete's waist. "Where are your guns, Sylvester?"

Frank dropped low. "Now!"

Gunfire ripped the night.

A spatter of rounds struck one of the uniforms, rupturing his head.

Herb and Nadine darted from cover, firing their T5s in precision bursts.

The second uniform deftly dodged bullets streaming his way until he was hit in the back and side. Despite his wounds, he raced toward Herb, transforming in the process.

Herb held steady, took aim, and sent two more rounds through the cop's chest.

The uniform tumbled to the ground, yowling in pain.

Bleeding from a bullet wound to the arm, the detective leaped over Pete's car and landed in the street. His eyes glowed silver fire from the beginning stage of transformation. He zeroed in on Nadine and sprinted toward her.

"Hold fire, Herb!" Nadine pulled out a tranquilizer gun. She leveled the weapon and calmly pulled the trigger. The gun whispered. One dart . . . two darts . . . three darts struck the detective's midsection. His legs gave way and he hit the pavement, rolling to within six feet of Nadine. The detective brushed at his chest and stomach in a frantic effort to remove the darts. But enough tranquilizer had been pumped into his body to bring down an elephant. It also aborted his transformation into a wolf. The detective was very much a man when unconsciousness seized him.

Herb stood over the injured uniformed cop. Though incapacitated, the cop was close to transforming into a full wolf, at which point his injuries would be healed.

"You just got a raw deal," Herb snickered with a ruthless gleam in his gaze. "We only need one of you alive." He shot the werewolf twice in the head.

Jericho came from behind the parked car, looking and feeling mesmerized by what he witnessed.

Frank knelt beside the unconscious detective and gestured to Herb. "Call in the cleanup crew."

"Cleanup crew?" Jericho asked.

"We have specialists who come in and pick up the bodies after a confrontation. They do what they can to minimize evidence of our existence." Frank gave Jericho a knowing wink. "Did you notice that there was nothing in the news about those dead cop-werewolves in the park yesterday?"

Jericho raised a brow. "I hadn't been paying attention . . . but now that you mention it, two dead cops should have been headline news."

"A UTC clean-up crew arrived shortly after we left and removed the bodies," said Frank. "So, in actuality, someone in the police department doesn't want the disappearances of two cops to be publicized."

"You mentioned 'someone.'" Jericho shot a grim gaze at the knocked-out detective. "What if the entire CPD is in on this? What if there's a plot, extending to the mayor's office, to swarm Negro neighborhoods with werewolves?"

Frank put a hand on Jericho's shoulder. "If there is, UTC is here to stop it, bet on it. You can be a part of that effort. Have you made up your mind?"

Jericho pressed his lips decisively. "Oh yeah."

*   *   *

Two hours later, Jericho had an opportunity to see more of UTC headquarters when he accompanied Professor Neal to the interrogation room. They walked through brightly lit intersecting corridors, passing offices occupied by UTC personnel. Walking past a larger room, Jericho paused, his attention drawn to a metallic box, approximately seven feet tall, six feet wide. Prongs, buttons, and switches layered the box. A technician in a white lab coat adjusted functions on the box, while another perused data on a printout disgorging from a horizontal side slot.

Jericho pointed. "Is that a . . ."

"Computer," Neal finished.

"Aren't they supposed to be much bigger than that . . . like room-size?"

"We've found a way to streamline the hardware, while optimizing processing speed," said Neal. "Vacuum tubes, diodes, resisters and capacitors have been drastically miniaturized and they're powered by plasma energy as opposed to electricity. It's a far more efficient machine than the current monstrosities in use. Of course, for reasons of security, our innovation must remain restricted to a UTC setting." The professor beckoned Jericho along. "Come, time is precious."

*   *   *

"His name is Jeffery O'Malley," Frank announced when Professor Neal and Jericho entered the interrogation room.

The werewolf cop sat in a metal chair that was bolted to the floor, his wrists and ankles bound with chains.
Frank and Nadine flanked the prisoner.

Jericho tensed.

"Not to worry," Neal said, sensing Jericho's trepidation. "The detective has been injected with an inhibitor, preventing him from transforming."

Jericho relaxed slightly. "Well, if all it takes is a drug to keep them in human form then that's a relief."

Neal brushed the detective with a cool, appraising gaze. "Indeed. Science spawned these abominations. Science is one of the tools in our arsenal that we will use to combat them."

"Your nigger science will fail!" O'Malley snapped, tugging at his chains.

"Nigger science is what's keeping you in our custody, idiot." Nadine countered dryly.

"Detective, please enlighten me," said Neal. "How many werewolves are on the force?"

O'Malley's hatchet face contorted in an ugly mask of hatred. "Enough to make a full course meal of every coon in the city."

Neal ignored the insult. "Our doctors performed autopsies on your fellow officers. They discovered massive amounts of a chemical substance in their bodies which they believe triggers the change from man to wolf. I assume that there exists a stockpile of this chemical somewhere and that you know the location."

"Sure," O'Malley replied with a crooked grin. "I know the location. But I ain't tellin.'"

The professor tsked. "This would be so much easier if you simply cooperated.

O'Malley spat a glob of spittle at the professor's feet. "I've never made anything easier for a nigger. No reason for me to start now."

Neal shook his head. "Detective, I'm afraid you misunderstand. I don't speak of making this process easy on me. I preferred that you made it easier on yourself. But since you choose otherwise . . ."

Nadine produced a syringe filled with a blue fluid and plunged it into O'Malley's neck.

The detective screamed in pain, his cries elevating in pitch as the blue liquid forged a fiery path through his body. He bucked like a mad bull against his restraints.

"You've just been administered an experimental truth serum based on a formula developed by the late Dr. Carver. It's derived from a peanut extract. The serum is supposed to be extremely effective in spite of its rather unpleasant side effects. Since it's never been tested until now." Neal shrugged. "We'll see."

* * *

The truth serum worked beyond Neal's expectation. When the pain subsided, O'Malley lapsed into a trance and sang like a bird, truthfully answering every question Neal posed to him. The cop revealed how a German scientist named Klein had introduced werewolf serum to extremely bigoted elements in the CPD. The serum had been the result of Nazi research efforts to create super soldiers. The war ended before Klein could unleash his creation on the Allies. But why let years of painstaking research and development go to waste?

Three months after the police obtained the serum, an abandoned apartment building on the outskirts of the Bronzeville neighborhood had been converted into a police station.

Jericho drew the connection. Within a month of the new station opening, Negroes began disappearing. O'Malley confirmed that werewolf cops were operating out of the Bronzeville station. He also recounted how he approached Two-Gun Pete and asked him to supply Negroes to the werewolf cops. It took no prodding on O'Malley's part to get the Negro cop to agree to that despicable proposition.

Jericho's stomach turned.

Most importantly, the cop revealed that vials of werewolf serum were stashed in the police station.

As it turned out, the experimental truth serum had another debilitating side effect: death.

O'Malley expired an hour after the interrogation.

* * *

Two days later.

Jericho sat in the sterile briefing room; beset with jitters he hadn't felt since the war. He watched Frank, Herb, and Nadine banter lightheartedly with each other.

Although he wasn't formally a part of UTC, when Professor Neal asked him to join the upcoming mission, Jericho jumped at the opportunity. Frank and Herb exuberantly endorsed the idea. UTC operatives were stretched thin across the country, leaving Frank's team painfully shorthanded for the mission. Even reticent Nadine conceded to Jericho's participation.

Professor Neal walked briskly into the briefing room, followed by a thin, light complexioned Negro man in a rumpled tweed suit and a loosened black tie.

"Jericho, you haven't met Dr. Omohundro, one of our top scientists. He was part of the Manhattan Project."

As Jericho and Omohundro exchanged greetings, Neal gave printouts to the team members and began the briefing. "Dr. Omohundro assembled an emitter that shoots x-ray pulses.

Mounting the device on a remote operated helo-pad, he used the emitter to saturate the police station with those pulses, producing over a thousand images of the building's interior. The images were fed into our computer which tabulated them into composite floor plans of the areas relevant to our operation: the first floor and the basement. That is what you hold in your hands."

The team members glanced at their printouts.

"As Detective O'Malley so willingly divulged, the vials are in the basement, in a safe next to the evidence room. It is absolutely imperative that you destroy those vials. Do not leave as much as a drop of serum to be salvaged. Any questions?"

"No questions," said Herb. "I'm just ready to go wolf hunting."

Frank and Nadine cracked smiles of agreement.

"Do all the hunting you like," Neal cheerily encouraged. "As long as those vials are destroyed. In the meantime, study your printouts and develop a mission plan."

* * *

A two-day crash course in the use of UTC firearms had reacquainted Jericho with military skills that had only minimally eroded in the absence of war. The T5 was quite a different animal from the M1 rifle. T5s were manufactured in a secret facility on the Tuskegee University campus. In addition to conventional and explosive rounds, the rifle fired shock, incendiary, and fragmentation mini-grenades. It was equipped with digital targeting and cryon gas dispensing nodules to keep the weapon from overheating.

Jericho easily mastered the weapon, reveling in its sheer killing power. He also trained with the T51, a heavier version of the T5. The T51 possessed a Gatling barrel and fired larger rounds. Jericho became equally proficient with the T51 and made it his weapon of choice for the mission.

The field gear on the other hand took some getting used to. He wore black ballistic coveralls lined with steel weave, a steel mesh-reinforced flak vest, steel-toed black boots, hard rubber knee and elbow guards, goggles, respirator, and a fitted combat helmet. Grenades, a UTC-issue ceramic knife as well his trusty trench knife dangled from the utility belt around his waist.

Five minutes later, Jericho boarded a vehicle parked in the church parking lot. The vehicle was designed to resemble a CPD paddy wagon down to the last marking. Jericho appraised the flawless paint job, commending the artist.

He joined Frank and Nadine in the rear compartment, both similarly garbed. Herb sat at the wheel. He started the vehicle and eased out of the lot onto a quiet street bathed in darkness.

"Remember" Frank reminded Jericho. "Stick close to me, cover my back. Nothing fancy."

"Right," said Jericho. "Will do." He studied Nadine for a moment. Other than stories he had heard of Soviet women fighting Nazis during the war, Jericho wasn't aware of any American women, Negro or white, who fought in combat.

"Nadine, how did you become a part of UTC?"

Nadine clapped a magazine into her T5. "Little over a year ago, my father and uncle were killed. They were successful businessmen in Troy, Alabama, too successful for jealous white folks to cope with. One night, the Klan kidnapped them. My father and brother were tortured, hung, and set on fire. My mother and sister fled North, but I remained behind. I tracked down most of those Klan bastards and slaughtered them like pigs." Nadine's eyes grew frightfully cold at the recollection. "One of the Klansmen I sent to hell was the police chief. Afterward, I made my way North and rejoined my mother and sister. A month or two later, Professor Neal knocked on our door. He told me he was impressed with my work. For the life of me I don't know how he found out. Anyway, he signed me up for the NAACP. The next day I was training for the UTC. The rest is history."

Jericho gazed admirably at the woman, hoping and praying that he acquitted himself well enough in the mission to earn at least a smidgen of her respect.

"She's a natural," Frank said with a wink.

Nadine shot a part amused, part scolding glance his way.

DIESELFUNK!

Ten minutes later, Herb parked the vehicle in front of the police station. "We're here," He called out.

Frank, Nadine, and Jericho slipped on their goggles, respirators and helmets. They checked weapons and made necessary adjustments to their gear.

Frank opened the rear door and the three stepped out of the vehicle.

The police station was a large, bleak structure with a weather-worn Gothic façade. Abandoned buildings flanked the station. In fact, the surrounding neighborhood appeared desolate, darkly foreboding as if it was never meant to accommodate normal human activity. A few police cars occupied reserved spaces in the front, but there were no officers present. That worked in the team's favor. No one saw Frank, Nadine, and Jericho racing up the steps toward the colonnaded entrance.

Herb remained in the vehicle. "Godspeed," he whispered.

Frank entered the building, Jericho and Nadine close behind.

An officer sitting at the lobby reception desk looked up, gawked and promptly died in a sheering hail of bullets delivered by Frank.

Nadine joined her fire to Frank's, peppering three more cops behind the desk with lead.

Jericho riddled a cop in the hallway, the smooth whir of his T51's triple barrels, registering as a sweet melody to his ears. He pumped additional bullets into his instantly dead target.

"Control your fire," Frank admonished. "Conserve ammo."

Jericho jerked a nod, his heart drumming with exultation. The T51 was a most intoxicating weapon.

Eight cops, two full werewolves, the rest in various stages of transformation bounded toward the team from the hallway.

Nadine triggered a fragmentation grenade in the cops' midst. The resulting blast shredded bodies, splattering walls and ceiling in a glistening tapestry of blood and gore.

Frank tossed a pop-can size canister into the gutted-out hallway. Thick black smoke billowed from the canister.

The team scurried through the smoke-smothered hallway. A pair of fully formed werewolves ran toward the team, but stopped short, wagging their heads fitfully.

Werewolves possessed exceptional vision, enabling their oculars to cut through any visual obstruction, from total darkness to haze. The smoke from Frank's canister, however, contained a chlorine compound designed to sting wolf eyes.

The werewolves tried to backtrack, their eyes smarting from the chlorine-riddled smoke.

Nadine and Jericho took aim. Their goggles switched from normal vision to infra-enhanced. The werewolves became large, red heat sources across their visuals. Short bursts from their rifles skewered the werewolves, knocking them off their feet.

The team emerged from the hallway into a wide-open space filled with desks and chairs. Cops who had not transformed fired guns at the intruders.

Jericho was struck in the arm, and he stumbled off balance from the impact. His field wear's ballistic weave repelled the bullet, but he still felt like he'd been blindsided by a mallet. He sprayed fire in the shooters' direction, hitting three cops.

Nadine launched a pair of frags across the room. Frag blasts obliterated desks and sent partially to fully transformed werewolf cops flinging in every direction on a shock wave current.

Frank led the way through the room, darting toward a door that led to the basement. A werewolf leaped toward him, arms spread wide, teeth poised to rend flesh and crush bones.

Frank leveled his T5 and poured hot lead into the creature's chest. The werewolf fell, but another one took its place as Frank opened the door. Nadine opened fire, and the werewolf's head snapped back, its right eye and much of the face around it blown off.

Nadine gestured to Jericho. "Go with Frank! I'll stay here and keep them off your backs!"

Jericho nodded and followed Frank through the doorway.

The two operatives raced down three flights of stairs to the basement. They ran through a corridor, coming across a large empty space, enclosed by a chain-linked gate. That was the evidence room, O'Malley spoke of; except nothing was there, further compounding the fact that this place was not an actual police station in a functional sense. It was nothing more than a werewolf lair.

There were five rooms across from the supposed evidence room. Frank pointed to the third room. "There."

Suddenly, the barrel of a shot gun jutted from the room and the muzzle blossomed fire to the accompaniment of an ear-ringing boom.

Frank and Jericho dove to the floor, eluding the shotgun blast.

Two armed cops emerged from the room, firing wildly. Frank killed the one with the shotgun, sending bullets tearing through throat and sternum.

The second cop wielded a Tommy gun. Heavy slugs chattered from the weapon, and Jericho scrambled sideways as bullets pockmarked the ground he just vacated.

Jericho returned fire, striking the cop in the gut. The cop dropped to his knees, blood bubbling from his wound. But he was transforming, face expanding, lengthening, teeth sharpening; eyes darkening, sinking beneath a scowling overlapping brow, grayish fur sprouting from bare skin . . .

Jericho approached the wounded wolf cop with his ceramic knife in hand. A blade, sharper than a barber's razor laid the cop's throat open as easily as a chef filleting fish. A second stroke carved a deeper gash into the werewolf's neck. The lupine creature slumped face first to the floor, his head connecting to his body by mere strands of flesh.

Jericho took a satisfied couple of seconds to assess his kill, and then followed Frank into the room.

The place was cluttered with boxes, old newspapers, pieces of dusty furniture, metal pipes, and electrical wiring. In one corner stood a lopsided wooden table with an assortment of guns laid out on its care worn surface. Ammo, loose and in boxes, lay scattered among the weapons. Next to the table sat an open safe.

"Jackpot," said Frank.

* * *

A half dozen police cars skidded to screeching halts in front of the station. Herb watched the arriving vehicles from the driver's seat of the fake paddy wagon. Obviously, the besieged cops inside the station had radioed for assistance. When cops emerged from the vehicles, Herb pressed a button in the middle of his steering wheel.

Instantly, two sixty caliber guns on spring-mounted turrets arose from niches within the paddy wagon's hood. Herb pressed another button and a fire control panel with a joystick jutted from the dashboard. Herb wrapped his fingers around the joystick, pressed the trigger and unleashed hell. A stuttering fume of uranium tipped rounds blazed from the 60 cals. Cops death-danced to the clamorous tune of bullets perforating their bodies from head to toe. An unremitting stream of armor piercing rounds punched through the police cars, shattering windows and pulping cops still in the vehicles.

Five more squad cars raced to the scene.

Herb decided to try a new weapon. He flicked a lever on the fire control panel and a third turreted gun rose from the hood. The weapon's silvery, bulbous breech gracefully tapered to a narrow muzzle. Herb manipulated the joystick, swiveling the weapon toward the inbound police cars. His finger tapped the trigger. Intensely bright light emitted from the weapon in terrible, slashing doses. The light lanced into the forward police car. The vehicle glowed red very briefly before erupting in a fiery fount of molten debris and charred body parts.

Herb whooped in delight. He had always wanted to fire the death ray . . . or incandescent light beam . . . as the weapon's developers at Howard University formally termed it. He smirked. He preferred death ray. Herb targeted another police car . . .

* * *

Seventy-five vials of clear liquid sat in a plastic container inside the safe. An open packet of syringes rested beside the vials. The two cops were about to dope themselves up with werewolf serum when Frank and Jericho interrupted their party.

Jericho eyed the serum with disgust. "Burn that crap."

"Way ahead of you." Frank removed a tubular applicator from his belt and squirted a thick, green combustive gel inside the safe, lathering the vials. He took out a detonator, twisted its timer dial and placed it in the safe. He gave Jericho a pat on the arm. "Let's go."

The two rushed out of the room, making their way back to the stairwell. When they entered the vast room, they saw Nadine hunkered down behind an overturned desk trading fire with half-formed werewolves in the hallway. The werewolf cops had abandoned their surge tactics, resorting to gunfire in efforts to bring down the UTC operatives.

Nadine glanced at her colleagues and gave a thumbs up. Bullets chewed the floor around her, gouging splintered divots out of the desk.

"On three!" Frank shouted. "One . . . two . . . three!"

Frank and Jericho burst from the stairwell at the same instant that Nadine scrambled from behind the desk. The trio advanced on the enemy in rapid strides, their T5s and T51 pulsing on full auto.

Four wolf cops collapsed to the floor; their bodies tattered to wet strips in a welter of bullets.

Seconds later, a thunderous explosion from the basement roared up the stairwell, and punched through the door with the savage force of a giant flaming fist.

A shock wave rippled across the floor at hurricane velocity, sucking oxygen out of the room, temporarily producing an airless vacuum.

Two wolf cops at the front entrance fired .357s at the UTC operatives. Nadine yelled out and lurched to the floor as .357 slugs smacked into her ribcage and left leg above the knee.

Jericho grabbed Nadine's arm, pulling her upright while launching an incendiary. The grenade spiked at the cops' feet and erupted in a blistering gale, dousing them in writhing shrouds of fire. A hammering back draft from the incendiary blast blew out the lobby windows.

Frank and Jericho lugged Nadine between them and hustled to the exit.

Herb saw his comrades leaving the building and jumped out of the paddy wagon. He rushed to the back and opened the rear doors.

Corpses and burning police cars littered the street and sidewalk in front of the station. Frank and Jericho lifted Nadine into the vehicle and climbed in after her. Herb shut the doors and ran to the driver's side, hopping inside.

A hail of bullets pattered the windshield. The bullet-resistant glass held.

Wolf cops charged from the building, their guns cracking. More bullets struck the glass.

"You freaks are really aching to dance with the devil!" Herb grabbed the joystick and triggered a sweep of sixty cal fire, clearing the entrance of wolf cops. "That's a dance you didn't want!" He slammed his foot on the accelerator and gunned the fake paddy wagon down the street.

Nadine unstrapped her helmet and tore off her goggles and respirator. She eased painfully out of her flack vest, wincing as she dabbed lightly at the area on her rib where she was hit. There was no penetration thanks to the vest. Her rib may have either been bruised or cracked at worse. Plus, her leg hurt like the dickens.

Frank and Jericho removed their helmets, goggles, and respirators and immediately tended to their colleague.

"How bad is it?" Frank asked.

Nadine managed a shaky smile through clenched teeth. "Not nearly as bad as what we did to those damn wolves." She looked at Jericho. "Good job."

Jericho sat a little straighter, his face beaming. "Thanks."

Frank burst into laughter at Jericho's expense. "You've got this guy floating on clouds," he said to Nadine.

Jericho's ebony brown skin hid his blush. He looked away, an embarrassed smile tugging at his lips.

* * *

Jericho sat in Professor's Neal office. A tingling excitement still gripped him from the previous night's mission. When he returned home from the war, he told himself he'd never fire a gun in anger again. Until last night, he never realized how much he missed the action. Better yet, as a UTC operator, he felt he was fighting for a truly worthwhile goal . . . for which he would get no public recognition. If there were medals to be awarded in this secret conflict, Jericho could never reveal them to the world. From this point on, he existed in the shadows. He was fine with that. He'd always thought he was destined for far more relevant endeavors.

"It's unanimous," Professor Neal began. His office was a little larger than the interrogation room and bereft of any personal adornments. Papers and folders were stacked neatly on his plain wooden desk, next to a simple lamp and a hardbound book titled *The Souls of Black Folks* by WEB Dubois.

Neal took a pipe from his inner blazer pocket and lit it, suffusing the office with a headily sweet tobacco aroma. "The team had wonderful things to say about you. Of course, I expected all along that you would be a worthy operative."

"Thank you," Jericho said quietly. "I'm glad I didn't let anyone down. I just hope we resolved the werewolf problem."

"I think we have," Neal replied confidently, taking puffs from his pipe.

"I've been listening to the news all morning," said Jericho. "A police station attacked, heavily damaged, dozens of cops killed, squad cars destroyed and nothing is mentioned. The press may not be aware of the existence werewolves, but what happened last night should have drawn some kind of attention."

"I can only speculate that powerful interests wish to keep this matter under wraps." Neal frowned thoughtfully.

"How powerful are we talking?" Jericho wondered. "Are they in the government, or perhaps we're dealing with a filthy rich cabal that controls the government?"

"Either or," Neal stated, uncertain of which, but more than certain that werewolves in police uniforms, running rampant in Negro neighborhoods did not result from low-level plotting. "Whoever is pulling the strings, we have to always be on hand to disrupt what they are planning. That's why we need good, capable people like you on our side. Starting tomorrow, you'll begin formal training as a UTC operative."

Jericho smiled. "That's swell, Professor. Not that I'm ungrateful for the opportunity, but I'm still interested in being a lawyer at some point in the future."

"That's in the cards as well, Jericho." Neal clapped his hands in emphasis. "The NAACP needs plenty of lawyers to wage war on behalf of the Negro on the legal end."

Jericho rose to leave. As he shook the professor's hand, a question came to him. "Professor, what's going to happen to Two Gun Pete?"

"Actually, he disappeared," Neal replied casually.

"Disappeared?" Jericho gazed intently at the professor, awaiting an elaboration.

Neal had none to give. He displayed a circus master smile. "Yep. Disappeared."

Jericho's face dawned with understanding. "Oh."

* * *

A bit of news did make the headlines in the wake of UTC's attack on the police station:

German Scientist Perishes in Hyde Park House Fire. House Completely Burned, Research Destroyed.

BONREGARD AND THE THREE NINNIES

BY

CAROLE MCDONNELL

Bonregard James Kirby Stewart was trying not to think. Trying not to weep, more like it. He tightened the iron and leather strapping of his jetpack and looked down at the city, the city where his estranged father, Cleveland George Stewart, lived.

In the mist of the dark night, tears began to fall. The same old humiliation, the same blast of disdain, from his younger days assaulted him. He tried to put aside the inundation of deadening memories, days when he would come in from the fields and listen to his Momma's old Victrola and ponder his father's cruelty. He wondered if he should continue his downward descent. If the past had been full of human cruelty, wouldn't the future be as well?

The mechanical hum of the jetpack and the growing heat of the iron nuts and bolts against his back reminded him that there was little time left. For this latest trip and or his dying father. He glanced in the distance at the setting sun, then at the rising moon.

"The sun rules all day, and the moon rules all night," he whispered to himself. There was order in everything, even in the darkness.

For more than fifteen years, he had traveled across state lines, across national borders. He had put on humility and shuffling and met other famous spies in hidden bunkers and sent missives from President Roosevelt to American undercover agents in France, New York, and England. He had walked proudly with such noble freedom fighters and spies like Josephine Baker, Zora Neale Hurston, and Billie Holiday. And he had kowtowed and aw-shucks and uncle-Tom'ed his way into the kitchens of fifth column Ku Klux Klan groups, Aryan American Nazi soirees, and American Communist leaders. At those times, he had thought of Cleveland George Stewart, the father who had abandoned him and divorced his mother when Bonregard was two. Soon, if he could build up the courage, he was meeting him again.

Below him, just one-hundred-and-eighty-feet to his left, was the city's red-light district. Bonregard studied the bright neon lights and remembered the third and last time he met his father, some thirty years ago when Bonregard was fourteen years old. At that time, Cleveland had driven into town in his Roadster, wearing a white suit, and two watches set to two different time zones. He had talked about his travels, of the "women of the night" he had encountered in big cities. "The women live in pretty houses," he had said. "Not like here. And they have such white pretty hands. Sweet-smelling, too." He had gestured with his hand. "And you can just pick them like you pick a flower from a garden."

In spite of his desire to be respectful to the father he had only met twice, Bonregard had raised a questioning eyebrow. Cleveland George Stewart had seen it and had responded, "You ninny! Why am I wasting time with you?"

Later, when Cleveland married up, to a fine educated lady younger and classier than Bonregard's mother, he sent Bonregard a letter.

"You are no longer my son," he said. "You and your sister are nothing to me now. My only children are here with me."

So that was that; Bonregard accepted that he no longer had a father, no one to honor and help him and claim him as his very own.

Cleveland had been the first person to call Bonregard stupid, and ninny had been the only assessment his father had given him. After that, a strange thing happened: almost everyone –the headman at the logging company, the pastor and music teacher at his mother's Christ Prayer Warriors Church, the dean of the Negro college-- everyone began calling him stupid.

The last person to assume Bonregard was an idiot – although he hadn't come out and actually said it – was Dr. Stadlen, his mother's general practitioner. He had asked him to reconsider the prescription he had given. "It makes her woozy," he had said. "She says when she takes it, she can feel pain in the Circle of Willis."

The doctor had laughed "The Circle of Willis?" he had asked. "Is that one of those new-fangled driveways?"

Bonregard had wanted to say, "No, it is a part of the brain. My mother was a nurse before she took sick." But he hadn't said everything on the tip of his tongue and in the back of his mind. Dr. Stadlen was white and educated, after all; he was also the only local doctor who attended to Negro patients. Bonregard thought it best not to cause trouble, even though the idea that this white man was so dismissive dug at his very soul. As his mother lingered on her walk toward death, Bonregard had lain in his bed, angry and feeling doomed. It seemed to him that in addition to the sorrow of being black, he himself was cursed. Or, why had so many people—black and white, male and female—treated him so disdainfully?

At last, after thinking about his strange lot all night, he began to think that he should visit Miss Joanna.

Miss Joanna was old but she was educated and she had befriended Bonregard when he was a child. More than all that, she respected him. If anyone could help him, she could. So he travelled to her yard and there he told her all his heart. About how his Daddy had called him a ninny and how he must be because everyone treated him like an idiot.

"I don't know why your Daddy said that to you all those years betimes," she told him, rocking in her chair. "He wasn't no saint. Maybe he sensed you could see through him. So he said it to make you feel dumb. Some grown folks ain't grown at all. And some folks just plain mean. Whatever the reason, for good or bad, the curse done stuck and you gotta lift it offa you.

And, after it lifts, you go out into the world and do great things! Hell, expect great things! Cause now people gonna see the smart boy you always was."

"So, my Daddy made me dumb?" Bonregard asked.

"No!" Miss Joanna shouted. "He didn't curse you with foolishness, boy! Ain't nobody can curse what God done blessed and God ain't never made anything foolish yet. It's not foolishness that's your curse. It's the appearance of foolishness!" She pointed her fat index finger in his face. "That there the curse your Poppa done put on you."

Bonregard pondered the old woman's words and sipped some more sweet tea as he peered out her window at the hillside in her back yard.

The old woman sipped her tea as well and thought of her younger days, days when she could've been somebody if she'd been more educated, more beautiful.

"Bonregard," she said after they'd both been silent a long time. "I know whereof I speak. My Momma done did the same thing to me when I was young. And my life was hard acause of it. Everywhere I go, North or South, Eastern or West, somebody be thinking I'm stupid. I could see it in their eyes whenever I said anything, suggested something, or put forth my opinion. 'Who is this fat Black uneducated woman think she be?' I got the look everywhere. And it compounds the problem, you know. Cause you know how it be in the world. You Black, folks think you dumb. You a woman? Men folk be thinking you got no sense. You a Christian? Educated folks be thinking you believe in fairytales. So, compound that with the ninny-curse and my boy, life gets hard. Lotsa disrespect you gotta wade through."

Bonregard looked at Miss Joanna and was like to cry for her; he had a soft heart that boy.

"And you live like this alla your life? Ain't no way you ever freed yourself?" he asked her.

"Oh, I freed myself at last," the old woman answered. "From the ninny curse at least. Not that life got noticeably better. It's the South, after all. And slavery been over with a mere eighty years. And women just got suffrage. And, well, folks will always think Christians are dumb for believing some Jewish carpenter rose from the dead and is God. So, all that . . . remains. But yeah, you gotta have that curse lifted offa you. By the blood o' Jesus, just renounce it. The only words your Daddy said about you? Hell, no, Bonregard! Don't make 'em part o' your life. Not anymore!"

So Bonregard washed away his father's curse by the blood of Jesus and walked down the hill from Miss Joanna's yard. As he strolled down the lane, he heard her calling out to him and turned around. She was standing up on the porch, her bottle of sweet tea in her hand. "That be a pearl I just told you!" she shouted to him. "Be careful who you share it with. Lotsa swine out there!"

"I'll remember, Miss Joanna," he shouted back.

"And watch who you're kind to!" she shouted again. "Be wise as serpents but harmless as doves! You hear me, Bonregard?"

"I hear you, Miss Joanna," he shouted back. Then, after bidding her goodbye a second time, he continued along his way, his feet still heavy and his heart aching. Still, now he understood part of the cause of all the cruelty that had assailed him.

When he reached his own yard, he told his mother all that Miss Joanna had told him. His mother listened and after he finished, she said, "Now look here, Bonregard! I ain't got no time for none of your foolishness! You get inside and clean up. That's the only thing you're good for, you sorry-ass excuse for a human being."

Bonregard had looked at his mother and understood, sadly and too late, that he had shown her a pearl she could not appreciate. Still, he reminded himself that the curse was now lifted; yet shame was a switch in hand; ready to beat his hide because he was an unloved, disowned son. Bonregard surmised that the effects of the curse were still powerful with those who knew him from the past. Future friends and acquaintances would be different, he reminded himself. They would see him as he is. Race, of course, would remain a problem. From the looks of things, race-hatred would take a long time to die down. But he told himself, at least he wasn't a smart woman like Miss Joanna.

Smart women, he figured, had it way harder than smart men. Of course, there was the matter of religion; Miss Joanna had said people thought you were dumb if you were a Christian. Bonregard walked into his house and picked up a broom. He pondered if he should change his outlook on life, maybe become a follower of Mohammed or even an atheist. Something that would make him look less bumpkin in the eyes of people he needed to impress.

That night he got to thinking about all the folks who had treated him like dirt. But the thoughts were too much for him so he put them aside and, forgetting what was past, he looked ahead to his high calling. What was he to do with his life? He had looked about his room at all the doodads, do-hickeys, and what-nots he'd been fussing with. As a boy he'd wanted to be an engineer and he had succeeded. He had wanted to fly to the stars even though he was black and poor and with no one believing in him. Now, on this present night, he was beginning to think again about his past and with so much fervor it was obvious to Bonregard that the shame of the past had never left.

In fact, it occurred to him that much in the present was mirroring the past. On a morning twenty-three years ago, Bonregard had gone down to the city newspaper office.

"I'd like to buy an ad," he had said, trying hard to make the white spectacled lady behind the counter trust in his intelligence.

She didn't seem to; she rolled her eyes to some unseen person behind him and gave him a form to fill out, hovering over him like a teacher helping a stupid kindergartener.

Bonregard reminded himself that her behavior wasn't personal; the curse was no longer in effect because it had been washed away by the blood of the lamb. It was race-prejudice and maybe class prejudice as well. He had worn his best shoes, his business suit that the church folk had saved up and bought for him last year at his high school graduation, and his father's Sunday hat. Still, the lady had sniffed out his poverty. Nevertheless, she was one of those genteel, hypocritical, patronizing sorts. So Bonregard accepted her "help."

His ad read, "If you've ever been called a ninny and you know you're not, please meet Bonregard James Kirby at the public Library on Saturday noon, June 21st. He will be standing in front of the magnolia tree. I am specifically interested in those who love engineering and building stuff."

As Bonregard looked down at the ad he'd written, his bespectacled helper counseled, "Perhaps you ought to tell them you're a Negro boy," and wondered aloud if perhaps he hadn't spelled his name correctly. "Are you sure it's Bonregard?" she queried. "And not Beauregard?"

"It's Bonregard," Bonregard answered, politely.

To which the woman said that the name was "a might too country-sounding. But perhaps it's best because you don't want some white boy to show up thinking your ad was from white folks. Also, Saturday most people work. Maybe you should change the date to Sunday after church."

Bonregard hadn't considered the possibility, but now that the idea was presented to him, he thought it discriminatory to only ask for black boys. Or even only for boys. But he understood how cruel disappointed white boys might become so he rewrote the ad: "If you've ever been called a ninny and you know you're not, please meet Bonregard James Kirby, a colored man, at the public Library on Sunday at 3:00, June 22nd. He will be standing in front of the magnolia tree. I am specifically interested in those who love engineering and building stuff. Women and all people of good will accepted."

The woman took the ad, Bonregard's hard-earned cash, and his grateful, "Thank you, Ma'am" and once again eyed some unseen person with a conspiratorial patronizing glance. Bonregard pretended he didn't notice her supposed superiority and walked out into the street.

He glanced back at the library and thought of the librarian. He shouldn't have been so damn polite, he told himself. When you pretend that ignorant deluded people were good people, when you ignored how they slighted you, they never think that you're tolerating them. They just think you're stupid. And when you ignore the cruelty of mean-minded people, they think they've won. Cause they know they cowed you into bowing down to them. Bonregard hated bowing down to mean-minded people.

That Sunday afternoon so long ago had found Bonregard standing under the magnolia outside the library. A white woman sat on the bench below the tree but didn't seem to mind him being there. Bonregard studied her, waiting to see if she would demand that he take his Negro self out of her shade. But she just leaned on the bench, pushing at the cobblestones with a white-tipped cane. After a while, Bonregard realized she was blind. And he began wondering if she also had moments of shame.

Shame was the hard thing, Bonregard thought, as he hovered over the city. Here, in his father's city, there were many people –like Governor Smith alias Governor Lynch—who had turned their shame into their glory. There were others who had conquered shame but who did not live in glory. Those were the women of the night whom his father reportedly still encountered. There were others who still struggled against shame like the shoeshine men and door keeps who had to kowtow to rich matrons and flyboys, rich folks whose pride seemed to depend on how much they could humiliate others who were unlike them. And there were others, like Bonregard, who could ignore humiliation and use the pretense of shame to conquer their enemies. The enemies, then as now, were those of a Nazi fifth column; good-old-boys who worshiped Eugenics because they were descendants and products of the Master Race.

More often than he cared to remember, Bonregard had flown into the City with his jetpack, hidden his gear within the bowels of some church basement that was akin to a modern-day Underground Railroad. After that, he would put on his costume --the torn, tattered outfit of a poor Negro houseboy—and meet his other counterparts of the spy alliance. He limped, of course, which made the costume all the more convincing. And no one ever looked under his crumpled woolen trousers to see what lay beneath. Dressed for shame and humiliation, he had managed more than once to pass important information along to others equally dressed-for-shame. The network was large and global, filled with the great and the small, the famous, the infamous, the holy, the lowlife, men, women, married, unmarried, Blue-black, near-black, red bone, good brown, and high yellow. Its primary goal was to make the world safe for Black folk of all kind. Unlike the goal of the white spies who simply wanted to make the world safe for democracy. And it was certainly not the goal of sycophants like Cleveland Stewart who used their education to benefit from their fellow Blacks or to leech off the whites. Democracy hasn't helped the Black man much, Bonregard mused as he searched for the house where his traitorous father dwelt. His own goal, his own mission, loomed nearer as he jet packed behind the house. Would he be able to do it or not?

It had been a long journey. So long that the gear caused the bolts to burn red with heat. Even the leather burnt hot. Bonregard had gotten used to it. In the earlier days of his experiments, before the device had been perfected, he had burned himself more than once. He looked down at the metallic prosthetics that would soon be covered over by the clothing he had brought. He thought again about his lost legs and how he had come to lose them.

He turned his thoughts again to that Sunday, the day he went out to meet others who were like him. He stood under that magnolia until sometime around two-thirty when two Black men approached. They stood afar off; their look wary. They were dressed in Sunday-go-to-meeting suits that appeared faded but never-the-less well-kempt. Bonregard recognized them from the church; they nodded to him but did not approach. Around a quarter to three, two Black boys around the age of sixteen or so arrived, along with a white boy. All three wore overalls and although they were familiar, Bonregard was hard put to remember where he'd seen their faces. It didn't surprise him, however, that none of his neighbors or kin from around town had shown up. After all, he reminded himself, they think I'm dumb. Only strangers will believe in me from now on. He glanced back at the library. Strangers who ain't nothing like that library missus.

The young boys were the ones who approached him; the older men still kept themselves in the background. After Bonregard told them his great dream of building a jet-pack fuel rocket, the boys told him their dreams. The older men, who were within earshot, would laugh occasionally. Bonregard's new companions were David, the white boy who said he wanted to have a garden on the moon; Malcolm, the taller Black boy who said he wanted to build an underwater submarine to circumnavigate the globe; and Thomas, the shorter Black boy who said he wanted to build a train that would burrow through the earth.

Bonregard asked his new companions if they'd ever been called "stupid" in their lives; each responded in the affirmative. And just after Bonregard had told them where he lived, but just before he said they were all going to learn to expect great things and to do great things, a group of four white men appeared on horses.

"You guys early!" one of the men, a blonde man in a brown hat, said. "Negras don't ever meet on time!" He turned to his fellow horsemen. "Guess we shoulda come early, uh?"

He indicated the other riders. "Know what they call us?" he asked.

Bonregard and his three friends respectfully shook their heads.

"They call us the Four Horsemen," the man said. "You know us now?"

Bonregard nodded. Since his childhood, he had heard tell of a group of men called the Four Horsemen of the Apocalypse. The men had the reputation of destroying the farms, the water-holes, and the churches, or Black folks who were thinking of "organizing" in the county.

"We don't gotta say any more, do we?" the man asked Bonregard. "So, you and your little advertisement gonna be for-gotten soon, right?"

Bonregard lowered his head.

"Good boy!" the man said. He pointed to David, the white boy. "And what're you doing here? Don't you got a home to get to? Come on, over here, son."

The white boy walked over to the two men. Some minutes later he returned to Bonregard and the group.

"What they ask you?" Bonregard asked.

The boy replied, "I told them I wanted to meet other folks who were stupid."

"And what he say?" Bonregard asked.

"He say, 'You go take your stupidity committee somewhere else,'" the boy answered.

The older Black men drifted away and Bonregard and his three ninnies kept their heads low until the Four Horsemen left. Still, now they knew each other's dreams.

Even then, suspicion was pretty much Bonregard's bread and butter. It was the mother's milk Black folks had learned to suck on and the bitter-tasting honey each Black child had had to sup on since boyhood. It was something Black folks always had to manage and balance as one would balance a keen word. Because Bonregard had a kind heart and a morbidly-introspective spirit, he always wanted to see clear and not be overtaken by suspicion. He did not want to turn into a cruel, judgmental, dismissive person. But neither did he want to return to a simple benefit-of-the-doubt doormat life.

So, when Malcolm suggested they meet secretly in spite of the Horsemen's threats, Bonregard insisted that David be allowed in the group. Thereafter, they set to work creating those dreams and calling themselves "The Tinkerers." Day after day, week after week, month after month, in cold and heat, in wet and dry, they could be found tinkering away in the old barn at the back of Bonregard's mother's house.

Even the Four Horsemen seemed to understand that the Tinkerers weren't aiming to cause any kind of uprising. The boys delighted the townies with what they called "Little Delights." There was the sub-mariner they built and dragged to the gulf so children could look at the watery world in the Gulf of Mexico. There was the jetpack they built and, to the amusement of the crowd, flew over the county fair. There was the jaunty motorbike they roared in across the fields and roads.

As for David, Bonregard battled suspicion when he found himself making negative assumptions about the white boy who spoke so easily and equally to Black boys. Often the boy would say or do something questionable that would make Bonregard's ears prick up and his heart wonder. But then he would excuse the questionable thing. Whenever he got a whiff of contempt from anyone, he would give the person the benefit of the doubt. It's only my own heart-wound, he would say to himself.

Sometimes he'd even say to himself, *or maybe it ain't me and David really does hate Black folk. But he seems to be trying hard to be one of us. If so be, we can just accept him until he finds his way.* Besides, he reminded himself, he had spoken to the white boy long enough to know that David was just a wounded soul as he was.

Then one night an explosion destroyed the little barn that was the studio of the young men. The three tinkerers had gone home but Bonregard had been working late into the night. Because of this, he suffered great bodily harm. Three days after the accident when he had returned to consciousness, Bonregard lay in his bed, looking at the places where his legs and arms had been.

After he returned to his mother's house, two neighbors built him a wheel chair, a poor-looking thing made up from discarded tires and a couple planks of lumber. The thing was humiliating and uncomfortable to sit in, and after a while the humiliation and the discomfort so chafed Bonregard that he would lie in bed imagining his funeral and what-all his coffin would look like and what-all folks would say. The thought often occurred to him that even in the grave he would be consigned to idiocy. Wouldn't folks say that "that idiot Bonregard done blowed himself up."

As he thought of these things, of the flowers that would bedeck his dead head, of his dead man's suit, and of the shoes that would be placed on his feet, he got to thinking how mad he was. Mad at the explosion, yes. But more than anything else, mad at that father who had cursed him. And even if all that talk about father curses wasn't just mystical silliness, there was truth in Miss Joanna's words. Because so many years ago his father had dismissed him and had made him seem smaller than chawed-up-tobbacky under his feet: *Who in the hell*, thought Bonregard, *gonna tell his own son that he ain't nothing?*

So Bonregard was angry as hell. Then word came around that the Four Horsemen of the Apocalypse had been bragging up and down the county that the explosion "weren't no idiot mistake but we done it!" And "let that be a lesson to uppity Negras who think they got more sense than God gave 'em." But worst, it turned out that David had been a false friend sent to spy out what Bonregard had been doing.

It was that incident that set Bonregard to thinking of betrayal and treachery and spying. Sometimes there is no greater fuel than anger and Bonregard found himself suddenly fueled up enough to live. He was mad at himself too, because he had had a suspicion about David and had ignored it because Old Pastor John had pretty much hammered out of his congregation every human tendency to trust their intuition. It seemed to be lost on the old minister that wolves often appeared to be better sheep than real sheep, or that wolves who thought they were sheep were more dangerous than wolves who know themselves to be wolves.

So, after that, when someone in the network came to his bedside and told him he was needed, he was both excited and suspicious. Excited because he liked the notion of spying on the likes of The Four Horsemen and knocking their horses out from under them. But suspicious too because he couldn't quite get it into his head that his silly-ass tinkering was that important to the federal government.

But it was. And soon, with the help of the two remaining former ninnies, he was outfitted with diesel-fueled prosthetic arms and legs of his own making. Heck, when he wore it, he felt human again. More than human. And the trouser pants covered the gears as well as the long-sleeved shirt covered those armless stumps of his. When he walked around town, heads would turn. Because everyone had pretty much given him up for dead. After a while, word got around that this Black boy had done made himself arms and legs. And the ma's and pa's of soldiers who had lost arms, legs, and themselves in the first world war kept showing up at his door begging for iron legs and steel arms.

Bonregard thought long and hard about their request but he couldn't help thinking that somehow these soldiers would return to their own superior ways. Still, he just couldn't bring himself not to help them. So, in addition to helping the poor Black farm boys who had lost arms and legs in farm accidents, he helped the sons of white racists and bowed to them and kowtowed and hid the fact that he knew they were just using him and, although they were grateful, they didn't respect him at all. He helped them all, from near and far. Then, when they were all on their feet and using their new arms and legs, Bonregard and his friends built the jetpacks and the submarines.

That was when his daddy, Cleveland George Stewart, showed up. Him who had never showed one ounce of interest in the boy he left behind. He came into the shed, looking around like he owned it. He talked a good talk, that it was good what Bonregard had done, that yes, we ought to share our gifts with the white folks, that it was truly Christian to help those poor white boys who had lost limbs to save Democracy, that it was possible the white world would like Black people after they saw all the gifts God had graced us with, but shouldn't he give the patent to larger firms that could do the job better?

He sat in his former wife's house with his two watches and his patent leather shoes talking about the same things he had talked about. He drank up Bonregard's sweet tea and biscuits and asked for more. He walked around the house marveling about everything he saw and when Bonregard angrily avoided him by setting his mind to work, he said, "Ain't no never mind, you don't have to show me around. So, he went into all the sheds and studios where Bonregard worked. Around the end of the day, he asked Bonregard once more. "You sure you won't sell that copyright? Fifty dollars is a lot of money for a Negro boy. And I'm your daddy. I wouldn't take advantage of you."

But Bonregard wasn't interested. Worse, he was angry that his father had appeared only when the possibility of money had reared its head. So, Cleveland George Stewart left with the check for $50 the white engineering company had given him to get the patent, instructions, methodologies from his son.

However, some five or six days after that, Bonregard went upstairs to where he had kept his papers and found that many of his drafts, instructions, and work papers had been stolen. Of course, it was his daddy who had done it.

Soon enough, some months later, a white company in the city began advertising prosthetics that looked very much like Bonregard's. Worse yet, they created his submarines and jetpacks as well. Money and government contracts flowed in for them, and Bonregard was left with nothing but the knowledge that he had been the original creator. But some good that did. The worst part of it was that the company was owned by The Four Horsemen. They had no desire to help poor Black boys; they cared only for the soldiers who had allied themselves with creating the Aryan Nation of the United States.

As Bonregard put up his jetpack and pulled on his tattered pants over his iron legs, he looked up at the night sky. It would be the last time he would see it, he told himself. For inside his father's house, his father — like the lackey that he had always been — was sitting with one of the women of the night. It was a woman Bonregard knew well, the blind white woman he had met all those years ago, a woman who had become a fallen woman because she had no other choice, a woman whom men often mistreated because they thought she was dumb and didn't know much. A woman who was a particular favorite with Cleveland George Stewart even though she herself hated him. She was one of the few women in the network and she was waiting for Bonregard now.

Bonregard dragged his iron legs out of the shoddy building and into the neon-lit street in front of his father's house. He looked ahead of him at the city, then to his right at the house. With his iron fingers, he grasped the laser gun in his vest. He had never murdered a man before, he told himself. Not a white man, not a Black man. But tonight, tonight, he would murder his father. And the only witness would be a blind white woman. He stalked toward the front steps, lowered his head and said a prayer for his soul. At the top of the stairs, the door opened and the woman's blind eyes peered out behind it.

"Is he alone?" Bonregard asked.

"He's always alone," the woman answered. "Even when he's got company."

"It's like that?" Bonregard said.

The woman nodded. "It's like that. Today his wife is gone to Church meeting. Praying for his soul as usual. That's why I'm here." She pointed to a room. "He's in there."

Bonregard entered a room that was silk and satin to find a frail old man sitting on a chair. "Daddy," he said, "Can I call you Daddy?"

Cleveland George Stewart chuckled. "You ain't no son of mine," he said. "Don't even understand the value of money! But your Momma was always stupid. You're like her people, dumb ninnies."

At this, Bonregard removed his laser and pointed it at his father. "A Ninny?" he repeated.

Cleveland George Stewart sat up in his chair. "You ain't got the balls!" he challenged, "Now me . . . if I had to kill my own kin, I could do it. But you! You're nothing like me."

At those words, Bonregard lowered the laser gun. He realized his father had just blessed him. The only kind thing his father had ever said to him. The only blessing he needed now. And now he could go on. The curse was a blessing. "Yes," Bonregard answered, "I ain't nothing like you."

DOWN SOUTH

BY

MILTON J. DAVIS

Roscoe Hill removed his chauffer's hat as he entered Miss Liza's mansion, patting his hair in place with his free hand. Although he worked for Miss Liza almost 10 years, he'd never set foot inside the expansive home on East 127th Street, New York City. Whatever she summoned him for must be special.

The maid led him through the antique laden foyer then through the gauntlet of oil portraits hanging on the hallway walls on the way to the parlor. Miss Liza sat before the picture mirror; her ecru skin radiated by the sunlight reflected from the window opposite the mirror. She took a sip of tea then placed the gold inlaid teacup on the matching saucer on the table before her.

"That will be all, Celia," she said.

"I'll be right outside if you need me," Celia said as she cast a distrustful glance at Roscoe.

"There's no need for that," Miss Liza replied. "Roscoe drives me every day. If I can't trust him, I can't trust anyone."

Celia glared at Roscoe.

"You behave yourself, boy," she whispered.

Roscoe glared back. "Mind your own business, you old bitty."

He smiled as he turned his attention to Miss Liza.

"You asked for me, ma'am?" he said.

"Yes, I did, Roscoe. Have a seat."

Roscoe sat in the chair next to the door.

Miss Liza turned toward him. "How long have you worked for me, Roscoe?"

"Ten years come this May," he said.

Miss Liza laughed. "You've outlasted all my husbands."

Roscoe lowered his head, hiding his grin.

"I reckon so, ma'am."

"Aren't you from down South?"

"Yes ma'am."

"Where?" she asked.

"Alabama, ma'am. A little place called Seale."

"I've never heard of it," she said. "My parents are from the South, Atlanta to be exact. But you know that."

"Yes, I do, ma'am."

"You fought in the war too, didn't you Roscoe?"

Roscoe tensed. "Yes, I did, ma'am. I was a Hellfighter."

Miss Liza knew about his time in the army. He fought in Verdun and earned a medal from the French. He came home thinking the medal and his time served would make a difference, but it didn't. The Klan almost lynched him outside of Phenix City, so he got out the South as soon as he could. If he'd had the money, he would have gone back to France. Instead, he ended up a taxi driver in New York, where he met Miss Liza. She was so impressed by his manners she hired him as her personal chauffer.

"Miss Liza, excuse me for being direct, but why did you ask me here?"

Miss Liza's smile faded. "Roscoe, I need you to pick up a package for me, a very special package."

"That ain't no problem ma'am," he said, somewhat relieved. "Where do I need to go? Brooklyn? Manhattan?"

Miss Liza looked at him square in the eyes. "Savannah, Georgia."

Roscoe shook his head. "I don't think . . ."

"Listen to me, Roscoe," she said. "You're the only person I can trust to do this. You're from the South so you know to behave down there. If I sent one of my New York men they'd be lynched before sunset. You're an ex-soldier so you can handle yourself. I'll pay you one thousand dollars up front and one thousand dollars when you return with the package plus all your expenses."

Two thousand dollars would set Roscoe straight for quite some time. But he knew his answer long before Miss Liza began her persuading talk.

"I'm sorry, Miss Liza," Roscoe said. "I can't do it."

"Roscoe, please," Miss Liza pleaded. "This is very important to me."

Roscoe put on his hat. "The last thing I want to do is disappoint you ma'am. You've been good to me. But this is one thing I can't do."

"Roscoe . . ." Miss Liza said.

Roscoe backed out the room.

"I'm sorry, ma'am. I'm sorry."

Roscoe turned then walked away,

"Roscoe, wait!"

Roscoe kept walking. Celia waited at the door, a grin on her face.

"You done messed up now, boy," she said. "Ain't no way Miss Liza going to keep you on now. Good riddance to bad rubbish, I say."

Roscoe pushed by the old maid then continued on to the garage. He trudged up the stairs to his room. Celia was right. He would have to leave and find another job. He was fond of Miss Liza; she reminded him of the daughter he never had. But there were some things he just could not do. Going back down South was one of them.

He opened his closet then dragged out his trunk, the same trunk he was issued when he enlisted. He opened it and was engulfed in memories. He gazed upon his uniform, neatly folded and pressed; the Cross de Guerre still pinned to the pocket. Atop the uniform was his bolo knife sheathed in the army issue canvas sheath. He picked up the knife then pulled it free, studying the long, razor-edged blade. The last time he held it in his hand was in Phenix City, Alabama. It was the only thing that stood between him and a lynch mob. He closed his eyes then shook the memories from his head. A man who fought for his country shouldn't be treated that way. He had the right to defend himself.

He sheathed the knife, and then placed it back into the trunk. Roscoe shuffled over to his dresser, opened the drawers then began removing his clothes and placing them neatly into the trunk.

"And where to you think you're going?"

Roscoe turned to see Miss Liza standing in his doorway.

"Well Miss Liza, I figured since I turned down your request, you'd be ready to fire me."

Miss Liza sat in his desk chair. "You figured wrong. You're like family, Roscoe, and Lord knows I don't have much of that."

Roscoe sat on the foot of his bed. "I appreciate you think of me that way. But I don't . . ."

Miss Liza grabbed his hand.

"Listen to me, Roscoe. I'm going to tell you the whole story. After I'm done, if you tell me you won't do it, I'll never bother you again."

"I'm listening," Roscoe answered.

Miss Liza swallowed. "When I was 15, I got pregnant. The father was a white boy, Leonard Shuman."

Roscoe leaned back stunned, almost pulling Miss Liza from her seat.

"Pregnant? By a white boy?" Roscoe felt anger rising inside. His grip on Miss Liza's hand tightened.

"It's not what you think, Roscoe," Miss Liza said quickly. "Leonard and I loved each other. Leonard's parents were prominent in New York politics, just like my parents. But Leonard's parents weren't about to let their son marry a colored girl, and my parents weren't about to let me throw my life away on some weak-minded white boy. We fought them, but in the end our parents won. Leonard's parents sent him to Europe; my parents sent me to Atlanta where I lived until I gave birth. They took my baby from me, and then put her up for adoption."

Miss Liza's eyes glistened. Roscoe took a handkerchief from his drawer then handed it to her.

"I held her in my arms, Roscoe. She was so beautiful. I made a promise that day that I would find her, no matter where they took her. Five years ago, I did."

"In Savannah?" Roscoe asked. Miss Liza nodded.

"It took a long time and a lot of money, but I discovered her living with foster parents. I sent them a letter explaining who I was and what I wanted to do. I promised I would not try to take her from them. I only wanted to communicate with her. They agreed."

"So, you ready to break your promise now," Roscoe said.

Miss Liza nodded. "About three months ago my letters started coming back. I've been going crazy ever since. I think she's still in Savannah, but for some reason her family decided to stop the letters."

Miss Liza opened her purse, reached inside then took out a picture. She handed the picture to Roscoe.

"Her name is Mary Ann," Miss Liza said.

"She looks just like you," Roscoe replied.

"I want my baby, Roscoe. I want my baby home. I'll pay you whatever you want. Please do this for me. Please."

Miss Liza bent over then cried into her hands. Roscoe leaned toward her, placing a gentle hand on her shoulder.

"I'll do it," he said. "I'll go get your baby, Miss Liza."

Miss Liza lunged toward him, wrapping her arms around him.

"Thank you, Roscoe. Thank you!"

Roscoe held her, stroking her hair. He imagined if things had been different for him his own daughter asking him the same question. There would be no doubt he would do it, even if it meant returning to the South and risking his life again.

"It'll be alright, Miss Liza. It'll be alright," he said.

* * *

Roscoe took the subway to the train station. He paid for his ticket then took a seat in the cabin. Once they crossed the Mason-Dixon Line he'd have to move to the colored section, but for now he sat where he chose. The train left promptly; Roscoe settled into his seat then quickly fell to sleep, lulled by the rocking rhythm of the train. He dreamed of the day he discovered what he possessed. He was twelve. There was a storm that day, the worst storm he'd ever seen. He, mama and daddy crouched in the kitchen under the table, mama praying like a preacher on revival Sunday. They heard a loud crack then everything when black. When he woke, they were still under the table, except the large white oak that grew beside the house was on top of them. Daddy was still, but mama moaned and prayed. Roscoe pushed against the tree, straining with all his might, but the tree was too heavy. He cried out for help until he was hoarse, but no one answered. In a fit of rage, he pushed against the tree again and it shifted. Roscoe kept pushing until they were free. He picked up Daddy and took him outside, and then he returned for mama. She looked at him with wonder.

"God done sent us an angel," she said. "An angel!"

Weeks later, after the excitement and tragedy of the storm had passed, Daddy and Mama called him to their room.

"The Lord done gave you a gift, boy," Daddy said. "And it ain't one to be trifling with."

"You have to keep it secret, unless other folks find out and try to get you to do bad things with it," Mama said. "It's bad enough being colored in this world. What you have will only make it worse."

"But I can help people!" he said.

"Listen up boy!" his father said. "You promise that you'll let no one know about this, you hear?"

"Yes, sir," Roscoe said.

"Swear on the Bible," Mama said.

Roscoe placed a trembling hand on Mama's Bible.

"I swear I won't use my strength or let anyone know," he said.

Mama smiled then kissed his forehead.

Roscoe jumped awake. He halfway expected to see Seale, Alabama. He settled into his seat. It was hard, but he kept that promise for most of his life. It wasn't until the Great War did he use his powers again. That was another nightmare.

The train eased into the Savannah station in the afternoon in the midst of a hot humid day. Roscoe peered out the window, his stomach churning with emotions. During the journey down he'd spent his time lending a hand to the porters, chatting with the Negro men who served the passengers and kept the train running smoothly. Most were from the south like him, fleeing Jim Crow or seeking a better life in the North. From the conversation nothing much had changed. One discussion with the men warned him to keep on his guard, even though the men didn't realize the warning in their words. They were playing Spades when it began.

Moses Jeffry, a tall light-skinned man with slick-backed hair dropped a seven of diamonds on the table.

"You fight in the war?" he asked Roscoe.

Roscoe nodded.

"Yeah. I was there, but I wouldn't call it fighting," he lied.

Mike Stevens, a thick muscled man with skin like onyx and glittering white teeth, flashed an easy smile as he cut Moses' seven with a three of spades.

"I think I dug more holes in France than I did in Arkansas," he said.

'Pepper' Lewis, another light-skinned man with freckled cheeks, cursed as he dropped a two of hearts.

"Them boys from the 369th gave them hell, though," he said. "A few of them won medals from the French. You meet any of them, Roscoe?"

Roscoe dropped an eight of spades and everyone moaned.

"No," he said. "I heard they were something else."

"Sho' were," Mike said. "Gave them Huns hell."

"Shoulda stayed in France," Pepper said. "You heard about that one that got lynched in Alabama?"

Everyone but Roscoe shook their heads. Roscoe picked up the cards and shuffled them.

"Say he was coming home and a bunch of Klansmen met him getting off the train in Phenix City, Alabama. Dragged him back in the woods and lynched him."

"That's a damn shame," Moses said. "A goddamn shame."

"You ain't heard the rest of it, though," Pepper said. "Story is every last one of them Klansmen showed up dead. Every last one of them."

Mike folded his arm across his chest. "You a damn lie."

"Kiss my ass, Mike," Pepper said. "If I'm lyin' I'm flyin'. Some say it was that soldier boy's ghost."

Roscoe quit shuffling the cards, the memory of that night paralyzing him.

"Hey boy, you gonna shuffle them cards?" Pepper said.

Roscoe placed the deck on the table.

"Got to go," he said. "This is my stop."

Pepper laughed. "That story scared you, didn't it?"

Roscoe peered over his shoulder. "Something like that."

As Roscoe trudged back to his cabin, the images of that day in the Verdun filled his head. The French officer had sent him and Thaddeus Jones out to scout the trenches north of their position. Thaddeus was always a joker, making fun of everything and everyone. They laughed as they walked the narrow, filthy gully, Roscoe taking point. As they rounded a sharp turn in the trench, they came face to face with a column of Germans reoccupying the abandoned trench. The Germans fired immediately; Roscoe heard Thaddeus grunt then fall into the mud. Bullets struck Roscoe in the back, spinning him around. He dropped to his knees as more rounds battered his chest. But he didn't die. Roscoe shot back, emptying his Bethier rifle, then throwing it aside for his .32 Ruby. Germans fell before him, replaced by more as they came closer and closer. When his Ruby was empty, he snatched his US issued bolo knife from his waist then charged, a rebel yell escaping his lips. The rest of the fight was close quarter carnage, Roscoe hacking and slashing like a madman. The Germans finally had enough of the black devil that would not die. They fled the trench, leaving Roscoe alone with his dying friend. When the rest of his unit reached him, he cradled Thaddeus's head in his arms, the wounds that hadn't healed still bleeding. In the medical tent they marveled at his recovery; if anyone thought it was unusual, they didn't say. Weeks later he was awarded the Cross de Guerre amidst the protests of the American Expeditionary Force commanders. A colored man didn't deserve such an honor. The French thought different.

Roscoe shook away the memory. He went back to his seat and gathered his things. The porters had been good company on the way down, but it was time to get serious. He waited until he was off the train before opening the leather pouch Miss Liza gave him before the trip. Inside was the address of her daughter's last known residence and a map with directions. Roscoe ventured into the old city, falling into familiar habits drummed into him since he was a boy. He kept his head down, making sure not to make eye contact with any white folks, especially white women. He was a man of average height, so physically he didn't draw any attention. He deliberately wore his clothes two sizes too big. Most people saw him as overweight; in truth Roscoe was nearly three hundred pounds of hard muscle on a 5 -foot 8-inch frame.

He hesitated as he came within a few blocks of his destination. This was a neighborhood for rich white folks. There was no way he could enter without being noticed. What would a colored girl be doing living in this kind of neighborhood, he thought. He shrugged. Miss Liza was light-skinned, and with her daughter being half white she could probably pass. Roscoe checked the directions one last time.

"Yeah, this is it," he said. "Lord help me."

He proceeded down the manicured street until he reached the address. He was walking up the walkway when the voice startled him.

"Hey boy! Where the hell you think you're going?"

Roscoe turned around to see the policeman standing on the sidewalk, his billy club in his hand. He was a lanky white man with straw blonde hair and a snarl.

"I'm sorry sir, but I was told the people living here were looking for a gardener," Roscoe said.

"They might be, but you know damn well you ain't supposed to be on this walkway. Git on around back!"

Roscoe silently cursed himself. He shuffled down the walkway toward the officer.

"You better be glad I'm in a good mood today, boy," the officer said. "Otherwise, I'd take you downtown."

"Much obliged to you, sir," Roscoe said.

"Git on now before I change my mind," the officer said.

"Yes, sir," Roscoe replied. "Yes, sir."

Roscoe walked across the grass then worked his way up the side of the house to the rear entrance, all the while clenching and unclenching his fists. By the time he reached the back of the home he was trembling.

"What you doing back here?" a husky female voice asked.

Roscoe looked up to see a dark brown woman dressed in a sky-blue maid uniform hanging clothes on the wire clothes line.

"I came back here to wait on the owners," he said. "I'm looking for yard work."

"Well, you a day late and a dollar short," the woman said.

Roscoe ambled to the fence.

"What do you mean by that?"

"The Finches moved out two weeks ago," she said. "Flew out of here like they owed somebody money. But that ain't so, because they got old money."

"My name is Roscoe Hill," Roscoe said.

"Lucinda Jones," the woman said. "Nice to meet you. Where you from?"

"New York," Roscoe said.

Lucinda laughed. "If you from New York I'm the Queen of England. You sound like you from right around here. Why you trying to be uppity?"

Roscoe laughed. "I'm originally from Alabama."

Lucinda smirked. "I thought so."

Lucinda walked back to the clothesline and began hanging the wash.

"Were they expecting you?"

"Apparently so," Roscoe whispered.

"What?"

"I said I guess not. My boss man said they'd be here."

"Looks like your boss man was wrong," Lucinda said.

"You got any idea where they went?" Roscoe asked.

"I don't, but Mrs. Henderson might. He's who I work for. You got a place to stay?"

Roscoe pushed back his hat. "No. I just got here."

"There's a place called Lulabelle's down by the marsh," Lucinda said. "It's a juke joint, but they have a couple of rooms upstairs they rent out to colored folks. It's loud but the food is great and it's far enough out of town so no white folks will bother you. Now come over here and help me hang up these clothes. The sooner I'm done, the sooner I can leave."

"Your boss won't mind?"

"Hell naw," Lucinda said. "As long as he ain't got to pay you he's fine. He'll probably think you some old buck sweet on me."

Roscoe grinned as he made his way next door. Lucinda wasn't a bad looking woman, but she was way too young for him. Besides, he was in Savannah on business. He helped her hang the rest of the laundry then went out front to wait for her. She came from around back, a wide smile on her face.

"Give me your arm," she said.

Roscoe extended his arm and Lucinda wrapped hers around it.

"Now we're sweethearts until Mrs. Henderson can't see us no more."

Roscoe glanced at the house. The curtain was pulled aside; a white woman with a blonde bun on top of her head glared at them.

They strolled down the road until they were far from the house and into the city. Lucinda let go of Roscoe. The two strolled to Black Savannah, a section of town that was in complete contrast to the newer section north and south of the city. Though the boll weevil destroyed the cotton crop, Savannah still thrived on shipping naval stores. The city had grown because of the prosperity, but like most cities that prosperity barely touched Negroes.

Lucinda walked up to a grocery store then went inside.

"I thought we were going to Lulabelle's," Roscoe said.

"We are. I got to pick up a few things before I go home."

"I need to get something too, come to think of it," Roscoe said.

They entered the grocery store. Lucinda strolled about the little store picking up items here and there; Roscoe went straight to the tool barrel. He searched through the tools until he found a sturdy long handled shovel. When he met Lucinda at the counter her eyes went wide.

"Now what in the devil's name do you need that for?"

"I'm a yard man," Roscoe said. "It always helps to have a good shovel."

Roscoe and Lucinda strolled down the street until they reached the edge of the colored district.

"This is as far as I go," Lucinda said. "Keep walking that way. You'll smell the marsh before you see it. Once you get inside ask for Slow Tom. He owns the place."

"Slow Tom?"

Lucinda laughed. "We call him that because he's the smartest man in Savannah."

"Thank you, Lucinda."

"You'll thank me by buying me dinner once you finish your business."

Roscoe looked puzzled. "My business?"

Lucinda tilted her head. "You might fool them white folks, but you ain't fooled me. I know you ain't no yard man. I don't know what business you got with the Finches, and I don't want to know. All I can say is be careful. This ain't New York."

"I'll be getting on then," Roscoe said.

By the time Roscoe reached the marsh the moon had risen over the humid night. The muted moonlight wavered on the high tide; the air heavy with the wetland organic aroma. The sound of raucous laughter spurred on by a teasing melody of guitar and piano drifted toward him as he neared Lulabelle's. The large barn-like structure sat on a piece of land jutting into the marsh, surrounded by ancient live oaks heavy with Spanish moss. A tall man in coveralls leaned against a pickup truck, cradling a double-barreled shot gun in his thick arms. Roscoe hid the shovel before stepping into the open. The man stood up straight as Roscoe approached.

"Who that is?" the man said in a thin, high pitched voice.

Roscoe walked into the light with his hands raised.

"Roscoe Hill," he said. "Miss Lucinda told me I could find a place to stay the night here."

The man motioned Roscoe forward with the shotgun.

"Where you from?" he asked.

"Alabama, by way of New York."

The man smiled. "I'm Percy Green. My niece lives in New York. You know a girl named Corliss Lewis?"

"Can't say I do. New York is a mighty big place."

"Yeah, but all the colored folks live in Harlem," the man said. "You sure you don't know her? Tall, yellow gal with big teeth."

"No, I don't know her."

The doorman shrugged. "Go on in. Slow Tom will be behind the bar. Can't miss him."

Roscoe nodded then went inside. The blues band was playing a slow, heavy tune, the dancers slow dragging to the beat, grasping and grinding. Roscoe made his way across the packed floor toward a wide dark brown man with a bald head, a cigar protruding from the side of his mouth. His thick hands worked on a large beer mug as he rocked to the music.

"You Slow Tom?" Roscoe asked.

Slow Tom looked at Roscoe and his eyes narrowed.

"Who's asking?" Slow Tom's voice flowed like the folks he'd met from Jamaica.

"Roscoe Hill," Roscoe said. "Miss Lucinda told me you rent rooms to colored folks."

Slow Tom placed the mug on the bar then extended his right hand. They shook, Slow Tom attempting to crush Roscoe's hand with his grip. He yelped when Roscoe returned the favor. When he finally let go Tom jerked his hand away as if he'd touched fire.

"Damn, boy! Where'd you get a grip like that?"

"Grew up on a farm," Roscoe replied. It was half the truth.

"Rooms are a dollar a night. Might as well stay up until I close. Won't get much sleep with this going on. You play cards?"

"No, sir," Roscoe replied.

"Quit with that sir stuff. Just call me Tom."

Roscoe reached into his pocket then handed Tom a dollar.

"Now that's the kind of boarder I like!" Tom said. "Man pays up front. You hungry?"

"Yes, I am," Roscoe replied.

"I'll fix you up. Sit on down and I'll have Hattie mix you up a bucket."

Slow Tom turned then pushed the swing door behind him open.

"Hey Hattie! Fix up a bucket! I got paying folks out here!"

Roscoe took a seat at the bar just as the music tempo picked up. Some of the couples reluctantly let go of each other, others took their business outside. Tom dropped a mason jar in front of Roscoe and grinned.

"Good stuff," he said. "Made it myself."

Roscoe picked up the jar then took a swing. It was good moonshine, stronger and smoother than most. He would need some liquid encouragement for what he was about to do.

"Good stuff," Roscoe said. "How much?"

"First one is on the house," Tom said.

Roscoe finished the glass then wiped his mouth with his sleeve.

"Hey Tom, you know anything about a white family called Finch?"

"I don't," Tom said. "But their maid Nadine does. She came in here two weeks ago mad as hellfire. Said the Finches let her go without even a warning. Said they were moving."

"When did that happen?"

"About three weeks ago. She said they got a letter then lost their minds. Rumor is they went to hide out in the marsh. Mr. Finch's daddy owns a house there. Uses it when he goes fishing."

"Any idea where that house is?" Roscoe asked.

The kitchen door swung wide and Hattie came out with a steaming bucket, a wash towel wrapped around the metal wire handle. She dropped the bucket between Tom and Roscoe. Her eyes lingered on Roscoe as a grin came to her face.

"You gonna have to teach that boy how to eat crabs," she said. "He ain't from around here."

Tom took a crab out the bucket then instructed Roscoe the proper way to crack a crab.

"Why you trying to find them white folks so bad?" Tom asked.

"I have a special delivery for them," he said. "My boss man told me to deliver it directly to them, nobody else."

"He picked a colored man for the job?"

"My boss man is colored."

Tom sucked the meat out of a crab leg.

"They're hiding out at the old Wallace Plantation about five miles from here. But you better have business with them. They got some local rednecks standing guard. You might mess around and get lynched."

"I'll be alright," Roscoe said. "That's been tried before. Didn't work out too well for them."

Tom began to laugh until he saw Roscoe's serious face.

"Do me a favor; when you get caught, don't mention my name. I gots to live here."

Roscoe was working on his third crab.

"I won't."

The men finished their meal as the band slowed down the music again for another round of slow dragging. Roscoe laid two dollars on the counter for the meal, but Tom waved him off.

"You don't make a man pay for his last meal," he said.

Roscoe chuckled as he took the bills.

"You think your man can take me close?"

Tom laughed. "You give Percy five dollars and he'll take you to the moon."

"Much obliged," Roscoe said.

He tipped his hat then went outside. Percy leaned against the pickup truck, whistling.

"Hey Percy, Slow Tom says you'll take me anywhere I want to go for five dollars."

"Hell yeah!" Percy replied.

Roscoe handed Percy the five-dollar bill.

"I'll give you another five if you'll wait for me," Roscoe said.

"It's a deal. Where we going?"

"The Wallace Plantation," Roscoe said.

Percy hopped into the truck. They drove a few feet then Roscoe touched Percy's shoulder.

"Stop here."

Percy stopped the truck. Roscoe got out, grabbed the shovel then threw it into the truck bed. He climbed back into the truck.

"What's that for?" Percy asked.

"Don't you worry about that," Roscoe replied.

Percy shrugged. "Ain't none of my business. I'm just the driver."

They drove deeper into the marsh. After a few more miles Percy stopped the truck.

"This is as far as I go," he said.

Roscoe climbed out the truck then took his shovel from the bed.

"I'll be back," he said.

He trotted down the narrow road through a gauntlet of live oaks. A few minutes later a large house came into view. Roscoe counted six white men in the front, four standing guard near the gate and two on the porch with rifles or shotguns. Roscoe slowed to a saunter as he walked into view.

"Who's there?" one of the men shouted. Roscoe didn't answer.

"God damn it, who is it?" the man said again.

Two of the guards approached him, their guns still cradled under their arms.

"Boy, what the hell are you doing out here this time . . ."

Roscoe smashed the man in the face with the shovel. He knocked the gun from the other guard's hand, then reached behind his back for the knife. As soon as his hand touched the hilt he was back in Phenix City, surrounded by the sights and sounds of that horrible night. He cut the guard across his throat then sprinted for the house.

He heard a rifle report then flinched as a bullet struck his shoulder. He gritted his teeth, and his body expelled the bullet then commenced healing. Other men appeared from behind the house. Roscoe counted twenty in all. He had worse odds in France. He waited until they were all close before he went to work. Roscoe stabbed, cut and slashed his way through the bodyguards, every blow a killing blow. Thirteen bodies lay sprawled on the ground before the others realized this was no ordinary man they were dealing with. They tried to run, but Roscoe caught them then dragged them back to his blade. He managed to glance toward the house; he saw a car pull from the back then speed up the narrow road. He looked about; five men were still alive, each running in a different direction. If he wanted to get Miss Liza's daughter, he would have to let them go.

He wiped his knife then tucked it in the back of his pants. Roscoe started with a slow gait then picked up the pace with each step. He ran down the dirt road then onto the paved street, increasing his speed. Soon the rear lights of a car came into view. He assumed by how fast it traveled it was the car he sought. Roscoe ran faster; in a few moments he was side by side with the car, peering into the passenger's window. A young woman sat there; she looked up, saw him then screamed. The driver swerved then looked at him as well. Roscoe lowered his shoulder then rammed it into the car. The driver lost control, then spun across the road and into the surrounding marsh. Roscoe hurried to the car. The driver leaned over the steering wheel rubbing his head. The girl looked at him as if he was death. He reached for the door, but the girl locked it. Roscoe gripped the door handle then ripped the door free. The girl cowered; Roscoe smiled then extended his hand to her.

"Don't be afraid," Roscoe said. "Your mama sent me."

The man in the driver's seat pulled out a gun. Roscoe snatched the woman from her seat then turned his back as the man fired. The bullets struck him hard and he fell forward. He caught himself, hovering over the young woman. He heard the man grunt as he exited the car.

"Get up and turn around," the man ordered.

Roscoe sprang up and spun around, knocking the gun from the man's hand. He wrapped his hand around the man's throat then lifted him off his feet.

"Now you listen to me Leonard, and you listen good," Roscoe said. "I'm taking Mary Ann to her mother where she belongs. Y'all could have worked things out, but I guess it's way beyond that now."

"I'm her father!" Leonard managed to say.

"You done took everything from Miss Liza. You ain't going to take her daughter, too. Now I'm going to put you down and you're going to get in that car and keep driving until you get back to where you came from. And you ain't never going tell anybody what happened here. If you do, I'll find out and I'll find you. And the next time I won't be so nice."

Roscoe set the man down on his feet. He glanced at Mary Ann then scrambled to the car, started the engine, then sped into the darkness. When Roscoe turned to the woman she cowered.

"Don't hurt me!" she said.

Roscoe reached into his jacket then took out the letter Miss Liza sent with him.

"This is from your mama," he said.

Mary Ann reached out with a trembling hand then took the letter. She opened it; as she read it her fear gave way to joy. She folded the letter.

"So, you're Roscoe," she said. "Mama told me a lot about you, but I guess not everything."

Roscoe nodded. "You can't tell what you don't know. I'm trusting that you can keep a secret."

"I can," Mary Ann said.

"Good. Now let's get you to New York."

Roscoe picked up Mary Ann.

"Hold on tight," he said.

Mary Ann held his neck tight, and Roscoe sprinted down the road back to Percy's truck. The man was snoring.

"Percy!"

Percy jumped, his eyes wide.

"Where? What?"

He looked at Roscoe and Mary Ann and his eyes got bigger.

"Where the hell you get that white girl from?"

"I'm not white," Mary Ann said.

Roscoe walked over to the passenger's side opened the door. Mary Ann climbed inside.

"You'll be alright now."

"Thank you, Roscoe," she said.

Roscoe nodded then walked back to the passenger side. He gave Percy ten dollars.

"Percy, this is Miss Mary Ann Pritchard. You take this girl to the train station and stay with her until she boards," Roscoe said.

"Where you going?"

"I got some cleaning up to do."

"Got it."

Percy sped off down the road. Mary Ann looked back at Roscoe with a warm smile, waving as the pickup truck disappeared into the darkness.

Roscoe returned to Wallace Plantation. He found his shovel then proceeded to dig a deep hole. He piled all the dead mean into the hole and covered it the best he could. The sun was breaking the eastern horizon as he finished. It was a sloppy job, but he didn't have time to make it right. Word would spread soon on what happened at Wallace Plantation and he would need to be long gone by then. He heaved the shovel far into the marsh, and then ran into the forest shadows.

* * *

Franklin Stevens took off the blood-stained apron then washed his hands. Working at the slaughterhouse wasn't the best job he'd ever had but it definitely wasn't the worst. He was working, which during these times was a blessing. He trudged to his locker, taking out his coat, hat and scarf. Chicago winters were brutal, and this winter was no exception. Despite the cold he walked back to his flat, relishing the quiet time. Sometimes a man just needed to be alone with his thoughts.

His landlord stood in the lobby as he entered the building. He had a sly smile on his face that bothered Franklin.

"Rent due?" he asked.

"No," the landlord replied.

"So why you looking at me like that?"

The landlord grinned. "You'll see."

Franklin shook his head then climbed the stairs to the third floor. He opened his door then stepped inside. He took off his coat and scarf, hanging them on the coat stand near the door.

"Roscoe?"

He stiffened at the sound of an old name from a familiar voice.

He turned around to see Miss Liza sitting at his table.

"Miss Liza?" he said.

"It took me a long time and a lot of money to find you," she said.

Roscoe took off his hat. Miss Liza stood then rushed him, wrapping him in a tight hug.

"Thank you so much for sending my baby back to me!"

Roscoe held Miss Liza for a moment then let her go. He walked over to the door then opened it.

"You're welcome. Now I think you best be leaving."

"Leaving? I just found you! I have so much to tell you, so many questions to ask . . ."

"I can't answer your questions and there's nothing I need to hear," he said. "I know the both of y'all is alright. You know I'm alright. That's got to be enough."

"Roscoe, please."

Roscoe shook his head.

"I'm suspecting Mary Ann told you everything."

Miss Liza's face became serious. "Yes."

"The more you know about me, the less safe you are. There are people out there looking for me and I'm trying my best not to be found. You understand?"

Miss Liza nodded. "I found you."

"Which is why I got to leave this place."

Miss Liza gathered her things then walked to the door. She placed her hand on Roscoe's cheek then kissed him.

"You take care of yourself, Roscoe. If you ever get tired of hiding, you have a home with me and Mary Ann."

Roscoe closed his eyes hard to cut off the tears he knew were coming.

"Goodbye Miss Liza."

Miss Liza's hand lingered on his check a moment longer before she left his flat. He closed the door then sat hard at his table. He gave himself a moment, letting a few tears fall before wiping his face. He went to his closet then opened his trunk, gazing at the old uniform and the bolo knife.

"One day," he whispered. "One day."

He took his clothes off the hangers and began to pack.

BIG JOE VERSUS THE ELECTRO-MEN

BY

JAMES A. STATEN

Baltimore, July 1949

FBI agent Joey Calhoun was running for his life. The storm wasn't helping; it had knocked out the power, so he was running blind. He had lost his flashlight in the ambush. The wind whipped what was left of his jacket around him, his left arm hung bloody and useless, his lungs burnt from the exertion. Yet despite the pain, he still ran as if the devil was pursuing him. He tried not to think about what they'd done to his partners back in that warehouse; he just ran between the buildings trying to lose them. But he heard the whirring of gears and pulleys, and the scrape of metal on concrete as they relentlessly followed him. He cursed when he saw that he had turned into a dead end. There was a flash of lightning and he saw them gleaming in the rain. Their multiple limbs and large oval eyes made them look like giant praying mantises. He realized that they had been herding him to this spot. He started shooting, knowing that it would do no good, but kept firing until he'd emptied his gun. The last thing he saw was the glowing eyes as they closed in on him.

Somewhere in Arkansas, January 1950

A large Hudson sedan made its way along a rutted dirt road. The four FBI agents inside were not happy about the bumpy ride or their destination. The windows were down but it didn't help in the early afternoon heat. All of the agents had their jackets off and their ties loosened. Their armpits were stained with sweat. Special agent Dan Swenson drove quietly. He was a big beefy blonde man who'd been a boxer in his youth but was way past his prime and wasn't going to let the younger agents see how much he was suffering in the heat. Next to him a younger thinner blonde man, special agent Jack Addams held a microphone and fiddled with the dials of the agency cars shortwave radio. He had a worried expression on his face.

"Nothing but static, that's all we've been able to get since we turned off the main road. I don't like it!" His expression was getting even grimmer as he said it.

"This whole trip is senseless. Why are we even out here? These ignorant backwoods nigras won't know anything! How are they going to help us find this guy?"

That was agent Brandon Flynn, a tall gangly redhead from the Little Rock office, who Swenson, being a New Yorker, didn't particularly care for.

"Because he's one of them, some super Negro, didn't you pay attention during the briefing?"

That was special agent Mark Williams, a tall muscular man with dark eyes and dark hair and a large hook nose that gave him a menacing look. He reminded Swenson of himself when he was younger.

"Personally, I don't think he exists."

Swenson stopped the car and finally spoke as he got out of the car. "We're here. Let me do the talking."

On either side of the road were about a dozen buildings that were little more than shacks except for one. It was a nice house with a porch on which an old black woman sat as if waiting for them. There was no one else around. The agents reluctantly put on their jackets and trudged up the slight incline to the house.

"Good afternoon Madam. We're looking for a colored girl name of Mary Williams," Swenson said politely with a smile.

The old women didn't answer; she rocked in her chair as if she hadn't heard him. The agents came right up to the first step of the porch. Swenson spoke to her again.

"Mary Williams, ma'am. I understand this is her home."

She finally stirred turned her head and spat a stream of brown liquid into a can on the table next to her. She looked down defiantly at the men facing her.

"Who wants to know?"

That was too much for agent Flynn. "You watch your tone, nigra!" he screamed, striding aggressively toward the old woman. Only the sound of multiple shotguns being cocked stopped him. The agents suddenly realized that they were no longer alone. They found themselves surrounded by at least a dozen well-armed Black men.

Swenson very calmly said to his men. "Don't make any sudden moves if you want to see tomorrow." He then turned to the old woman, who he saw was now standing and pointing a double-barreled shotgun at his chest.

"Who are you, and what business do you have with my granddaughter?" she said.

Swenson raised his hands so that everyone could see them and motioned for his agents to do likewise.

"We mean you no harm and meant no disrespect ma'am. We're with the FBI. I'm special agent Swenson. My men are special agents Addams, Williams and Flynn. We just want to ask your granddaughter a few questions about a man we've heard she is associated with."

Sadie Mae Williams sat back down in her rocking chair and lowered her weapon, beckoning agent Swenson to come closer.

"Who is this man and what has he done that would bring four G-men all the way out here?"

Swenson let out the breath that he had been holding and relaxed a little. Not much though; he noticed that the men still had their weapons pointed at them.

"Nothing, ma'am. We just want to know how to find him. Well, you see we need his help, in a very sensitive matter. We're not sure what his real name is, but he goes by the name of Big Joe."

Sadie and all of the men broke out in laughter at that statement. "Big Joe? Boy you're about a year too late. Big Joe came by and offered her a job flying for him and she hasn't been back since. Even if we knew we wouldn't tell you. You government types broke my grandbaby's heart. She went to that Tuskegee program, flew rings around those boys, then you wouldn't let her fly. White girls got to fly in that other program, but my baby was sent home. Big Joe lit the spark in her soul again. Now I suggest you leave while you still can."

Eastern Tennessee, February 1950

Charles "Lucky" McKnight, the overweight white man behind the desk in the office of the Alston raceway dirt race track, wiped his brow in relief with a handkerchief that had seen better days. At one time it used to be white, now it was dull gray. The four agents weren't there about his moonshine running business.

"Speedy Sam? You want to know about Speedy Sam? Samuel Lincoln was the best colored . . . forget that, the best driver that ever raced here, period. I made a lot of money off of that boy. I cried like a baby when the army snatched him up. Heard he served with Patton as part of the colored brigade."

Special agent Swenson was sitting across the desk from him, his men waited patiently around the cramped office.

"What about after the war? It's our understanding that he came back here and started racing again."

Lucky wanted to get the agents out of there; if they stayed too long, they might become interested in him instead of Speedy Sam.

"Yes sir, he came back alright. Didn't stay long though. After all I'd done for that boy too. Treated him like a son I did.

He stayed about six months then some big fancy nigra came by and he couldn't leave fast enough."

Swenson and his men sat up straighter and leaned in when he mentioned the big man.

"What was this man's name? Where were they going?" Swenson asked.

McKnight held his hands up "Now hold on fella, give me a minute, it's been four years you know. I think Lincoln called him Big Joe or something like that. They didn't say, but I thought I heard something about New Orleans."

Houston, Texas

The port of Houston was burning. Swenson's team watched as the firemen tried to extinguish the blaze.

"What happened here?" he asked the local section chief, Tommy Cochran, a man of medium height, thinning sandy blonde hair. Cochran wore the look of a man who hadn't slept in weeks. He looked up at Swenson.

"Part of the weird shit that's been going on around here lately. There's been lights in the sky and people disappearing. I've lost three agents down here myself; fishing boats sinking for no reason, strange mechanical noises from the water and now this happens. See that ship there" — he pointed to where the bulk of the fire crews were — "it just rammed the dock. It never slowed down, never radioed in, just headed right in and wham! Some of the witnesses said that it actually sped up as it got closer."

Swenson looked around and saw his men helping the locals question small groups of people.

"Anything else happen?"

Cochran leaned in closer so he could be heard over the noise of the sirens and hoses.

"Yes, there's nobody on board. My men say the witnesses swear about a dozen men in strange shiny metal suits leaped off the ship and ran away into the alley ways."

DIESELFUNK!

New Orleans, March 1950

The French Quarter was jumping. Not unusual for a Saturday night in New Orleans, especially at Big Dolly's club. The four agents felt awkward in their grey suits as they pushed their way through the colorful crowd of revelers to the door. They showed their badges to the two men who barred their path. One of them was a large bald white man with a nasty scar that ran from just above his right eye down to his left cheek and the other was an equally bald large black man with an eye patch. If they thought the street crowd made them seem dull, the crowd inside made them seem invisible. Even through the dim lighting and smoke the colorful suits and dresses of Big Dolly's patrons stood out. This was the first time any of them had been to New Orleans so they were mesmerized by the house jazz band and the people dancing to the music. Only the arrival of the maître de snapped them out of their spell.

"May I help you gentlemen?" he asked. He was a thin man with slicked back black hair wearing a tuxedo.

Swenson showed him his badge and said, "Special agent Swenson of the Federal Bureau of Investigation to see Dorothea Davis. We have some questions for her about her son and daughter."

The maître de looked at him like an insect. "My wife isn't here tonight, she's ill. My name is Daniel Davis. What have my children done?" He gestured for them to follow him. They went up the stairs to the balcony that encircled the entire large room and into the office. He sat down behind the desk and pointed at some chairs indicating that they should take a seat.

"It's a good thing Dolly isn't here tonight. She'd be quite upset about law enforcement looking for her children. So, gentlemen, please tell me what kind of trouble they are in."

Swenson shook his head before saying "None that we know of. We just need to know their whereabouts, or more explicitly the whereabouts of the man we're assuming is their employer."

Daniel Davis smiled then laughed. "Big Joe, you're looking for Big Joe? Good luck with that. He's not been known to stay in one place to long. No one finds him unless he wants to be found. How long have you been looking for him?"

Swenson hadn't expected that question but answered anyway. "Three months. He's been quite elusive."

Davis laughed again. "I bet. Sorry gentlemen, I can't help you. It looks to me that he's not ready to talk to you yet. When he's ready he'll let you know. Now if you excuse me, I've got customers to relieve of their money. Enjoy the rest of your evening."

They left feeling just as frustrated as they had when they came in. They didn't notice the three men standing in the shadows watching them make their way back through the crowd to their car.

An hour later, the phone rang in the office of Big Dolly's. Dorothea "Dolly" Davis answered it right away. There was a reason they called the place Big Dolly's. There was nothing small about her. She was a tall, full figured Creole woman with dark hair, fair skin and green eyes like her husband and children. They could have easily passed as white. That had come in handy over the years.

The voice of her daughter came through the phone. "Did you deliver the message?"

Dolly smiled then spoke into the mouthpiece. "Not even a hello for your poor old mother, just right to business?" She heard her daughter's laughter, something that had been rare in their conversations lately.

"Yes, your father told them, but he doesn't think they got it. Another thing, Dorothy, they're being followed." There was a second of silence.

"We know. It's being taken care of. Love you, goodbye."

Chicago Railyards

They'd expected it to be a routine raid. They received a tip of some foreigners meeting at odd hours of the night and freight cars going missing. They thought it was another group of Communist infiltrators. They weren't prepared for the nightmare they blindly walked into. There were twenty agents involved in the raid; only two remained. Agents Bruce Clark and Tony Rogers had their weapons drawn and nervously scanned the tops of the boxcars they ran through. They could hear them skittering across the cars in pursuit of them. They stopped and crouched down close to the nearest car when they heard the explosions. Suddenly it rained four-armed metal men. They thought they were dead. Then they noticed that they weren't jumping down, they were falling from the roofs of the box cars, and most of them were missing their heads.

Amos and Jackson Smith continued firing from the water tower until there were no more of the mechanical men following the FBI agents. They took out most of them with head shots, a few had their upper bodies blown apart. Big Joe wanted some more specimens to examine. The FBI raid was an unfortunate coincidence, so the brothers had to improvise to salvage the mission. They signaled for their men to move in and clean up. Amos called in the completion of their mission, while Jackson signaled their rides home. Two gyrocopters were there within minutes and they vanished into the night.

Dearborn, Michigan, April 1950

The work floor of the Ford assembly line was a noisy place. Shift supervisor Jeb McFarland was used to it though. He led Agents Swenson and Williams into his office and then closed the door. He could barely fit behind the desk. He was a middle-aged man with thinning hair and a considerable waistline. He poured himself a cup of coffee, offering some to both men who politely declined.

"Let me tell you gentlemen, I really admire the fine work that you do protecting the citizens of this country. So how can I help you?"

Williams took a large manila envelope out of his jacket and slid it across the desk to the foreman.

"What can you tell us about these two men?" Swenson just sat quietly and observed. Jeb had a look of astonishment on his face and let out a slow whistle before answering.

"The Smith boys? Really, you're here about the Smith boys? He was holding the pictures from the envelope and looking at them with disbelief.

"You sure you got the right men, Amos and Jackson Smith? If you're telling me they've done something wrong I don't, I can't believe it."

Williams looked at his superior before answering.

"Why not? What's so special about them?"

Jeb didn't hesitate with his answer. "You'll never find more honest and upright men than those two. They wouldn't hurt anyone or let anything bad happen to another person. No sir, you've got the wrong men."

Both agents stared at the man standing across the desk from them who was now bright red. Williams held up his hands.

"Calm down now, Mr. McFarland, you'll give yourself a stroke. They haven't done anything wrong."

McFarland looked at them with a puzzled expression. "Then why are you looking for them?"

It took them thirty minutes to calm the foreman down. It took another thirty minutes of listening to him sing the praises of the Smith twins, before he told them that they never returned to work after the war and the last thing they heard was they had moved to LA. They paid no attention to the men sitting in the black Lincoln that they passed as they drove away from the factory. The police later reported the three men as victims of a gangland shooting when their bodies were found three days later.

Los Angeles, April 1950

A warm breeze was blowing into Sun Village from the desert. Alfred and Paulette Malone drove with the windows down on their old Studebaker. Paulette was using her church fan to stay cool. Despite the heat, there were many well-dressed black families making their way home from church on the street. The four white men leaning on their car in front of their house looked distinctively out of place. Alfred told Paulette to stay in the car. He got out, put his jacket on and straightened his tie. Alfred wasn't tall but he was big. Twenty-five years of Paulette's cooking saw to that, but he walked up to the strangers like it was just a normal Sunday afternoon.

"Isn't a fine day that the Lord has given us? Pastor Jones was really inspirational today. Many people were skeptical that he'd be the right pastor for our church, being so young and all. But not me, I had faith that he'd be the right man to deliver the word of Jesus to the congregation."

He paused in front of agent Swenson as if he was really seeing him for the first time.

"Excuse me. I'm sorry, where are my manners? You boys look lost. Something wrong with your car?"

The agents were thrown off guard by the casual way he approached them. They were expecting hostility and suspicion. Agent Addams moved forward so that he was in between Swenson and Alfred.

"Are you Alfred Malone?" he asked.

"Why yes sir, I am. What can I help you with?" Alfred's face never lost its smile. Addams continued.

"We'd like to talk to you about your daughter Pearl." At the mention of her daughter's name Paulette shot out of the car and almost bowled the agent over.

"Pearl? You know something about Pearl? Where is she, where's my baby? Is she alright? She's not hurt, is she?"

Alfred pulled her away from Addams and wrapped his arms around his now hysterical wife. The stunned agents just stood there with their mouths open. Alfred looked around their neighbors were starting to gather on the sidewalk.

"Come inside, and I'll explain. You'll have to excuse my wife. Pearl is our only child." He took his sobbing wife by the hand and led her into the house, beckoning the agents to follow. He pointed to his right as he went down the hallway.

"Have a seat at the table. I'll be right out." The agents took a quick look to the left and saw a neat living room with two armchairs, two end tables, a couch, and a fireplace. There were pictures of a gorgeous, dark skinned round-faced young woman with a beautiful smile and bright eyes everywhere.

They filed into the kitchen and sat down. He came back poured a glass of water and then went back to the rear of the house again. Alfred returned, and then poured each of the agents a glass of water.

"She's lying down; you gave her quite a shock."

Agent Addams apologized for the team.

"I'm sorry. We didn't mean to upset her, but we're a bit confused. What happened here?"

Alfred sat down before he spoke. "You'll have to understand, mister. It's been 2 years since we've seen or heard from our daughter. Pearl was always smart as a whip, headstrong and impetuous too. She lied about her age to sign up for the war. She was only 15, but because she was a big girl and it was wartime they didn't check too closely. We didn't hear from her for the entire time. Paulette almost died of heartache. Anyway, one day she was back, and it was like she'd never left. She never talked about what she had done for the army. She got a nice job with the phone company and was home almost every night."

The agents looked at each other; they had tried checking her file, but only Swenson had a high enough security rating to see it, and he wasn't telling. Alfred continued telling the story.

"Well, one night she told us that one of the other girls was sick, so she was working her shift for a little extra money. She never made it there. Her car showed up out front two days later. There was nothing in it except a map of Nevada. So why are you here? Have you found out something new?"

Swenson spoke up then. "No, Mr. Malone, somehow this information never made it to the bureau. We're looking for her in connection with a man called Big Joe."

Alfred leaned back in his chair. "Lord Almighty!" He was smiling now; you could see the resemblance between him and his daughter in that smile.

"Ain't that girl something, running with Big Joe? That news will cheer my wife up a bit. Well gentlemen, I don't have any more to tell you, except that you aren't going to find her here or anywhere else unless they want to be found. Do a favor for me when that happens; tell my daughter to at least send a postcard so her mother won't worry so much."

Flynn spoke up as they walked back to their car. "How come the coloreds know all about this Big Joe fellow and none of us have ever heard of him?"

Addams looked at him with disgust. "Maybe it's because people like you don't want to know? I've heard of him, rumors mostly. They've been floating around since the First World War." Before he could continue they all noticed that there was something on the windshield of their car. Flynn grabbed it and handed it to Swenson. It was a map of Nevada.

The Nevada Desert, May 1950

The Hudson engine roared as it sped down the highway. Agent Swenson had it opened up all the way as he tried to lose his pursuers. He wiped the blood away from his eyes that flowed from the cut on his forehead away with one hand and said a silent prayer. Flynn was dead and Addams was on his way to join him.

"I didn't particularly like the boy, but no one deserves to die like that; they just tore him to pieces." He looked over at Addams, who was pale as a sheet from blood loss. His right arm had been ripped off at the shoulder. Williams was still alive and returning fire from the backseat. He had been hit several times, but he was still fighting.

The Hudson had definitely seen better days. The roof and half of the passenger side were missing. It had one headlight left and it was riddled with bullets. He was surprised that it was still running. However, the men firing on them from the black Mercedes behind him were the least of their problems. The things that they had been searching for had come for them. There were metal men with four arms each riding motorcycles trying to kill him.

There was a loud whooshing sound and an explosion. He looked in his remaining mirror to see the Mercedes disappear in a ball of flame. Swenson heard the propellers and high-powered machine guns that flooded the air. He shielded his eyes from the spotlights that suddenly blazed to life. The metal men were cut down by a hail of bullets. He knew that those had to be high-caliber bullets because regular ammo just bounced right off the mantis men. A quartet of heavily armed gyrocopters came down and took up positions around the car. The pilots, who all wore black flight suits that had a black triangular patch with a green skull and red crossed bones on it, motioned for him to turn off the highway and follow them across the dessert.

They rode for about an hour before Williams broke the silence.

"Boss, am I hallucinating or are you seeing this crap too? Who are these guys and what are those things?"

Swenson turned to look at the remaining member of his team. "Glad you're still with me. Yeah, they're real. From the propellers and rotors, I'd say they were gyrocopters. They used to be popular about ten years ago. But they're not like any gy-rocopters I've ever seen. They're bigger, looks like they can car-ry 3 people, and sleeker. Plus, they didn't have machine guns and whatever those tubes on the side are. I think they're bazoo-kas. Since they just saved our asses back there, I'd say these guys are on our side. You know, I'm seriously considering re-tirement if we make it through this."

Williams coughed then said "Don't make me laugh, it hurts too much. Shouldn't you keep your eye on the road?

It was Swenson's turn to laugh. "We must have both passed out at some point, because they've been carrying us for about half an hour. We aren't on the road."

Williams looked around; there were cables running from all four gyrocopters to the battered automobile. The desert floor was passing by ten feet below them.

"How's Addams doing?"

Swenson shook his head. "Sorry he didn't make it. This looks like our stop."

The gyrocopters had made a turn into an area between two mesas and were lowering them down.

"Well, that explains why nobody can find this guy." Moored between the mesas was the largest dirigible he had ever seen. The gyrocopters released their cables and flew into a hangar at the rear of the dirigible's gondola. There were long cables coming down from the dirigible linked to a platform on the ground. The entire area was illuminated by spotlights on the underside of the airship. A dozen people suddenly surrounded the car. They lifted both injured agents onto stretchers and began tending to their injuries as they wheeled them to the platform. A booming voice was giving commands at the foot of the platform.

"Get them aboard quickly." Swenson saw another group of men rush by.

"Dispose of the car then meet us at the rendezvous point in an hour."

Swenson sat up on one arm to get a look at the owner of the voice. He turned and looked at him. Whatever the medics had given him for the pain had started to kick in because his vision was getting blurry. However, he would always remember the man he saw. He was one of the largest men he had ever seen; he looked like he had been carved out of a block of mahogany. A large smile appeared on his chiseled features.

"Good evening Agent Swenson," Big Joe said. "I understand you've been looking for me."

Three days later he was escorted through the corridors of the airship, whose name he had found out was the Sojourner Truth, into what appeared to be a briefing room. The first things he noticed were the pictures. There were pictures throughout the room of Big Joe with many of the most prominent scientists of the time. Albert Einstein, Enrico Fermi, Robert Oppenheimer, and Edward Teller were all shown working alongside Big Joe. The largest picture in the room was one of Big Joe and a group of Black men in lab coats in front of Fat Man and Little Boy, the atomic bombs dropped on Hiroshima and Nagasaki.

"Who were those men and why hadn't that picture been classified?" Swenson hadn't realized that he'd said it out loud.

"Those fine gentlemen are Doctors, Jasper Brown Jeffries, William Knox, Lawrence Knox, Harold Delaney and J.

Ernst Wilkins. Let's just say I had the authority to take it and leave it at that."

The distinctive voice of Big Joe came from behind him. He turned to face the man who he had spent almost half a year trying to find. He realized then that all the people seated in the room were the people he had been trying to find. Seated from left to right were Mary Williams, a short brown skinned woman who wore her hair in a short bob; next to her sat Sam Lincoln, a scarecrow of a man with light brown skin, a mustache and slicked back curly hair. Next to him sat Dorothy Davis, a tall voluptuous woman with long dark hair and green eyes that reminded him of Ava Gardner. Across from Dorothy was her younger brother David, the spitting image of his father Daniel. Next to him were the Smiths, Amos and Jackson, whose slight stature, large eyes, bald heads and large noses made them look like brown skinned Jiminy Crickets. Sitting very close to the Jacksons was a large dark-skinned woman whose pictures didn't do her true beauty justice, Pearl Malone. They were all dressed in the same well-tailored black flight suit with red trim. Standing at the head of the table was Big Joe. That was the only name that appeared in the rather thin file he'd been handed by the director himself, J. Edgar Hoover. Hoover wasn't happy about having to rely on Big Joe, but the situation called for the agency to officially stay as far away from it as possible.

Big Joe pointed to the foot of the table "Have a seat, Mr. Swenson. First, I'd like to apologize for the loss of your men. We were cleaning out a nest of those vipers under Lake Superior and met with more resistance than we'd expected. I was hoping that Die Reiche Hammer would back off a little after we thwarted their attacks on you in Dearborn and New Orleans."

This came as a shock to Swenson. He'd been unaware that he and his men were targeted.

"Die Reiche Hammer, the Empire's Hammer? You already knew about them? Wait a minute, you've been watching us? You've had me crisscrossing the country looking for you, but you've been right there all along!"

Big Joe, whose real name of Dr. Joseph Jackson M.D, PhD, looked at him solemnly.

"A necessary deception I'm afraid. It kept the enemy looking in the wrong direction. However, to be truthful, you were told to back off. This is war, and we do have other things to do besides protect you."

Swenson was on his feet, his face was bright red. "Now I don't know what kind of game you're playing, but it cost the lives of two good men. We were never told to call off our search."

Dorothy Davis spoke up. "My father told you. He told you we'd contact you when we were ready."

Swenson sat back down. He was mentally kicking himself for not picking up on what now was a very clear message that he had been given. Big Joe waited for him to calm down before continuing.

"I believe you have some information for me."

When Swenson had woken up in the infirmary, he found his battered leather briefcase on a chair next to his cleaned and pressed suit. He'd assume they had read the files inside. But when he checked he found the envelopes were still sealed. He slid them over to Big Joe, who unsealed them and spread the contents on the table.

"You probably know that at the end of the war we obtained certain human assets from the Nazis and brought them into the country. They were some of their top scientists, whom had been working on their most advanced projects."

He looked around the room and saw that they all had knowing smirks on their faces. Sam Lincoln spoke up.

"We know. We helped get some of their ungrateful asses out of Europe. The Jewish guys were okay, but some of the other Germans seemed to be insulted by having to be rescued by us."

Swenson continued. "Most of these scientists were truly happy to have the chance to come to America. A few it seems were just trying to stay alive and were still loyal to the Nazi cause. In addition to the scientists, we also gained the services of many of the German intelligence officers. Their services have proven invaluable against the Reds."

It was Pearl Malone's turn to interrupt him. "But you found out that the same problem applied to the former SS agents." Swenson found himself wondering just how much they actually knew.

"Yes, several of them have gone rogue and have joined up with the scientists. They formed the Die Reiche Hammer, along with some Nazi sympathizers. Their goal is to get revenge for the Axis powers defeat and to create conditions here that would lead to the establishment of a fascist government in this country." He paused and Mary Williams chimed in.

"Former members of the Bund, Americans of German descent. They were pushed out during the war to prevent an anti- German backlash from developing." Swenson was becoming frustrated.

"Due to the sensitive nature of the people involved and how they came to be in this country, my superiors want to keep this as quite as possible, which is why we've come to you."

Big Joe leaned back in his chair. "Of course, since the government also doesn't want the existence of Negroes like us to be known. After all, average White Americans are told is how superior they are to us. Heaven forbid that it be known that they had to depend on us to protect the country."

He motioned for Swenson to continue. Swenson held up one of the pictures. It showed a dour well-dressed man with a thin mustache, with whose face resembled a bird of prey.

"This is Doctor Aaron Rosenthal, an expert in the field of robotics. He was developing artificial workers for the Third Reiche. We believe he is the man behind the machines that have been wreaking havoc across this country."

Amos Smith raised his palm for Swenson to stop. "That isn't Dr. Rosenthal. Dr. Rosenthal died in Vienna in 1943. We were sent to retrieve him, but a blizzard delayed us. The SS got to him and his family first. That is a picture of Dr. Rosenthal."

He pointed to a picture of Big Joe towering over a short portly man with thinning hair and round spectacles. Swenson was stunned by this revelation.

"You wouldn't happen to know who it really is would you?" he asked sarcastically. Swenson was getting the feeling that they were humoring him. Pearl Malone pulled a picture from the folder that he now noticed was in front of her.

"Doctor Conrad Beyreuther. He was the SS scientist in charge of Rosenthal's division. He was conveniently reported killed in an avalanche in early January of 1944."

Swenson was getting angry again and stood up. "If you know all of this, what did you need me for?"

Big Joe waved him down. "We knew someone claiming to be Rosenthal was said to be involved. However, we didn't know who it was. We have been given files on the scientist who were involved with Hitler's quest for technical superiority. Unfortunately, a great many of them contain inaccurate or false information. The additional resources of the FBI were needed to provide us with further information. As you know, Pearl and the Davis siblings were involved with Allied intelligence during the war. So was I. Our mutual contacts alerted me to Die Reiche Hammer when it was formed four years ago. I alerted the bureau, but they didn't see fit to act upon it until last year. That's when the results from what they dubbed 'Project Electro-men' started appearing."

Swenson sat down, "So what is our next move?" From the look on Big Joe's face, he knew he wasn't going to like the answer.

"You and agent Williams will be dropped off at Roswell, New Mexico. There are some items there that we don't want falling into the enemy's hands." He was right, he didn't like it.

"What about you and your people?" Big Joe was gathering the documents and papers off the table.

"We are no longer your concern."

Lake Superior, Michigan

Patriots Point Resort, formally the Rhineland Resort, was well hidden by the forest surrounding it. Only the stairway that led down to the lake gave any indication that it was there. Doctor Conrad Beyreuther sat in the darkened theater getting angrier and angrier with what he saw on the screen. It was film footage of the attack on the FBI agents in the Nevada desert. The flickering image showed that the initial attack by his men and machines was a success, catching the agents completely off guard. It had been sheer luck that they were able to get away. That part didn't really bother him. It was the appearance of Big Joe's people and their rescue of Swenson and Williams that made his blood boil.

"Stop the film!" He strode to the front of the room with a long wooden pointer in his hand. He tapped the image of the gyrocopters assuming their protective formation around the Hudson that was frozen on screen.

"Who are these men? Can you identify those uniforms?" The other men in the room all looked down afraid to speak, knowing they had no definitive answer to his questions. Finally, the man on his furthest left mustered the courage to speak up.

"No sir, however, we are certain they are the same men who have been following the agents and who were responsible for the disappearance of our men in New Orleans and Dearborn. We also believe that they are the ones who destroyed our underwater facility on the eastern shore of the lake."

Beyreuther marched angrily back to his seat. "Resume the film."

He watched as the car was escorted off the road into the desert and then the film ended with a flash.

"What happened? What was that flash?" he demanded to know. The lights came on and the projectionist spoke up.

"Apparently there was a fifth aircraft, sir. The observation plane was shot down. This is all we could recover from the wreckage."

Beyreuther started pacing the room. "The government's strategy makes no sense. In the last year they've dispatched four teams of agents to investigate our activities. Three of these teams focused solely on us. The fourth seemed to have a secondary objective of locating a group of missing Negroes. This same group of agents is also being followed by another group, who doesn't seem to like competition and is eliminating our teams." He paused and stopped pacing. One of his aides, Herman Mueller, interjected.

"They also appear to be behind the destruction of our Lake Superior manufacturing facility."

Beyreuther sat down when he heard this news. "This means that they are not with the government. They appear to be well trained and well equipped. Those aircraft are more advanced than anything the government has."

He looked sternly at the other five men in the room. "We need to find out who these people are and what plans of theirs we seem to threaten. Take the steps necessary to protect our remaining facility and the shipment. I want results on my desk in 8 hours. We are too close to achieving our goal. Dismissed." He watched them file out of the room.

He was troubled by the turn of events. He spent years transforming Rosenthal's crude worker prototype into an efficient weapon. The war of revenge against the Americans was succeeding quietly; they had infiltrated both the state and federal governments. The legal mechanism for the succession of Wisconsin, Michigan, and Minnesota from the United States and form the republic of New Rhineland was being slipped into various bills that were soon to be voted on in the statehouses and Congress. This new enemy made things complicated.

Two weeks later-

The diesel locomotive hurtled along the tracks of the Pacific Northwest corridor at top speed, its train of twenty boxcars whipped behind it like a great man-made snake. Ordinarily, its operator Henry Miller enjoyed this part of his route. It had some of the most breathtaking scenery in the world. However, this was no ordinary run. For one thing he usually didn't share the cab with an armed guard standing next to him. He tried not to think of the metal monstrosity crouched on the roof of the cab, or its brethren riding in pairs on top of each box car protecting more of their kind. His superiors had moved the shipment up and were pressing for a quick delivery. They were nervous, according to his tight-lipped escort; there was a new player in the game. They'd been known to use small aircraft in attacks on the Order.

"So now I have a flying guard dog?" he thought. Winging alongside of the train was a German aircraft; his silent companion had identified it as a Focke-Wulf Fw-190. It came complete with a swastika on the tail. He turned to the man next to him and pointed to the plane.

"The fact that we can fly that plane in broad daylight proves how weak the government is. We will do well out from under their thumb."

The higher ups had figured that no man would dare attack the train. Unfortunately for them the pilots of the gyrocopters weren't men. Mary Williams and her Valkyries (her crew of handpicked female pilots) rose up from the valley floor undeterred by the fighter plane. Miller could only stare in astonishment as it exploded in a ball of flame. Suddenly, the headless body of their metal guardian tumbled off the roof in front of them; it was crushed under the wheels of the train. A half dozen of the custom craft strafed the box cars. The armor piercing explosive rounds cleared them of the robots. They came around and fired rockets into each car. The last sight he had was of one of those rockets speeding towards the cab.

The Shores of Lake Superior, Michigan

Doctor Beyreuther was screaming into the telephone.

"What do you mean you've lost contact with both LA and Baltimore?"

This was the last thing he wanted to hear today. He was already overseeing the evacuation of the lodge. His men hustled about loading trucks with records and equipment. He'd received word from his FBI informant that this location had been compromised and that the government would be raiding it soon.

"What about Houston?" he demanded from the man on the other end of the phone. His agent paused for a moment reluctant to be the bearer of more bad news.

"We just lost contact with them too." Beyreuther was furious. So, this was a coordinated attack. It couldn't be the government; it had to be their mysterious adversary.

"Contact the train. Tell them we are sending more protection."

Suddenly the smooth voice of a woman was on the line.

"Oh honey, it's way too late for that."

He almost dropped the phone. "What, how?"

Pearl chuckled. "I'm very good at what I do." And she was; she'd broken many Axis codes during the war, and had used his communications network to find Die Reiche Hammers headquarters. She hung up the phone and jammed all communication systems within a two-mile radius of the lodge.

Suddenly the lodge was shaken by the force of multiple explosions. Beyreuther glanced out of the window as he put on a harness that had a box covered with many dials and antennas attached to it. This was the control box for his electro-men guards. He saw armored vehicles moving quickly across the grounds pass burning trucks, broken electro-men and the bodies of his men.

Sam Lincoln shifted gears on the "Rhino" and pressed the gas pedal to the floor, it responded by accelerating rapidly after the speeding trucks. Rhino was the armored vehicles nickname; he couldn't remember if it was Amos or Jackson who came up with it. He smiled at the memory of the day Big Joe had presented them with the blueprints, the look on his face when they each whipped out markers and started crossing things out and drawing arrows to where they wanted to move certain components was priceless. They forgot about him and Big Joe standing there. They were lost in their own world. He could hear them muttering to each other.

"Eggheads complicating everything, doing everything the hard way, that's never going to work there, how someone that smart could be so stupid . . ."

It was hilarious; they didn't even notice them leave. The Rhino was the size of a regular armored car, but had thicker armor, a larger more powerful engine, a special suspension, oversized rear tires, machine guns and two cannons.   The front mounted one was what gave it the nickname. Amos sat in the front gunner's position; Jackson sat in the top position behind Sam. The brothers had been sharpshooters during the war. They never missed. It turned out that no matter what kind of weapon you gave them, handguns, rifles, cannons, they always hit their target. The drivers of the three-truck convoy had abandoned all sense of caution as they raced down the old logging road. Sam had no problem catching up to them. The men in the rear of the truck had started firing at them but were quickly dispatched by the twins. Someone had activated some of the Electro-men. They leapt toward the Rhino, but Jackson cut them to pieces in midair. Amos disposed of the truck with a shot from his cannon. Sam easily maneuvered around the burning truck, Jackson fired on it as they sped by on the embankment. Sam looked in his mirror and saw the truck lifted off the ground by the explosion and the flaming wreckage hurled into the trees. The driver of the remaining truck lost all control when he saw what happened to the others. He drove off the road into a stand of trees. He was already dead when the shells from both cannons hit his truck. Sam whipped the Rhino around and headed back to the lodge at full speed.

Beyreuther ran through his door and turned the dial to activate his two Electro-men guards. He heard the firefight growing closer. One robot took position in front of him, the other in the rear. The scene that greeted him filled him with dread. There was a squadron of men engaged in battle with the Electro-men. They were winning the battle and pressing toward him. They were led by a giant, who looked directly at him. The face-mask of his helmet hid his face, but he could tell he was determined to get to him. The giant wore a backpack, which clearly contained some sort of dynamo. He could hear the whirring and see the arc of power generated by its operation. Several of the other troops also wore them. Each man had a pair of meter long truncheons in each hand. The truncheons were throwing off arcs of electricity which disabled the robots whenever they came in contact with them. Those that weren't smashed by the giant and his shock troopers were being cut down in a rain of exploding shells. He was now very afraid.

His mind flashed back to the escape from Berlin, where he assumed the identity of the dead Jew Rosenthal. He'd shot his wife and daughter and used their bodies to gain sympathy from the American soldiers who had raided his laboratory. He was wondering how he was going to escape this time. The big man easily dispatched his guards. Beyreuther was running as fast as he could, but Big Joe was right behind him.

"Aaron Rosenthal was my friend; you are not worthy of saying his name."

Beyreuther turned and fired his gun at Big Joe. The bullets merely bounced off his body armor. Beyreuther screamed in agony as his hand and wrist were crushed when Big Joe grabbed the gun.

July, 1950; Somewhere over the Pacific Ocean

Big Joe sat back in his chair sipping from a mug of hot chocolate as he watched the members of his command crew who were on board file into the briefing room. He would brief Mary when she returned from dropping Jackson and Pearl off in LA. When they were all seated, he had David Davis begin.

"My team and I have finally uncovered all of the legislation that they slipped into other bills. Only about half of them would have withstood a court challenge. The rest would have been tied up in court for at least a decade. By then, they would have gotten complete control of all three state houses and governorships, making it harder to dislodge them. They have been withdrawn and their authors have resigned, committed suicide, or been arrested for corruption."

Dorothy Davis picked up from there. "We've identified a dozen groups like Die Reiche Hammer. We're preparing to move on the ones that present the most immediate threat. We have suspicions about two dozen more. We've alerted the FBI, and we'll let them do the leg work on those."

Amos Smith gave his report. "All copies of their files and blueprints have been destroyed. Of course, the originals and prototypes are sealed in our Arkansas vault."

Sam Lincoln reported on the fate of the enemy leaders. "They're all dead, executed on the spot by some very shady looking government agents. We're doing some careful probing into them; they may be a potential threat to us."

Big Joe took another sip then said, "Good job everyone. You've earned a well-deserved rest in Fiji. We'll be there in two days." He rose as if to leave, but everyone stared at him. Sam spoke first.

"So, where did Mary take Jackson and Pearl?"

Amos was next. "I've never seen my brother so nervous. What's going on? Where did you send them?"

Big Joe sat down, smiled and laughed. "Oh, that's what you're all looking so serious about? I sent them to LA. I figured that Jackson should meet her father. After all, they've been to-gether for two years. They'll join us in Fiji later."

* * *

Alfred Malone had just retied his tie for the tenth time. For some strange reason, he couldn't get it right today.

"Daddy, Momma says for you to stop fiddling with your tie and get out here. We're going to be late for church."

He reached for his jacket on the bed and answered back. "Pearl you tell your mother . . ." he stopped in mid-sentence. Pearl, he'd just been fussed at by Pearl? He grabbed his hat off the chair and hurried out the door. His daughter met him half-way down the hallway. After giving him a big hug, she adjusted his tie.

"There now, just perfect. Good morning, Daddy. Now I want you to listen carefully. There is a gentleman in the living room waiting to speak to you. We want to get married, but he's the old-fashioned type and wants your blessing. His name is Jackson Smith. He's from Dearborn Michigan; he has a twin brother named Amos. He can fix or build any type of machine you can think of. Albert Einstein called him a genius. He served with distinction in the war and has the medals to prove it. He's like you, a hardworking honest God-fearing man who loves me.

Don't give him too hard of a time." She hugged him and waited for him to say something.

"Baby doll, if you thought he was good enough to bring him here to meet your mother, he's already got my blessing. How's she taking the news?'

Pearl laughed "She's out there trying to fatten him up and she's already got names for her grandchildren picked out. She can't wait to introduce her future son-in-law at church."

New York City, December 1950

Special Agent Dan Swenson was glad to be back at home, despite the cold and snow. New Mexico was just too weird for him. He was speaking on the phone with the director of the FBI, J. Edgar Hoover himself.

"Thank you for the commendation, sir. I'm just glad to do my part in protecting our citizens. No sir, I don't know how to get in touch with Big Joe and his people. He said he'd contact us when he needed to and not to bother looking for him."

The director wasn't happy about that news. He decided to take advantage of the situation. "Also, sir, he said that he'd only deal with me and Williams from now on. I don't know why, sir, but that's his position. Yes, sir I'll let you know as soon as I hear from them."

He hung up then and sat down on his bed. The phone rang two minutes later. The voice of Big Joe came through the phone. "Lying to the director isn't a good career move, agent Swenson. I'll guess I'll have to make it official. We'll be in touch."

THE
DIESELFUNKATEERS

Day Al-Mohamed
Power Play: The Very True and Accurate Story of Eunice Carter, Mob-Buster

Day Al-Mohamed is author of the novel "Baba Ali and the Clockwork Djinn: A Steampunk Faerie Tale" and editor of the anthology, "Trust & Treachery. "She hosts the multi-author blog "Unleaded: Fuel for Writers" and is one of the hosts of Geek Girl Riot on idobi radio. In addition to speculative fiction, she also writes comics and film scripts.

Day's recent publications are available in Fireside Fiction, Apex Magazine, Sword & Laser, and Gray Haven Comics' anti-bullying issue "You Are Not Alone." Two of her films were recently shown on local Virginia cable television, and two more are in pre-production. Her current focus is on a Civil War documentary on the Invalid Corps and the Battle of Fort Stevens about group of soldiers with disabilities who saved President Lincoln from a surprise Confederate raid.

She is an active member of Women in Film and Video, a 2015 Docs in Progress Fellow, and a graduate of the VONA/Voices Writing Workshop. Her short story, "The Lesser Evil" was recently nominated for the WSFA Small Press Award for Best Short Fiction of 2015.However, she is most proud of being invited to teach a workshop on storytelling: "Strikingly Beautiful: A Celebration of Women & Girls with Disabilities" at the White House in February 2016.

When not working on fiction, Day is Senior Policy Advisor with the U.S. Department of Labor focusing on Youth Employment. She has also worked as a lobbyist and political analyst on issues relating to Health care, Education, Technology, Disability, and International Development. She is a proud member of the U.S. Coast Guard Auxiliary, loves action movies, and drinks far too much tea. She lives in Washington, DC with her wife, N.R. Brown.

She can be found online at DayAlMohamed.com and @DayAlMohamed

S.A. Cosby
Girl With The Iron Heart
S.A. Cosby is a writer from southeastern Virginia. His work has appeared in many anthologies and magazines including THUGLIT, Sound and Fury, Shakespeare goes Punk, Yellow Mama Magazine, and Crime Syndicate Press. His story "The Bandit King " was featured in the Rococoa anthology from Roaring Lion Publishing. His urban fantasy novel Brotherhood of the Blade is available from HCS Publishing. He lives with a neurotic pug named Pugsley and a cantankerous squirrel named Solomon.

Milton Davis
Down South
Milton Davis is a research and development chemist, speculative fiction writer and owner of MVmedia, LLC, a micro publishing company specializing in Science Fiction, Fantasy and Sword and Soul. MVmedia's mission is to provide speculative fiction books that represent people of color in a positive manner. Milton is the author of Changa's Safari Volumes One, Two and Three. His most recent releases are *Woman of the Woods* and *Amber and the Hidden City*. He is co-editor of four anthologies; *Griots*: *A Sword and Soul Anthology and Griot: Sisters of the Spear*, with Charles R. Saunders; *The Ki Khanga Anthology* with Balogun Ojetade and the *Steamfunk! Anthology*, also with

Balogun Ojetade. Milton Davis and Balogun Ojetade recently received the Best Screenplay Award for 2014 from the Urban Action Showcase for their African martial arts script, Ngolo. His current projects include *The City*, a Cyberfunk anthology, *Dark Universe*, a space opera anthology based on a galactic empire ruled by people of African American descent, and *From Here to Timbuktu*, a Steamfunk novel.

Milton resides in Metro Atlanta with his wife Vickie and his children Brandon and Alana.

Joe Hilliard
Angel's Flight: A Tale of the City

Joe Hilliard. Writer. Luddite. Teller of Tales. Grew up as a teen in Los Angeles on a diet of lucha libre, Doc Savage, Philip K. Dick, Philip Marlowe, film noir, Judge Dredd, 50s science fiction films, and the fringe of 80s Hollywood. Graduate of the University of Michigan, which only added Kawabata, Langston Hughes, Krazy Kat, and William S. Burroughs to the mix. His work can be found in APB: ARTISTS AGAINST POLICE BRUTALITY from Rosarium Press, THE LEGENDS OF NEW PULP from Airship 27, and HARD-BOILED SPORTS from Pro Se Productions. Marks time as a paralegal back in sunny Southern California.

Ronald Jones
Unusual Threats and Circumstances

Ronald T. Jones is a galaxy-renowned science fiction writer and author of four novels: Chronicle of the Liberator, Warriors of the Four Worlds, Subject 82-42, and Visitors to NeoAfrica. When not indulging his interest in history, science, current events, and whatever else catches his fancy, Ronald might be spotted in the skies over Northwest Indiana and Chicago practicing his hovering teleportation techniques. Do not be alarmed folks.

Carole McDonnell
Bonregard and the Three Ninnies
Carole McDonnell holds a BA in Literature from SUNY Purchase and is a writer of Christian, supernatural, and ethnic stories. Her writings appear in various anthologies, including So Long Been Dreaming: Postcolonialism in Science Fiction, edited by Nalo Hopkinson and published by Arsenal Pulp Press; Jigsaw Nation, published by Spyre Books; and Life Spices from Seasoned Sistahs: Writings by Mature Women of Color among others. Her reviews appear at various online sites. Her story collections are Spirit Fruit: Collected Speculative Fiction by Carole McDonnell and Flight and other stories of the fae. Her novels are the Christian speculative fiction, Wind Follower, My Life as an Onion, and the alternative world novel, The Constant Tower. Her Bible studies are: Seeds of Bible Study. She lives in New York with her husband, two sons, and their pets.

Malon Edwards
Into The Breach
Malon Edwards was born and raised on the South Side of Chicago, but now lives in the Greater Toronto Area, where he was lured by his beautiful Canadian wife. Many of his short stories are set in an alternate Chicago and feature people of color. Malon also serves as Managing Director and Grants Administrator for the Speculative Literature Foundation, which provides a number of grants for writers of speculative literature.

Balogun Ojetade
SOAR: Wild Blue Yonder
Balogun Ojetade is an author, master-level martial artist in indigenous, Afrikan combative arts and sciences, a surviv-

al and preparedness consultant, a former Communications and Asst. Operations Sergeant in the U.S. 7th Special Forces Group (Airborne) and a priest in several Afrikan spiritual traditions.

Balogun is Master Instructor and Technical Director of the Afrikan Martial Arts Institute, which has branches in the Unites States, England and Ghana, West Afrika, Co-Chair of the Urban Survival Preparedness Institute and Co-Chair / Founder of the State of Black Science Fiction Convention, the largest gathering of Black speculative fiction, film and fashion authors, filmmakers, cosplayers, designers, artists and fans in the world.

He is the author of the bestselling non-fiction books *Afrikan Martial Arts: Discovering the Warrior Within*, *The Afrikan Warriors' Bible*, *The Afrikan Warriors' Guide to Defeating Bullies and Trolls* and *Surviving the Urban Apocalypse* and ten novels, including the Steamfunk bestsellers, *MOSES: The Chronicles of Harriet Tubman (Books 1 & 2)* and *The Chronicles of Harriet Tubman: Freedonia*; the Urban Science Fiction saga, *Redeemer*; the Sword & Soul epic, *Once Upon A Time In Afrika*; the Action-Adventure novella, *Fist of Afrika*; the gritty, Urban Superhero series, *A Single Link* and *Wrath of the Siafu*; the two-fisted Dieselfunk tale, *The Scythe*; the "Choose-Your-Own-Destiny"-style Young Adult novel, *The Keys*; and the Sword and Soul Horror novel, *Beneath the Shining Jewel*. Balogun is also contributing co-editor of three anthologies: *Ki: Khanga: The Anthology*, *Steamfunk* and *Dieselfunk* and contributing editor of the *Rococoa* anthology

Finally, Balogun is the Director and Fight Choreographer of the Steamfunk feature film, *Rite of Passage*, and the short dark fantasy films, *A Single Link*, *Rite of Passage: Initiation* and *The Dentist of Westminster* and co-author of the award-winning screenplay, *Ngolo*.

James A. Staten
Big Joe and the Electro Men
'Big Joe vs. the Electro-men is my first published work. Certain genies should never be let out of the bottle. I'm the 2nd oldest of 7 children. I was born at the old military hospi-

tal on Fort Ord in Monterey California, but grew up in New Jersey at the real Jersey shore. I'm the divorced father of 3 daughters and 2 sons, whom I consider my greatest achievement in this world.

I have a Bachelor's degree in Biological Science from Kean University of New Jersey and a Master's in Education from National University.

I've worked in the pharmaceutical industry, retail industry and in the High-tech industry here in Silicon Valley. I've been in education for 15 years and warping young minds on a full-time basis for 10. I am currently a high school Biology teacher in San Jose, California.'

EDITED BY MILTON DAVIS AND BALOGUN OJETADE

Editors Milton Davis and Balogun Ojetade have put together a masterful work guaranteed to transport you to new worlds. Worlds of adventure; of terror; of war and wonder; of iron and steam. Open these pages and traverse the lumineferous aether to the world of Steamfunk!

cyberfunk!

edited by milton j. davis

What is Cyberfunk? It is a vision of the future with an Afrocentric flavor. It is the Singularity without the Eurocentric foundation. It's Blade Runner with sunlight, Neuromancer with melanin, cybernetics with rhythm.

Nineteen amazing Black Speculative Fiction authors have come together to share their visions on the pages of this book. Prepare to be mesmerized by their stories.

For more exciting Black Fantastic books, visit our website
www.mvmediaatl.com

CPSIA information can be obtained
at www.ICGtesting.com
Printed in the USA
JSHW040048070721
16656JS00006B/129